Lust, desire, tenderness, a fierce masculine need to possess, all passed across his face. And, yes, perhaps even love. His blue-gray eyes raked over me and made me shiver with expectation. Would he be gentle or fierce? Did I care as long as I could feel him next to me? The setting sun bathed the balcony and splashed a pool of light across the floor of my bedroom. He stopped a few feet from the deadly sun and held his hand out to me.

Such a simple gesture, but it meant everything. If I went to him, I would lose myself, everything I'd ever known I was. If I lay down on that bed with him, it wouldn't be me who got up again but someone new, someone different. I would never again be exactly who I was at this moment. He would take my innocence, and my life.

I looked at that chiseled face, at that strong, battle-scarred hand reaching out to me, and I walked forward. I reached my hand out, placed it in his, and he pulled me out of the sun and into the shadows.

"Are you sure, lass?" he asked, his voice harsh with emotion.

I pressed myself against him and felt him shudder. "Don't I feel sure?" I purred.

He grabbed my hips and lifted me, my legs wrapping around his waist. I leaned down and pressed my mouth to his. His tongue plunged in, and then he was walking toward the bed, every step moving me against him in delicious ways, and we fell to the sheets in a tangle of limbs...

Wages of Sin

Jenna Maclaine

St. Martin's Paperbacks

This is a work of fiction. All of the characters, organizations, and events portrayed in this novel are either products of the author's imagination or are used fictitiously.

WAGES OF SIN

Copyright © 2008 by Jenna Maclaine.
Excerpt from *Grave Sins* copyright © 2008 by Jenna Maclaine.

For information address St. Martin's Press, 175 Fifth Avenue, New York, NY 10010.

ISBN: 0-312-94616-3
EAN: 978-0-312-94616-6

Printed in the United States of America

St. Martin's Paperbacks edition / August 2008

St. Martin's Paperbacks are published by St. Martin's Press, 175 Fifth Avenue, New York, NY 10010.

10 9 8 7 6 5 4 3 2 1

To my wonderful parents, Dan and Lynn. Thank you so much for your unwavering love and support and for never letting me give up on my dreams. This book would not have been possible without you. And to my grandmother, Phyllis Jean, because I made you a promise.

Acknowledgments

I owe special thanks to so many people for making this book possible. To my wonderful agent, Miriam Kriss, for finding me. To Rose Hilliard, editor and friend, for believing in this series and taking a chance on it. To Jennifer, for being brave enough to be the first one to read and critique it for me, and for our girls' nights out when I needed a break. To my cousin Donna, who helped me via many late-night e-mails when I had those "this doesn't look right" moments. To my cousin Cecily, for the reference books, music, working lunches, and for helping me with All Things Opera. To James, who said "follow your bliss" and inspired me to do just that. To my dear friend Moray, for helping me with the Gaelic. Any mistakes are entirely mine. To the man who stole my heart, your support and encouragement mean more to me than you will ever know. And most of all to my readers, especially those of you who believed in this book when it was nothing more than a self-published work by an unknown author. Without you, these characters are simply voices in my head and words on paper. It's the reader who gives them life. I hope you enjoy reading this book, and the ones to follow, as much as I enjoyed writing it.

Chapter One

My name is Cin. It's an unusual nickname, one that always incites speculation about how I received it. Some say it's because of the color of my hair, blood red and sinful. Others, the ones who whisper behind their hands, or cross the street rather than pass me on the sidewalk, say that it's because of who I am, of what I am. Ah, what is that, you ask? I am a witch . . . among other things.

They are all wrong, of course. I remember well how I got the name, who gave it to me, and why. So long ago, and yet sometimes it seems like only yesterday. I have been Cin for a great many years but I was not always her. Once I was young and sweet and innocent, just a girl with her whole life ahead of her.

I was born Dulcinea Macgregor Craven. My mother called me Dulcie. . . .

Ravenworth Hall
Surrey, England 1815

"Dulcie, my dear, are you sure you won't come tonight?" my mother asked, looking lovely as ever in an emerald satin ball gown, her copper red hair piled atop her head in a glorious mass of curls.

"The Anworthys always throw a magnificent party,"

my father said. "The punch is actually drinkable and there will be no end of eligible young men there," he added with a wink.

I laughed. "No, truly, my head aches. Besides, we've just returned from the Little Season and I've had quite enough of dancing and eligible young men for the moment. I think I'll have some hot chocolate and retire early tonight. Do give my best to the Anworthys though."

"Darling, are you sure you aren't staying home just to avoid Lord Montford? I hear he's returned home."

"No, Mama, I just don't feel up to going tonight. Lord Montford is a pest but he's harmless."

"Can't like the man by half, Dulcie," Papa humphed, straightening his already impeccable cravat in the hall mirror. "If you know what I mean."

I did. My mother was a Macgregor witch and my father came from a long line of men who married Macgregor witches. Sometimes he could, well, *sense* things. My mother was always trying to get him to develop his skills but he always waved a hand and said it was nothing. Two witches in the family were quite enough, he'd say.

Sebastian, Lord Montford, was a handsome, if somewhat overzealous, suitor of mine but he'd never been anything but a perfect gentleman with me. Heavens, we'd played together as children, though our friendship had taken a header later, as childhood friendships often do. I'd loved him as a child, hated him as an adolescent, and was surprisingly entirely indifferent to him as an adult. However, if Papa said he didn't like him, then I had to respect that. I'd never known his intuition to be wrong. To tell the truth, there was something about Sebastian, something in his eyes, that made me uneasy also.

"I know, Papa. I'm trying to dissuade him politely but he doesn't seem to take the hint. Perhaps I should be more forceful, though I do hate to hurt his feelings."

"His feelings will mend," Mama said. "It's you I don't want to see hurt."

"Posh," I scoffed.

"I want you to watch yourself around him, my dear," Papa said. "Even the Devil can be kind when he goes courting."

"I can take care of myself. I am not a child," I mumbled.

"You are *my* child," Papa said and wrapped his arms around me. I put my arms around him and rested my cheek against his frock coat. He kissed the top of my head and then ruffled my hair. "Now, any more of that and I'll have to go up and have Sanders tie another cravat."

"Oh, we couldn't have that," I laughed, thinking of Papa's starchy valet, Sanders.

"My lord, my lady," our butler, Masterson, said from the doorway. "The carriage is waiting whenever you are ready."

I hugged my mother. "I love you, Mama."

"And I love you too, Dulcie darling. Rest well and we'll see you in the morning," she said as she hugged me.

I watched them walk through the door, my mother's arm entwined with my father's. She laughed up at something he said and he looked down at her with a smile filled with love.

I awoke suddenly, my neck and the back of my hair slick with sweat, a stray drop running down between my breasts. What had woken me? A nightmare? No, no. I looked at the ormolu clock on my mantel. Three o'clock in the morning. My parents should have been home from the Anworthys' by now. My stomach clenched at the thought. Dear Lord, something was wrong.

I threw my thick velvet dressing gown over my night-rail and bolted out my bedroom door and down the hall-way. Stopping in front of the massive double doors of my parents' suite of rooms, I suddenly felt ridiculous. Slowly easing one door open, I looked inside. No lamps burned in the sitting room but there was a small fire laid in the grate in anticipation of their arrival. I passed by it and slowly pushed open the door to their bedchamber. My parents had married for love and had never seen the sense in keeping separate beds, as many of the aristoc-racy did. They always slept together, curled in each other's arms, but tonight the carved mahogany four-poster bed with its dark green velvet hangings was empty.

I turned and hurried down the hall, my feet flying lightly down the great staircase. Masterson was asleep in a chair by the front door. Gracious, I thought with a smile, the man even slept like there was a steel rod run-ning up his back, just his head lolling to one side. No matter how many times my parents told him he ought not wait up, he always did. Masterson took his duties very seriously. I touched his shoulder and softly called his name. He snorted and then looked up at me, not a wiry gray hair or a whisker out of place.

"My lady?" he asked, and then blinked a couple times. "Ah, no. Miss Dulcie. Whatever is wrong?"

I must have woken the dear man from a dead sleep be-cause he hadn't called me Dulcie since I had outgrown short dresses and pigtails. He creaked a bit as he got to his feet and straightened his waistcoat and jacket.

"Masterson, I—" Good Lord, how did I say what I was feeling without sounding like a complete lunatic? I decided to lie just a bit. "I had a nightmare. Please, would you send someone down to the stable and have one of the grooms saddle a horse and ride to the Anworthys'?"

He looked at me quizzically.

"I know I sound mad and I hate to wake anyone up at this hour and send them on what is probably a fool's errand but—"

"Never fear, Miss Craven," he said. "It shall be done."

"Thank you, Masterson. I'll wait in the green drawing room."

"Very good, miss. Shall I bring you a nice pot of tea?"

"No, thank you."

I walked into the green drawing room, poured myself a spot of my father's finest contraband whiskey from George Smith's distillery at Glenlivet, and walked to the terrace doors. Swirling the fiery liquid in the glass, I smiled. Masterson had not even blinked an eye at my request, but then he was well aware that ours was not exactly a normal household. Having been with the family since my father was a boy, Masterson was accustomed to the eccentricities of the ladies of the house.

I looked up at the two portraits hanging on either side of the fireplace. They were my family's two greatest ancestors. Ever since I was a little girl, looking at them had always given me a sense of calm and strength. I needed it tonight.

The portrait to the left was of a beautiful woman in the first blush of her youth, all raven hair and dark blue eyes. Her name was Lorraina Macgregor and she had lived during the mid-seventeenth century. Now, some women become witches and some are born with an innate magical ability. The Macgregor women of my mother's line are all natural, or hereditary, witches and Lorraina was the first to be born with the magic inside her.

As is usually the case with the women of my family, her magical powers didn't fully manifest until she was nearly twenty years old. Our magic is a patient thing, lying below the surface, waiting for the right moment to break free. I am a late bloomer. At twenty-two I still haven't experienced The Awakening, but I can feel the magic inside me, waiting.

Lorraina's magic hadn't come to her until after the birth of her daughter. Her husband had taken his men and gone to England to fight for Charles Stuart's restoration, hoping that the support of the clan would be rewarded with the lifting of the Act of Proscription against the Macgregor name. The husband disappeared during a skirmish and was presumed dead. Knowing how much of their hopes the clan had invested in her husband's plan, Lorraina left her baby daughter in her sister's care and went to London to the new court of Charles II.

Most people believe that Charles II lifted the proscription on our family name because of the Macgregors' service to his father; but the Macgregor women know that it was truly because Rainy Macgregor seduced a king. She sent one letter home from court and was never seen or heard from again. To honor her memory the MacGregors name the firstborn female in every generation after her. My mother is named Lorraina and in my generation my cousin Lori has that honor.

I walked to stand in front of the second portrait. She always made me smile. As is the case with many aristocratic families, we intermarry at an astonishing rate. My cousin Seamus's sheepdogs have a cleaner pedigree than at least four of my very closest friends and, by the sound of the Craven family tree, you'd think we were not much better. For the last three generations, and not without a vast amount of eyebrow-raising from the *ton*, Craven men have been particularly taken with Macgregor women. Thankfully, the Macgregors are a large enough clan that I can claim only the most distant kinship on my mother's side to any of my Craven ancestors.

Painted when she was in her early forties, the portrait to the right is of a brown-eyed redhead, much like myself, though I fancy I'm more classically pretty than Charlotte Macgregor Craven. Her beauty lay in her strength; you could see it in every stroke of the brush. She was an iron lady, my great-grandmother.

The letter that had come from Lorraina to her sister and infant daughter before she disappeared had been filled with prophesy. It was said that among her magics, Rainy Macgregor possessed the Sight. She warned of a great war between Scotland and England that would tear the countryside apart before another century had passed. Death would come to each and every door and the clans would be trampled under a butcher's heel. She knew the men would fight for Scotland and as always it would be the women who were left to pick up the pieces. For nearly eighty years the women of our family had kept the letter secret and planned for the day when they alone would take destiny by the throat and bend it to their will. And destiny had handed them Charlotte Macgregor on a silver platter.

A great heiress, Charlotte inherited fifty thousand acres of Macgregor land upon the death of her father. In 1740 the women of the clan fitted her out like a prize mare and her mother and aunt trotted her off to London to secure an English husband and ensure the survival of their family. Five short years later Bonnie Prince Charlie came to Scotland and the fields ran red with blood at Culloden as the Scots, Macgregor men among them, died for his cause. The clans were destroyed, their tartans and bagpipes outlawed, innocents murdered at the whim of the occupying English, but thanks to Lorraina Macgregor and the women of her line, a sanctuary awaited those family members who survived: fifty thousand acres of untouchable land belonging to the English Viscount Ravenworth and his beloved viscountess, Charlotte.

I refilled my glass from the decanter and glanced at the clock on the mantel. Surely they were safe. I had watched Mama put a protection spell on the new town coach not three days ago. I may have been able to accomplish only the simplest of glamours, or float a book or the tea tray, but my mother was a powerful witch, a direct descendant of Lorraina Macgregor's only daughter through the female line. Surely they were safe, surely.

I set the whiskey on a table and pushed open the

terrace doors, which led out to the small Winter Garden. I had to do something or the waiting would drive me mad.

The high stone walls kept the garden marginally warmer in the winter months but the chill of the October night still made me shiver and wrap my robe closer around me. I walked into the center of the garden, stood there silently gathering my energy, and then closed my eyes and raised my hands, palms up. Breathing in, I opened my mind to the world around me, to the smells and sounds of nature. I willed myself to be still, to empty my mind as I'd been taught from childhood and let the Goddess flow into me. I felt the wind, heard the crinkle of fall leaves, smelled the crisp autumn air. I was searching for peace. I didn't find it.

One moment the world was calm and the next it seemed to spin around me. Maybe it was the whiskey. I tried to open my eyes, to take a step and steady myself, but I couldn't. Not even my fingers would move. It was as if I were frozen, standing there in supplication, in darkness, the world whirling crazily around me, colors flowing and sparkling behind my eyelids.

I heard horses scream and I began to panic, trying in vain to turn my head and look around, to find out where the sound had come from. A man's shout and then the cracking of wood, loud as a gunshot. My eyes flew open. Whatever had gripped me was gone.

I was breathing heavily but I stood still, so very still, as if by not moving I could pretend it hadn't happened. The night around me was quiet, peaceful. The sounds had not come from outside the walls; they had come from inside my head.

And then I smelled it. Roses and violets, my mother's perfume, and in that single horrifying moment I knew she wasn't coming home. Her soul had flown free and it surrounded me now like an almost tangible thing. I could *feel* her with me. Spinning around I half expected to see her standing behind me. There was no one there, no physical body at least, but *something* was there.

Magic, her magic. I don't know how I knew it but I did. It moved against me, tingling like warm champagne on my skin. I held my hands out and my skin glowed, golden and iridescent in the moonlight. What was happening? I threw back my head as the magic pushed into me, filling me, and as it did her magic Awakened my own.

I should have experienced The Awakening, the gradual process of coming into my power, years ago but it had never come. It was as if it had been there inside me, patiently waiting for . . . something. The Awakening should have been slow, spread out over months or even years, but it burst forth within me like fireworks at Covent Garden. I could feel it mixing with my mother's magic and spreading through me. It was like water cresting the rim of a glass, one more drop, one false move, and it would spill over. The initial warmth was beginning to burn. The magic so filled me that there seemed to be no room for anything else, no room for me inside my own body.

I put my hands to my head as if I could somehow hold it all inside, but there was no way. It needed an outlet; it had to go somewhere or I would go insane. Screaming, I fell to the ground and the minute my hands hit the grass I felt all that power flow out of me.

A wave of iridescent gold left my hands and spread out over the grass, the flowerbeds, the trees—and the earth absorbed it like rain after a drought. I watched in horror as all the carefully tended plants in the garden were sucked into the earth as if jerked from underneath by some unseen hand and then just as quickly pushed out again, like watching several months' worth of growth spring forth in a matter of seconds.

The pattern of the garden remained the same but the flowers were all different: evening primrose, moon-flowers, jasmine, honeysuckle, night-blooming lilies and gladioluses, and a whole host of others, all in full bloom as they would never be in mid-October. Bloody hell. How was I ever going to explain this to the gardener?

The wave of magic, that sparkling gold, hit the walls of the garden and moved back in my direction. I was too tired to move so I sat there and watched it come, as if I were sitting on a beach as the tide rolled in. As the magic surrounded me and seemed to absorb back into me, I waited for the pain to come again, that unbearable fullness, but it never did. The magic resided in me now, comfortable as it should be, as I had always known it would be, but there was so much more there than I had ever expected, not only my power but my mother's as well.

Mama. She was still here; I could smell her perfume.

"Mama, don't go. Please don't go," I cried, the tears finally coming, streaming down my cheeks in torrents. "I love you so much, you and Papa."

I heard a carriage, the jingling of many horses' harnesses, but this time it wasn't in my head. It was out in the park, beyond the garden wall where no carriage should be. The wheels and hooves sounded as if they were traveling over packed earth, not the soft rolling grass I knew was out there. Mama's perfume grew stronger, as it always did when she hugged me.

"I'm so afraid," I whispered. "Don't leave me alone."

I shouldn't have felt warm out there in the crisp fall night, but as I smelled her scent so strong around me, I felt a peace and warmth that I hadn't felt since waking. She was saying good-bye. So many people never get that chance and I was humbled by it.

"I love you both," I said to the night sky.

I heard the ghostly sounds of the disembodied carriage moving again beyond the shadows of the garden wall, and then the night was silent.

I had no idea how long I sat there in the cold, damp grass, crying, thinking, remembering, but mostly waiting. Waiting for someone to come and tell me what I already knew. I would have to be strong, my family would expect it, my parents would have expected it. Arrangements had to be made, the funeral services planned, the paperwork handled. I would be strong and wait. When it was over I could fall apart. I could curl into a ball in the middle of their bed and stay there for a month. But not yet, not now. My grief would have to wait while I accomplished what was required of me.

And so I waited. It must have been several hours. I was numb all the way through, both physically and emotionally, when our housekeeper, Mrs. Mackenzie, found me. Her face was red and streaked with tears.

"Dulcie," she choked and swallowed hard, "there's been an accident. The magistrate's come."

I nodded once, stood with some difficulty, straightened my robe, and, running a hand through my hair as if I were always found sitting in the dew-covered grass in the middle of the night, held my head high and walked through the door.

Chapter Two

It was just past five thirty in the morning. It was silly that I should notice that when I had the magistrate, Lord Lindsey, in front of me with his hat in his hand, looking altogether like he'd rather be anyplace else on the face of the earth than in my drawing room. The door to the hall was ajar and Masterson stood just inside with Tim, one of the stable lads. He was a good boy, an Irish lad whom my mother had taken out of an orphanage in London, and from the look on his face I'd say that he must have been the one sent to the Anworthys'. After what I'd heard inside my head, I wasn't sure if I wanted to know what he'd found. I shuddered. Mrs. Mackenzie was pouring a glass of whiskey at the side table, and by the way her hand was shaking I thought she might need it just as much as I did.

"Miss Craven," Lord Lindsey started, shifting from one foot to the other. He was a squat, rabbity-looking fellow, but a good man nonetheless. "Miss, I'm so sorry to have to tell you but there's been an accident."

"Yes, my lord. Was it . . . that is to say, both of them?"

"Yes, miss."

I nodded. Mrs. Mackenzie handed me the whiskey and I took a stiff sip, the heat of it blossoming in my chest and taking off a bit of the chill. If Lord Lindsey thought it at all improper, he didn't show it.

"I knew something was wrong. Masterson sent Tim out to the Anworthys'. The carriage," I said. "Something happened with the carriage. What was it?"

There was an audible gasp and murmur from the doorway and I caught a glimpse of at least four or five maids and footmen standing about in the hall before Masterson shut the door in their faces with a scolding whisper. Lord Lindsey cleared his throat and collected himself. He pulled a small notebook and a pencil from his breast pocket and nervously flipped the pages, anything to avoid looking me in the eye. I wondered what exactly was scrawled in pencil on those pages that he didn't want to tell me. I wondered if I really wanted to know.

"Young Tim here was a couple miles down the road, just coming up to the big curve near the river," he said.

"Yes, I know the spot." I drained the last bit of whiskey and handed the glass back to Mrs. Mackenzie.

"As he came around the bend he saw a carriage on the road in front of him," he said, again looking down at the notebook, as if to make sure he got the telling of it right.

Tim spoke up, his eyes round as saucers in his small, pale face. "A big black carriage it were, Miss Craven, drawn by six horses all just as black as night."

A clatter of glass interrupted him as Mrs. Mackenzie knocked over the whiskey decanter and then righted it quickly. She looked at me and I looked at her, and then I nodded for Tim to continue.

"It was goin' entirely too fast, clatterin' down the road as if it was broad daylight. I seen his lordship's carriage comin' up the road but the blacks, they never backed down. Looked like they were aimin' to go right through his lordship's carriage. At the last minute the blacks somehow squeezed past on the shoulder but Bacchus and Zeus, they were mighty feared. Screamed and reared, they did, and John Coachman just a-shoutin' to 'em."

"And then the crack of wood breaking," I mused softly.

"Aye, miss. Looked to me like the rear wheel slid off the road an' broke the axle all to hell, beg pardon, miss. The horses somehow broke free and came at me down the road like the divil himself were a-chasin' 'em."

I looked up sharply. "The horses are alive?"

"Aye, miss, but by the way they was runnin' they're liable to be in London by now."

"Send all the grooms out at first light to search for them. They're . . . they were my father's favorites."

"Aye, miss," he said eagerly, as if here was finally something he could fix, something he could make right. "Don't you fret. We'll find 'em and bring 'em back home safe and sound."

"Then what happened? What of the other carriage? Did it stop?"

"Aye, miss, it stopped. Never did see the coachman though. His lordship's carriage, it . . . well, it teetered on the embankment and went over the side. John Coachman was thrown free."

"Is he . . . was he . . . ?"

"Naw, miss. Broke his leg all up and can't remember much of nothin' fer the knot on his head, but we got him back to his room in the stables."

"Masterson, you sent for Dr. Frady?" I asked. The least I could do was to provide the poor man the services of our family physician.

"Yes, Miss Craven," Masterson said with a small bow. "He should be here within the hour."

Now I had to ask the question I had been avoiding. I looked at Lord Lindsey. "And my parents?"

Lord Lindsey glanced back at Tim. "The lad found the, er, found . . ."

"Oh, Tim!" I exclaimed. The poor boy couldn't have been more than fourteen years old and to have witnessed what he had tonight was almost more than I could bear.

"Well, I had to, miss. If they was hurt an' needed help, although with as steep as that hill is . . ."

"Yes, I know," I muttered. I had always hated that stretch of road where the ground drops down to the river. Every time we went past it I'd look out and imagine the carriage falling over the edge. It had terrified me as a child and as an adult I wasn't much more rational.

"There weren't any blood, miss, well not much, leastwise. His lordship, he had his arms around her ladyship, like he were protectin' her. They looked like they was sleepin', miss. Truly."

"And your men, they're bringing them home now?" I asked Lord Lindsey.

"As we speak, miss."

I nodded. "Thank you."

I got up and walked to Tim. Forgetting all of my training as to what was right and proper behavior for a young lady of quality, I pulled him into my arms.

"Thank you, Tim. You're a brave lad and you'll be well cared for the rest of your days for the service you provided my family tonight. Now off you go. Get some food and some sleep, if you can."

His face flushed bright red and he smiled sadly up at me. As he reached the door I called to him.

"Tim? Who sent for Lord Lindsey? Was it the people in the black carriage?" I asked, even though I thought I already knew the answer.

"Naw, miss. The black carriage, it just sat there for a minute an' then went on down the road, kinda vanishin' into the mist like maybe I'd imagined it but I didn't, no, miss, I sure didn't. I'll remember that carriage an' them six black horses with their black plumed head-stalls 'til my dyin' day, I will. Bleedin' bastards—beg pardon, miss—never even got out to see what they'd done. It were Lord and Lady Bascombe from the next estate over came down the road a minute or two later. I guess they was comin' home from the same ball."

"Thank you, Tim," I said. When he'd left the room I looked at Lord Lindsey. "Did Bascombe's coachman see the black carriage?" I asked.

"No, Miss Craven, but rest assured I'll have every man I've got out looking for it. A carriage and horses that distinctive won't get far. We'll drag them in to pay for what their carelessness wrought this night, I promise you. It's unconscionable to be driving that way, and then after causing an accident to flee in such a manner. Unconscionable."

"Yes, it is. Thank you, my lord," I said.

"In fact," he said in a manner that clearly indicated he was looking for any opportunity to escape an uncomfortable situation, "I'll get the search up right now. I'm sorry for your loss, Miss Craven. Your father was one of the finest men I've ever met and your mother was a beautiful, devoted wife."

"Yes, thank you, Lord Lindsey. Thank you for coming to tell me yourself," I said, even though Tim had done most of the telling.

Masterson showed his lordship out, quietly closing the door behind him. Mrs. Mackenzie stood silent as a statue. I walked over and filled another tumbler with whiskey. Truly I'd drunk more tonight than I had in my entire life but, then again, no other night had warranted it as much as this one.

"They can search every stable, shed, and posting house from John o' Groats to Land's End," Mrs. Mackenzie said, "and they'll never find *that* carriage."

I swirled the amber liquid in the glass. "You think it was the coach-a-bower?" I asked.

"Don't you?"

The *coiste-bodhar*, or coach-a-bower, was a death coach. It was said to be a black coach drawn by black horses, although in some legends the horses were white. It came for the souls of the dead, to take them to the next world. This time it had come for my parents. Sitting out there in the grass tonight I had gone over and over the memory of my mother lighting the candles, speaking the words of her protection spell to ward the new carriage, trying to find some flaw, somewhere the spell had gone wrong, but I couldn't figure it out. Now I knew that it hadn't gone wrong at all.

"No," I said softly, "I don't think it was the coach-a-bower. I *know* it was."

I knew because I had heard it myself tonight. On my first summer in Scotland, where I began to learn my craft at the tender age of eight, my aunt Maggie had explained the rules and limitations of magic to me.

Ye canna cheat death, Dulcie, she had said to me. *Ye can use magic to heal and to protect ye but eventually the* coiste-bodhar *comes to claim us all and no magic among us can halt the hand of fate.*

The hand of fate. My mother was a powerful witch, I had felt that myself tonight as her magic had filled me. No mere accident would have befallen a carriage that was warded by one of her spells. It was the hand of fate. It was simply their time and they had gone together, as they would have wished.

The knowledge was not much comfort to me in my grief.

Chapter Three

I was curled up in the center of my parents' bed. As I watched the sun cast shadows on the carpeted floor, I dimly realized that I'd been lying here for nearly twenty-four hours. I couldn't sleep; every time I closed my eyes, I imagined what they must have looked like in death, lying at the bottom of that hill amid the splintered wreckage of our shiny new carriage. So I just lay there, watching the dust motes float through the air, counting the stripes on the wallpaper, staring at the loose thread in the top of the canopy. Thinking.

The house was unnaturally quiet. The day after the accident a quarter of the household servants had left the estate. Apparently the handful of maids and footmen who had lingered in the hallway and seen my reaction to Lord Lindsey's news had claimed that some sort of witchcraft was afoot. It wasn't natural, they'd whispered, that I'd known of the accident before it had occurred, that I'd sent Tim the stable boy out in the middle of the night, knowing somehow that something terrible was about to take place.

Those who had scoffed and said that I was a good and dutiful daughter without a hint of malice in my body had changed their minds later that afternoon when

William, the head gardener, had entered the Winter Garden to finish cutting back the rose bushes for the season. Of course there were no more roses; nothing in the garden looked even remotely like it had the day before when he'd last been there. Hastily crossing himself and backing out the gate, he'd told anyone who would listen what he'd seen and then had promptly taken himself off for parts unknown.

By the day of the funeral only Masterson; Mrs. Mackenzie and her daughter, Fiona; and Cook remained; the others had slipped out in the night. Perhaps they'd thought I would turn them into toads or some such nonsense. When I'd asked if they hadn't at least wanted their wages, Mrs. Mackenzie had informed me with pursed lips that the large, horribly ugly silver soup tureen that had belonged to my father's Great-aunt Gertrude had gone missing. I wished them well of it.

John Coachman was strictly confined to his room in the stables, bedridden with his broken leg. The first time I had gone to see him he was struggling to get up, wanting to check on Bacchus and Zeus, who had been found without much effort, having broken into Lord Bascombe's hay barn and made themselves quite at home. I had quieted John with the promise that I would see to them myself. I had also promised him a large pouch of gold and that as soon as he was able to travel I would send him to his mother's in Essex to recuperate. He never had remembered anything of that night beyond leaving the Anworthys', which was probably for the best.

My parents had been laid to rest in the family chapel at Ravenworth Abbey in Hertfordshire. It had been a lovely ceremony, as funerals go. I didn't fancy that

Mama would have particularly wanted to spend eternity at the Abbey, but it was the Craven family seat and the proper place for them to be buried. Mama had always preferred Ravenworth Hall, the smaller house and larger gardens, its closeness to London. It was our home. She had probably thought that there would be plenty of time to talk Papa into changing the instructions in his will, but there hadn't been, and the solicitor had been very specific about the details of the funeral. Papa had always been a man to know exactly what he wanted.

The reading of the will itself had held no surprises, as I'd long ago been well aware of my fortune. Being that I was my father's only child, the title, the London townhouse, and Ravenworth Abbey had gone to his late brother's eldest son. That was as it should be. My cousin Thomas would make an excellent viscount and his wife, Amelia, would be a credit to our family's title. They had two daughters who were just reaching womanhood, and a young son, all three of whom I positively adored. They called me Aunt Dulcie. I remember holding the eldest, Sarah Katherine, the day she was born. She would be having her debut in a few years.

Sighing, I rolled over and pulled the covers up about me, staring blankly at the wall.

When all my duties had been performed, when I didn't have to be strong anymore, I'd found myself wanting nothing more than to wrap myself in solitude and grieve. The servants disappearing had really been a blessing in disguise. I needed quiet and I needed to be alone.

I had even sent Masterson off to the London townhouse. He had protested that it wasn't right for me to be so alone here. I had argued that the new viscount would need his invaluable expertise in the running of the household in London since we left only a skeleton staff in place when we weren't in residence. I'd painted a vivid picture of the entire London *ton* showing up on Cousin Thomas's doorstep to pay their respects and there being no proper butler there to answer the door. *That* had sent Masterson off to his room to pack, clucking like an old mother hen. It was the only thing in days that had made me smile. I'd sent Cook with him for good measure. Mrs. Mackenzie was a fair hand with a skillet and it wasn't as if I'd be hosting dinner parties anytime soon.

I rolled onto my back and stared up at the dark green antique bed hangings. The redheaded ladies of my family were particularly partial to green.

Ravenworth Hall was still my home. The property and its contents were not entailed so it was now solely mine. The bulk of my father's fortune was also mine, more money than I could spend in several lifetimes. I was now an extremely wealthy young lady.

When my year of mourning was over I could go wherever I wanted. I could wear scandalous dresses and float in a gondola down the canals of Venice. I could be as eccentric as I'd ever wanted to be. For the rest of my life I could do exactly as I pleased.

Somehow I couldn't bring myself to care.

When I was sixteen I had fancied myself in love with one of the footmen, a horrible cliché, I know. He had quite properly not returned my affections and I had been despondent. Late one morning as I lay in bed nursing my broken heart, my mother had knocked lightly and entered.

Dulcie, dear, she had said to me, *the world does not stop for one broken heart. Life goes on and you must go on with it. There are people in this world, sick and dying people, who would give anything for one more day to be whole and well and walk in the sunshine or read under a tree or pick wildflowers in a meadow. I know you're hurting but you can be just as broken-hearted while doing something productive with your day, and you never know, perhaps at the end of it you'll feel better. At least it'll give you something to occupy your mind besides brooding over what will never be. Now, it's obvious you need some direction so I'll give you an hour to get yourself out of that bed and get packed. You and I are going to London for a few weeks. I think it's just what you need. All those marvelous shops on Bond Street have a miraculous way of lifting a woman's spirits, don't you think?*

It had been this stray thought that had gotten me up. I may be hurting, but I was being disrespectful of my parents' memory by lying around like a slugabed and accomplishing nothing. Mama would be horrified at my behavior. Since the sun had already set and I'd seen quite enough of the inside of the house for one day, I thought I would walk down to the stables and check on John and the boys.

I called for Fiona as I walked down the hall to my room. Once there I opened my wardrobe and frowned. I hadn't yet taken the time to go to my modiste in London to be fitted for mourning clothes, but I needed to go soon, desperately. I had absolutely nothing appropriate to wear. No one in my family had died since I had lost both of my grandmothers and Uncle William, my father's younger brother, when I was a child.

I had one mourning dress of my own, made of dove gray silk with black lace overlay, which I wore to funerals of acquaintances and family friends, but that wouldn't be acceptable for me to wear until I was in half-mourning. The black bombazine and paramatta silk that I had worn to my parents' funeral had been my mother's. It had been tucked away in a trunk since her mourning period for my grandmother had ended. Mrs. Mackenzie had altered it for me so that I could wear it to the funeral. I'd had a slight mishap with the dress afterward—in fact I still cringed at the thought—and it was no longer wearable. The only other garment I had in black, other than my cloak, was my riding habit.

I sighed and ran my hands over the dresses in my wardrobe. I had several dresses that were in acceptable colors for half-mourning and I supposed they would have to do for a few days until I could slip into London and visit Madame Rousseau's shop. There were two lovely afternoon dresses, one of lavender muslin and another of white muslin with lavender flowers and trim. There was a dark mauve evening dress which I'd bought against my better judgment and had never worn. The modiste had said it would complement my coloring, but the more I tried it on when I got it home, the more I thought it was simply horrid. I couldn't bear to put it on again so I pulled the lavender muslin out instead. It was a day dress, but if I threw my cloak over it, no one would know.

As soon as Fiona had laced my short corset and buttoned my dress, I descended the stairs and crossed the foyer, mentally planning the best time to drive into London to visit Madame Rousseau's. Just as I reached for the knob at the front door, a knock sounded from the other side. I jerked my hand back, startled, and stared at the door.

My first instinct was to look around for Masterson, but of course he wasn't there. Mrs. Mackenzie was in the kitchen preparing supper and Fiona had gone down the back stairs to join her. I was all alone. Well, there was no help for it; I would have to answer the door myself, though I couldn't for the life of me think who might be on the other side. All the neighbors had already paid their respects at the funeral. Everyone except . . .

I opened the door to find Lord Sebastian Montford on my doorstep. He looked immaculate as always, his clothing finely tailored, his shiny black curls artfully disheveled, the nails on his long, slender fingers buffed to a shine, his face very pale and proper and English. I cursed under my breath and then smiled sweetly.

"Lord Montford," I said, "how kind of you to come."

He bowed regally over my outstretched hand. "Dulcinea, we've known each other since we were infants. I think you can call me Sebastian while we're in private. Forgive me for the lateness of the hour but I've just returned home and heard the terrible news about your parents."

"Of course. I thought you'd returned from Yorkshire last week though?"

"Ah, well, I had, but I was ill for a time and didn't want to come pay my respects until I was fully recovered." He paused and looked at me expectantly. "Er, may I come in?"

Drat. "Actually, I've been cooped up in the house for days and was just about to take a stroll down to the stables before supper. Would you care to join me?"

He looked momentarily annoyed, which I thought was rather odd, and then he smiled and offered his arm to me. "I'd be delighted."

I didn't see a carriage but perhaps Sebastian's driver had pulled it around to the stables. We walked around the side of the house. There was plenty of light since Mrs. Mackenzie had just taken supper to John and the stable boys, and Tim had lit the lanterns between the kitchen door and the stables for her.

"Dulcinea, I wonder if you've had time to give any thought to what you'll do now?"

"Do?"

"Well, you're a young woman on your own without anyone to guide you."

It was rather annoying that anyone would think I needed guidance. I was not exactly a green girl just out of the schoolroom.

He cleared his throat. "I'm sure that it comes as no surprise to you that I have feelings for you."

"And I count you as one of my very best friends, Sebastian," I lied, patting his hand where it rested atop mine on his sleeve, hoping that would forestall wherever this conversation was going. Sebastian and I had been friends as children but it had been many, many years since I'd thought of him in those terms.

"Yes, well, my feelings for you go rather more deeply than that." He took a deep breath, drew himself up, and turned to face me. "I want to marry you, Dulcinea."

Oh, damn.

He continued, "It isn't right that you're here in this big house all alone, with no family."

"Sebastian, I'm in mourning. I can't possibly even consider marriage for at least a year."

"We can say that your parents had given their consent before their deaths. We can be married in a private ceremony here and live quietly until your year of mourning is over. Even the *grande dames* of the *ton* cannot find fault with that. It's entirely more fitting than you living here alone."

Oh, double damn. Did the man have an answer for everything? He had clearly thought this out.

"Sebastian, I appreciate your offer, truly I do, but there's nothing improper about my living here. It is my house now and I have Mrs. Mackenzie with me."

He scoffed. "A housekeeper is hardly a proper chaperone."

"Perhaps not but she was my nanny when I was a child, not to mention she is my mother's cousin. She's hardly a servant. And my cousin Thomas and his family are less than a day's travel to London. It's not as if I'm stuck out in the back of beyond with only a parlor maid in residence."

He stepped closer, taking my shoulders in his hands. I didn't like that by half.

"We would be good together, Dulcinea."

"Sebastian, I'm flattered by your offer, but the matter is closed."

He gave me a small shake and his fingers clenched. "Think of what your parents would want for you, then. They would want you to be settled with a proper husband."

"Actually, Sebastian, the last thing my parents told me was to stay away from you! Now take your hands off me."

He sighed and narrowed his eyes. "That's the way it's to be, then?"

"Yes."

He released me and I rubbed my arms, sure there would be bruises there tomorrow. Really, what had gotten into the man?

"Well, that's a pity. I'd wanted to do this the easy way." His right hand shot out like lightning, so fast I could barely see it, reaching across his body and grabbing my right arm, spinning me around until my back was pressed against him. "But I don't mind doing it the hard way if necessary."

I struggled but he was strong, far stronger than he should have been. "Sebastian, turn me loose or I'll scream."

His voice was soft and deadly calm in my ear. "Go ahead and scream, my dear. Call them all out here. I'll kill them all, your precious Mrs. Mackenzie, Fiona, that impudent stable boy, all of them."

I stopped struggling. There was something in his voice, something new and frightening. A week ago I'd have laughed at such a statement but now I was afraid. Afraid he'd actually do it.

"That's my girl. Now, don't worry," he said, unhooking the clasp at my neck and pushing my cloak down over one shoulder, "this won't hurt. Much."

His breath was behind my ear as he spoke, and then moved lower. His teeth grazed the throbbing pulse at my neck and there was a sharp, white-hot pain as he sank his teeth into my skin. *Vampire*, some age-old instinct in my brain shouted. I saw it all as if I were watching from somewhere outside my body. I couldn't move, couldn't scream, or he'd kill everyone I loved. All I could do was watch.

I watched his dark head bent to my neck. I watched

his hand, engulfing mine, pressed against my breast. I watched a small trail of blood run down my white skin and seep into the lace at the neckline of my dress, watched my eyes flutter shut . . . and something snapped inside me. This was not going to happen. By the Goddess, I would not allow it.

Reaching up with my free hand, I raked my nails down his face. He hissed, his grip slackening just enough for me to strike backward, hitting him in the throat with my elbow. He turned me loose, one hand reaching up to clutch his throat, and then he came at me again. *Stop, stop, stop,* I thought as I stumbled backward. Raising my hands, I called my power and pushed it outward through my palms. As it had in the Winter Garden a week ago, my magic flew free, surrounding Sebastian and holding him. He looked down at his feet, puzzled.

I ran. What I'd just done wasn't a spell, it wasn't any type of magic I'd ever been taught. I'd called it forth from pure emotion and I had no idea how long it would hold him. I had to make it to the kitchen door.

I saw Tim coming up from the stables with the dishes from supper. He saw me running and stopped on the trail. Looking over my shoulder I saw Sebastian struggling. It looked like he was making progress.

"Run!" I screamed to Tim, pointing to the kitchen door. "Run!"

There must have been something in my voice because Tim dropped the plates and bowls and sprinted for the door. I could hear my heels on the stone flags of the garden path, could feel my heart beating frantically. My neck was on fire and I was dimly aware that I was covered in blood. Maybe it had been the blood

Tim reacted to. Just as the boy reached the door, I felt
Sebastian break free of my magic. I didn't need to look
back; I could feel him coming. A howl of rage sounded
behind me and the wind picked up, scattering the leaves
and blowing dust from the path up into my face.

Tim had pushed the door open and was standing
there, frozen in fear, on the threshold. I didn't slow
my pace but put my hands on him and shoved him
through the door in front of me. I could almost feel
Sebastian's breath on the back of my neck as Tim and
I fell through the open doorway and sprawled in an in-
elegant heap on the stone floor. I heard female screams
above my head, Mrs. Mackenzie and Fiona. Rolling
quickly onto my back, I looked up at the doorway,
ready to do battle.

Sebastian stood there glaring at me, his fists clenched
at his sides, his canine teeth long and wickedly sharp. Yet
he made no move to cross the threshold. I laughed up at
him, faking a bravado I didn't come close to feeling.

"Vampire," I laughed, my voice sounding a little hysterical, even to my own ears. "You can't come in unless
I invite you."

The gleaming white teeth retracted to a normal
length as Sebastian seemed to gather his composure.

"Yes, well, I was invited in when I was human. I was
hoping that would be enough, but no matter," he said,
withdrawing a clean white handkerchief from his pocket
and dabbing at the blood, *my* blood, at the corner of his
mouth. "You'll have to come out sooner or later, my
dear. I can't touch you while the sun shines but darkness
is now my stalking ground. Eventually you will come
out after dark, you or one of the others," he said, glancing at Tim and the ladies as he neatly folded the hand-

kerchief and returned it to his pocket. "After all, I have nothing but time. I can be patient."

My temper flared at the thought that he would harm one of the others to get to me. He'd come back from Eton a mean-spirited bully, and the intervening years apparently hadn't corrected that flaw.

"You're nothing but a weasel, Sebastian!" I yelled. "That's all you've ever been and all you will ever be!"

His form shimmered iridescent gold. He looked down at his hands.

"What the—?" he said, and then he was gone. On the flagstones outside the kitchen door now sat a very large, very angry weasel.

"Oops," I squeaked.

"Dulcie, what have you done?" Fiona asked in a breathy whisper. She looked like a younger version of her mother with the same chestnut hair and heart-shaped face, a face that now stared at the snarling weasel in fascination and horror.

"I don't know," I replied. "It's the magic; I can't seem to control it. The day after the funeral I was in my room, crying and tidying up, and I wished that I could burn that horrid black dress and the thing went up in flames all by itself."

Mentally shaking myself, I leaped up and grabbed a stick of wood from the pile near the ovens. Wrapping what was possibly a small tablecloth around it and tying it tightly, I lit it from the fire.

"Tim, take this now and go back to the stables."

Tim was standing now, staring in horror at Sebastian the weasel. I grabbed his arm and shook him gently. "Tim, listen to me."

He flinched and looked at me wide-eyed.

"Don't," I said, my voice cracking on the word, "don't look at me like that. You know me. You know I'd never hurt you."

His face turned red. "No, miss. I'm sorry, I didn't mean—"

"It's all right. Now listen carefully. Are Lord Montford's carriage and driver in the stable?"

"No, miss. I assumed it was in the drive."

"Good. Now, don't tell the others what you've seen here. Go back to the stables and bar all the doors. Do not open them until sunrise, not for anything or anyone. Can you do that?"

He nodded.

"Good lad," I said, handing him the makeshift torch. "Come back up to the house in the morning, well after sunrise, mind you, and we'll talk about what's to be done."

"But, miss, I can't be leavin' you and the ladies here unprotected!"

"We'll be fine. He can't come in unless we invite him and we certainly aren't going to do that. Now, go quickly!"

Tim moved to the doorway. Sebastian the weasel hissed and snapped at him. Tim thrust the torch at the little fiend and he backed away, allowing Tim to move past and head down the stable path. I watched from the window to make sure that he got there safely.

"Dulcie?" Mrs. Mackenzie said, gesturing toward the weasel. "How did you do that?"

"As I said, I don't know," I sighed. "The Awakening didn't happen like it was supposed to. It's too much all at one time and I can't control it."

The three of us stood in a semicircle in front of the

open door, staring. Sebastian the weasel paced back and forth, looking at us, at me in particular, and spitting as he paced.

"Do you think you should . . . de-weasel him, Dulcie?" Fiona said in a small voice.

I shrugged and turned to her. "I don't know how I weaseled him in the first place," I said. "I truly don't know how I'd go about *de*-weaseling him. I suppose I could look through Mama's books, perhaps there's a spell of some sort."

"Then again," Mrs. Mackenzie said, "do we really want to change him back? Since it appears that Lord Montford is now a vampire and wishes to kill you, wouldn't it be best to simply leave him?"

"Frankly, Mrs. Mac, I couldn't give a badger's ass if Sebastian stays weaseled or not, but you know as well as I do that the first rule of magic is to harm none. I think turning someone into a weasel would be considered doing harm."

"I don't think that the 'harm none' rule applies to the undead, do you?" Fiona asked. I looked at her and she shrugged. "Well, they're dead. Aren't they already as . . . *harmed* as they're going to get?"

"Good point, my dear," her mother said, patting her shoulder. "Besides, he was trying to harm you first, and I think Lord Montford would make a fine weasel. Probably be very happy. And do watch your language, young lady."

I rolled my eyes. "My unwanted suitor has gone evil, I've been attacked in my own garden, I have two holes in my neck, I'm covered in my own blood, and there's a snarling weasel on my doorstep. I think the situation calls for a little strong language."

"If you ladies are quite through," a deep male voice said from the doorway.

We all gasped and turned. Sebastian stood there, back in human form. Well, not exactly human, not anymore.

"I guess that's settled, then," I said. In truth I was a little disappointed.

"You think you're so smart," he spat. "You have no idea what kind of power I have now, the things I can do to you now that I've tasted you."

"You've had quite a taste of my own power," I said, cocking my head to one side. "How did you like it?"

"Oh, you'll pay for that, never fear. I've wanted you for years, Dulcinea, and I will have you. We need you and no one can stop us now. Your blood is in me, flowing through me, and there is no chance of escape for you, not anymore. You'll be hearing from me soon."

And with that he was gone.

Chapter Four

We chose the dining room because it was the only room large enough to suit our purposes that didn't have any windows or outside doors. Inside of an hour my dining room came to resemble what I imagined the offices in the War Department looked like. Mrs. Mackenzie and Fiona brought down every book my mother had in her private workroom and piled them on the long mahogany table. I sorted them while Mrs. Mackenzie and Fiona looked through the stacks for any information about vampires.

I couldn't face Sebastian again with legends as my only weapons. Did a wooden stake through the heart really kill a vampire? What about crosses and holy water? I had to know for sure because one error could get us all killed. I placed another book on Mrs. Mackenzie's pile and continued sorting.

Mrs. Mackenzie was actually not a "Mrs." at all. When she was a mere girl she had allowed herself to be seduced by the blacksmith's handsome eldest son. Unfortunately he was already married with two small children of his own and had no more use for her when she came to tell him she was with child. The unfortunate situation was further compounded by the fact that she was the vicar's daughter. Her parents, horrified and ashamed, had been rather plain about the fact that she could not stay among their sainted flock and would have to leave Glen Gregor before her condition became apparent.

The good vicar had written my mother, a distant cousin, to see if she could secure a place for his daughter in one of the charity homes in London. Apparently Inverness was not far enough away to suit him. Mama had just learned that she was to be a mother herself so she sent the coach to Glen Gregor to collect young Jane Mackenzie. When Jane arrived at Ravenworth Hall, Mama introduced her as her cousin, the poor widowed Mrs. Mackenzie, whose young husband had been accidentally shot in the head in a hunting mishap. I always thought that both Mama and Mrs. Mackenzie relished the thought of the blacksmith's son being "accidentally" shot in the head. And so the unwed young mother had become Mrs. Mackenzie, first my nanny and later our housekeeper. I'd never known her as the frightened young girl she must have been back then; from my first recollections she'd always been the iron-willed supreme authority over everything that went on in our household. Fiona and I had never been able to get away with even the slightest mischief under her watchful gaze.

I sighed and plopped down in a chair, leafing through a book on protection spells.

"I'm going to have to send John and the boys away," I mused as I turned another page. "I'll have the boys harness Zeus and Bacchus to the old carriage first thing in the morning and take John to his mother's in Essex. She lives on a little farm by the sea and I think the boys would enjoy a holiday. I can get some lads from the village to come up during the day and care for the other horses."

"I thought they'd be safe out there," Fiona said. "Are they not safe, Dulcie?"

"The bunkhouse is in the stables. It's their home and Sebastian can't enter without an invitation. However, if he gets desperate enough, there's no reason he can't light the stables on fire to get *them* to come *out*."

Fiona looked up at me in horror.

I shrugged. "If I can think of it, he will too, eventually. Nothing useful here," I said, tossing the book aside and reaching for another one. "The two of you should go with them. It's not safe here."

Mrs. Mackenzie snorted. "You've never been a stupid girl, Dulcie. Don't start now."

"But it's not safe for either of you. You heard what Sebastian said tonight. He'll use you to get to me if he can."

Mrs. Mackenzie leveled a look at me that brooked no argument. "Your mother, God rest her soul, saved my life. I'll not abandon her only child and that's the end of it."

"Besides," Fiona said, reaching for another book, "what with you turning vampires into weasels on our kitchen stoop, surely we're safe as houses." She flashed me what I'm sure was meant to be an encouraging smile.

I knew not to argue further and, in truth, a part of me was glad that they were staying. Another part was terrified for them. A vampire was stalking me and I had no idea how to fight him, how to kill him. My only weapon was a font of powerful magic I couldn't seem to control. Life couldn't get much worse.

"You'd think in all these books on magic and the arcane that there'd be something useful about vampires," I

said, tossing another book onto the discard pile. I'd
cleaned the blood off me and changed my dress, but
the wounds on my neck were still raw. I ran my fingernails over them absently.

"Dulcie, don't scratch," Mrs. Mackenzie said, without even looking up from her book.

"I can't help it, they itch."

"Maybe we could cleanse them with holy water?"
Fiona suggested.

I arched a brow at her. "Do you happen to have any
holy water about you?"

She grimaced and looked back down at her book. I
continued scratching.

"You know who could probably help?" Mrs. Mackenzie said. "Mr. Pendergrass."

"Now, there's a thought," I replied. Mr. Pendergrass
was an apothecary in London and a dear friend of my
mother's. In a small back room behind his legitimate
business he supplied witches from miles around with ingredients for potions and spells. He also had a rather impressive collection of books himself. "If I took a horse
in the morning I could possibly make it back by sunset."

"I hate the thought of you being out by yourself,
Dulcie, but it looks like Mr. Pendergrass is our only option," Mrs. Mackenzie said grimly as she tossed yet another book on the discard pile.

"If I can't get back by sunset, then I'll have to stay
in London, and that leaves you two here, alone and
unprotected."

"We'll manage," she said firmly.

I shook my head and motioned to the books. "Keep
looking. I won't leave you both here alone unless it's
our last resort."

I rubbed my temples. My head was beginning to feel as though a bee were buzzing around in it. Getting up, I walked to the sideboard and poured myself a cup of tea. As an afterthought I dropped a dollop of whiskey into it. The buzzing was getting worse.

Dulcinea.

I looked around. "Did you hear that?"

"Hear what?" Mrs. Mackenzie asked. Fiona looked worried.

"Nothing," I replied, shaking my head and frowning down at my teacup.

Dulcinea. Come to me.

I rubbed my head.

Come come come. I have such wonderful things planned for us. Come out and play.

"He's here," I whispered, the teacup rattling as I set it down on the sideboard. "He's here."

Mrs. Mackenzie and Fiona both got up and came around the table.

"I have to go," I said, as if in a dream, and started for the door.

Mrs. Mackenzie grabbed me and shook me hard. "Dulcie, stop. Think what you're saying."

"I know, I know," I said, my head clearing a bit. "But he won't be quiet. He won't stop until I come out."

Dulcinea. Come, girl, don't make me hurt you. Come out . . .

I started for the door again and Mrs. Mackenzie dragged me back. We struggled. I lashed out, clipping her across the shoulder with my fist, and broke free. One of the dining room chairs flew across the room of its own volition and crashed into the wall behind us. I stopped and stood very still. I had done that.

"Help me," I whispered.

Mrs. Mackenzie righted the fallen chair and shoved me down into it. She rushed out of the dining room, returning seconds later with one of the thick silk cords that was used to tie back the heavy draperies in the green drawing room.

"Forgive me, child," she said and proceeded to tie me to the chair.

"If I leave this house, he'll kill me. Make it tight," I said. She looked up at me, a frown creasing her forehead, but she pulled the cords tighter.

Dulcinea. Don't let them keep you, not when you know you want to come to me. You have such power. Use it!

I screamed. "Let me go! I must go to him. Turn me loose or I'll—"

Fiona slapped her hand over my mouth before I could finish the sentence. "Shush," she said. "Mama? What do we do?"

Mrs. Mackenzie snapped her fingers. "Laudanum! If she's sleeping she can't hear the devil call to her. Stay with her and watch her like a hawk."

Mrs. Mackenzie hurried out the door. I looked at Fiona, my lifelong friend and companion, and she looked back at me, wary and frightened. "I swear, Dulcie, if you turn me into some sort of forest rodent I'll never forgive you."

Come to me. Come, Dulcinea. Come come come come come . . .

I moaned and stood as much as I could, tied to the chair as I was. With one swing of my body I caught the edge of the chair on the thick mahogany dining table, narrowly missing my hands and arms. The wood cracked and broke and within seconds I'd worked myself free.

Fiona leaped at me and we tumbled to the floor together. She landed on top of me and struggled to hold my hands to the floor. I got one leg out from under her and used it to push against the floor, the two of us rolling over and over. Her head hit the leg of the table with a heavy thump and I fought my way to my feet and headed for the door. Just as I reached for the knob I felt a hand on me, pulling me back with such force that I stumbled. Fiona moved between me and the door, her back against it.

"It hurts, Fiona," I said, pressing my hands to my head, "and I *will* hurt you to make it stop. I don't want to, but I will. Now, move aside."

I stalked toward her, my eyes never leaving her face, looking for some sign that she would give in and let me go. I had to go. I had to make it stop.

Dulcinea.

His voice in my head distracted me, just for a moment, but it was long enough. Long enough for me not to notice Fiona's hand snake out and grab the heavy Chinese vase on the pedestal next to the door.

Dulcinea, come.

"I don't want to hurt you either, but—"

I looked at her in confusion, not knowing whose voice I was hearing anymore, Sebastian's or Fiona's. And then there was pain and the tinkling of broken porcelain, and the world went black and still . . . and blessedly silent.

Chapter Five

I maneuvered my sorrel mare through the crowded streets. Missy did not care much for riding in London and I couldn't say as I blamed her. My head still pounded and my neck throbbed with every beat of my heart. Fiona, bless her, had been very apologetic when I'd regained consciousness half an hour before dawn. I didn't scold her; she'd done what needed doing and I would have done the same if I had been in her place. Still, I didn't think she'd needed to hit me quite that hard. It had worked though; I'd slept and not dreamed, of Sebastian or my parents or anything at all.

An hour after dawn I'd sent Tim and the other two lads on their way with John Coachman and Zeus and Bacchus. John had protested that his mother didn't have a barn fine enough to house my father's favorite horses for the winter. I'd pressed a purse with an obscene amount of money in it into his hand and told him to hire someone to build her one. John loved those horses and I knew they'd be well taken care of. Tim had been afraid, but I think he was more afraid of staying than he was of going. I'd promised I'd send for them as soon as the danger had passed.

The minute they cleared the gates I'd saddled Missy and headed for London. If I really pushed, I might make it back just before sunset, but I would still have to cool Missy down before I could put her in her stall with feed and water. As much as I hated it, I would have to stay the night in London. I knew that the knot wouldn't leave my stomach until I was home and certain that Mrs. Mackenzie and Fiona were safe.

I stopped the mare in front of a small shop on Panton Street near Piccadilly and dismounted. I earned disapproving glares from the matrons, turned-up noses from the young misses, and interested glances from more than a few gentlemen. To hell with them all; I really did not have time to be properly tricked out in a carriage, let alone chaperoned. The debutante in me was thankful, however, that my riding hat sported more than just attractive white peacock feathers; it also had a thick veil, which hid my features well.

I motioned to one of the omnipresent street urchins. The boy was about eleven or twelve years old, grimy and looking like he was in sore need of some funds. I pressed two shillings into his hand. That should buy his loyalty well.

"Hold my horse?"

"Aye, miss," he replied.

Even with my money in his pocket he still had the cagey look of the sort that would steal my horse the minute my back was turned. I stared at him for ten full seconds and then turned to go into Pendergrass & Company Apothecary Shoppe.

I heard a small voice behind me. "You goin' in there, miss?"

I turned. He'd obviously heard the rumor that Mr. Pendergrass was the local purveyor of all things magical.

"Yes, I am," I said, "and if you know why, then you know I'm not the type of woman you want to wrong."

"Naw, miss," he said quickly. "I'll 'old 'er right 'ere nice an' gentle like. Never you worry. We'll be right 'ere."

I nodded my head. The little blighter really would have stolen my horse!

The "company" of Pendergrass & Company was Mr. Pendergrass's partner and once-apprentice. He always looked rather ridiculous standing behind the glossy counter, more like a pugilist than an apothecary. He was a large dark-haired man, handsome enough in a rough sort of way, and possessing an air about him that would make any sane man reluctant to cross him. I always thought his size and looks must have been a great benefit to him, growing up as he did with the rather unfortunate name of Archie Little.

"Good morning, madam," he called out. "How may I help you?"

I lifted my veil.

"Miss Craven!" he greeted me warmly as he came around the counter. I was suddenly reminded that he used to slip me peppermints when I was all of ten years old and he was a very grown-up eighteen. It made me smile.

"Archie, how very nice to see you," I said.

"We heard about your parents. Tragic, simply tragic. Your mother was one of the finest women I've ever met."

"Thank you," I replied, not knowing what else to say because, quite honestly, I thought so too.

"So, what brings you to London?" he asked.

"Actually I need to ask Mr. Pendergrass for his advice on a bit of a problem I have. Is he in?"

"Certainly," he said, in a politely indifferent tone that belied the look of curiosity on his face.

He escorted me to the door at the back of the shop which I knew from experience opened into a small parlor where Mr. Pendergrass did most of his business. I walked inside and immediately spotted Mr. Pendergrass dusting and reshelving the bottles and tonics that lined the far wall.

"Sir?" I said.

He jumped and turned, a broad smile crinkling his face when he saw me. Truly, the man must have been a hundred years old. One would never guess to look at him that he was the distributor of the finest magical supplies south of Hadrian's Wall, and was quite a proficient wizard himself.

I had known Mr. Pendergrass all of my life. When I was a child he always had some shiny bauble secreted in his pocket for me when my mother came to the shop; when I was a young lady there was always a stray bit of satin or velvet ribbon he just "happened" to have lying around.

He came over to me now, his staff tapping against the wood floor. The staff was four feet of naturally twisting wood that had been glazed to a fine deep shine and topped with a sphere of polished amber the size of my fist. He'd had that staff as long as I could remember. He put his arms out and I sank into them, much as I would a beloved grandfather's.

"My dear," he said simply.

After a long moment he guided me over to one of two plump, overstuffed chairs in front of the small fire. As I sat, he turned to the tea service and poured us each a cup, his old, gnarled hands never shaking.

"My dear, I can't tell you how much it has grieved me to hear about your parents," he said as he slowly took his seat opposite me. "You don't often find two people who loved each other like those two did. And your mother was a very dear friend of mine for nearly thirty years. It just breaks my heart, it does. She was a fine witch, a fine witch indeed. I don't understand how such a thing could have happened."

I smiled and thanked him for his kind words and told him, briefly, what had transpired the night of the accident.

"Aye, well it's no comfort to you now that it was fate and that they weren't taken before their time, but one day it will be. When the grief begins to ebb, at least you'll be able to be thankful of that."

He took a sip of tea and looked at me but I couldn't think of a suitable reply.

"You say she passed her power to you? That's very odd. I've never even heard of such a thing, but it's my business to know that anything is possible. Your mother had a lot of power, she certainly did. Will you be staying in Town with your cousin? I'd be happy to help you work on your control, but you might be better served at Glen Gregor with your aunt."

"Actually, Mr. Pendergrass, that's not why I came."

He raised one bushy white brow.

"I'm in trouble," I said. "Big trouble."

"Well," he said, "tell me what's wrong and what I can do to help."

I ran my palms down the black wool of my riding habit and then reached up and pulled the fichu from about my neck. I pushed down the ruffled edges of the chemisette, tucking them inside the neck of the jacket. The Craven Cross hung at my throat, suspended on a short chain. It was a Celtic cross three inches long, intricately carved in gold and faceted with twenty-four blood-red rubies and many small, sparkling diamonds. I turned my head so that he could see the two puncture wounds and the nasty purple and green bruise that marred my neck. A look of pure horror crossed his face and he sucked in his breath.

"By the Goddess," he whispered, reaching out a hand toward me and then stopping, only to pull back as if afraid to touch me. "Archie!" he shouted in as strong a voice as I'd ever heard from the old man.

Archie came hurrying through the door, pushing back a heavy lock of dark hair that had fallen over one eye. He looked from Mr. Pendergrass to me, as if he'd expected some disaster to have befallen one of us.

"Lock the doors and put out the closed sign," Mr. Pendergrass said, never taking his eyes from me, "and then join us."

"Oh, Archie?" I said. "There's a grubby young man out front holding Missy for me."

"I'll see her stabled and cared for," he assured me.

"Thank you."

After Archie had left I nodded to the now-closed door and asked, "Mr. Pendergrass, do you think it's wise to bring him into all this?"

"I trust Archie implicitly in all things," he said, "and besides, he may be useful. He had a cousin who was a vampire slayer."

"Vampire slayer?"

"Aye, they are the stuff of stories on a long winter's

night, as are vampires themselves, but you and I both know that there is truth in most things that people regard as mere superstition. A slayer is usually the survivor of a vampire attack. Either their minds cannot accept what has happened to them or their anger consumes them, but they become obsessed with only one thing: executing vampires. It becomes their whole life and it is usually a rather short life. Slayers are driven to train in fighting techniques and weaponry. They do little else but fight, sleep, and eat. They are exceptional fighters, but in the end," he shrugged, "they are only human."

I thought about that and sat in silence, sipping my tea, until Archie came back, his keys jingling as they slid into his vest pocket. He looked questioningly at Mr. Pendergrass, who motioned him closer and then reached out and took my chin in his hand, turning my head so that Archie could get a good look.

"No," Archie whispered, his eyes wide.

"Tell me what happened," Mr. Pendergrass said.

I told them of Sebastian and the attack, trying to leave nothing out for fear any minor detail would be something of importance.

Mr. Pendergrass settled into his chair. "Well, clearly something must be done about your inability to control your magic, Dulcinea. We can't have you losing your temper and weaseling anyone who crosses you."

"I do not lose my temper," I said haughtily.

Mr. Pendergrass arched a brow at me.

"Very well, I rarely lose my temper, then. All in all, that's not the point."

"Yes, I daresay the point is that we must find a way to eliminate the threat to you."

"What about a slayer?" I asked. "Could we find one?"

Archie shook his head. "My cousin was a slayer, the only one I know of in London, but he was killed while on the hunt three weeks ago."

"Oh, Archie, I'm so sorry," I said. "Surely you know how to kill them though, the vampires? If only I knew how to fight him, how to kill him. I don't want to go up against him with an arsenal that consists of only legend and folklore."

Archie looked at me. "Could you really kill him? Cut off his head? This man you've known all your life?"

I swallowed and paused for one heartbeat, two, three. "Yes," I said, and I meant it.

"In the time it took you to answer that question he could have snapped your neck," Archie said. I didn't really care for his brutal honesty. I didn't want to admit that maybe I was that weak.

"What do you suggest, Archie?" I said, a little more coolly than I'd intended. "Perhaps Mr. Pendergrass could fight Sebastian? Or would you rather it be you? Should I leave your young wife a widow, all to save my hide? No, it has to be me. I can do what needs to be done, I swear it. I just need you to tell me *how* to do it."

He thought for several long minutes, pacing the room, and then he looked at me and shook his head. "It makes my skin crawl to suggest it but I think I have something that might help. It's incredibly dangerous but it just might work."

"Well?"

"Wait here," he said. "I need to get something."

He came back a few minutes later holding a small, battered, leather-bound journal in his hands. I couldn't be sure, but I suspected some of the stains on the cover were blood.

"This was my cousin's journal. I found it among the things in his rooms after he was killed. I, um, liberated it before my aunt could find it. I didn't think it wise for her to find out what he really was."

I nodded.

"There's a passage written about a month before he died. Listen:

"I fear I'm getting too old for this. Tonight I was one second off, one heartbeat too slow, and the beast was on me. She had me pinned to the cobblestones, her fangs lengthened, her head drawn back for the strike. I watched in horror, frozen for an instant . . . and then a booted foot came out of nowhere and connected with the side of her head.

"The impact threw her across the alley. I looked up at my rescuer. She was the most stunningly beautiful woman I'd ever seen. Her pale blonde hair was pulled back to hang in ringlets past her shoulders and her man's attire fit her slender body like a glove. The vampire got to her feet, hissing at the woman, and then charged her. They fought as I lay there, watching in fascination. The blonde was like some warrior goddess, every move perfect, every blow a work of art. She made fighting the undead look like child's play.

"The vampire fell before her and the goddess reached back and pulled a sword which had been sheathed down her spine, hidden beneath her frock coat.

" 'Do you know who I am?' she calmly asked the vampire.

" 'Betrayer!' the beast spat.

" '*I am the Devil's Justice,*' the woman said, and the sword fell, its blade taking the vampire's head in one clean motion. Nothing but dust and bone was left where the beast had been.

"The goddess sheathed her sword and turned to me. Reaching out a hand, she offered to help me up. I took her hand; it was cold. Recoiling, I realized what she was. Not a slayer, as I had thought. She was a vampire. She stared at me, her eyes sad for a moment and then going cold and distant. I sat there, unwilling to take her hand even though she had saved my life.

" '*Remember,*' she said, '*who it was that allowed you to see another dawn.*' And then she turned away.

" '*Who are you?*' I called to her.

" '*The Devil's Justice*' was all she said, and then she was gone.

"Two weeks later he wrote this:

"*I have asked those who would know. I believe she was one of The Righteous. They who would know whisper that The Righteous is a group of three vampires who slay the evil undead, those who take human lives. Their leader is a vampire called Devlin, or the Dark Lord. Supposedly in life he was one of Edward III's champions. He is invincible in battle and the undead fear him as they do the sunlight.*

"*His mate is a Frenchwoman called Justine; some call her the Devil's Justice. In life she was an actress and an opera singer without equal and the courtesan of kings.*

"*The third of the group is younger, less than a century old. They call him Michael, the Devil's Archangel. They say he is a Scot who fell at Culloden, and Devlin was so impressed by his skill in battle that he spared him true death so that he may fight forever as a vampire.*

"So, do I believe any of this? Before I saw her I would have said with absolute conviction that there could be no good vampires, and yet she saved my life, took the head of one of her own kind, and walked away. Do The Righteous really exist? Do I believe? Yes. Yes, I do."

I looked at Archie and then at Mr. Pendergrass. He had a thoughtful expression on his face.

Oh, dear.

"So," I said slowly, "you think that I should ask these vampires to help me? You think that they would?"

Archie shrugged. "There's only one way to find out. Besides, who better to kill your vampire than the undead themselves?"

"But that was written months ago! What if they aren't even in London anymore? And how do you go about finding a cadre of vampires in the City at any rate?"

"A summoning spell might work," Mr. Pendergrass said, one finger tapping idly on the amber globe at the top of his staff.

"But it would have to be done at night, so they would be able to travel," I said.

"Yes."

"And I can't go out at night or Sebastian will eat me."

"True," Mr. Pendergrass said slowly, as if waiting for me to come to some sort of conclusion on my own.

I leaped to my feet. "Oh, you can't be serious! You expect me to work a summoning spell, which I'm not even sure I can do, to call vampires into my home who may or may not be friendly? And even if they are friendly, they're more than likely to be very angry with me when they get there. Lord and Lady, I might as well just slit all of our throats!"

"Do you have a better idea?" Archie asked.

"Just tell me how to kill him!" I shouted.

"Dulcinea," Mr. Pendergrass said gently, "come child, sit down. Here's a nice cup of tea. Now, we have to be realistic here. I could possibly work a spell quick enough to incinerate Sebastian, but if he has reinforcements, then we're all dead. Archie's a fine, strapping lad, but he's only human and no match for the strength of a vampire. Besides, as you said, there is his young bride to consider. You have a great deal of power within you, but you have yet to learn to channel and focus it and, as Archie pointed out, if you hesitate for one instant, if you think for one heartbeat about the Sebastian Montford who was your childhood friend, then all is lost.

"Now, I don't like this idea any more than you do, and no one will make you do anything you don't want to do, but I think you should get some rest and consider it. Come, let me show you to the guest room."

As I wearily followed Mr. Pendergrass up the back stairs I thought about what Archie had suggested. It was foolish—foolish and horribly arrogant—to believe that I could fill a vampire with a compulsion to come to me, ask him to help me kill one of his own kind, and expect him to agree to it, or at the very least not to kill me out of pure irritation. It was ridiculous. Tomorrow morning I would take Missy and go back home. Mr. Pendergrass and Archie would stay in London, safe and sound, and I would think of something else. One thing was certain: There was no way I was ever going to perform a summoning spell to welcome vampires into my home. No. Absolutely not.

Chapter Six

"So how exactly does this spell work?" I asked Mr. Pendergrass as the carriage rumbled along the lane, a very cranky Missy tied to the rear.

"It's quite simple, really. You create a circle of power and open yourself up to the magic. Then you call the ones you seek to you. The closer they are, the stronger the magic will be. If the vampires are in London you should be able to call one or two of them, probably the Scot and the woman, since they are the youngest of the three. If they happen to be closer, you may even be able to call the Dark Lord himself."

"And we're assuming that if I can call one, the others will follow?"

"Yes," Mr. Pendergrass said.

Archie flicked the reins and scowled. "Then why didn't we do this last night while we were in London?"

Mr. Pendergrass sent him an arch look. "She was exhausted. I could have done it but it needs to be her spell, and she needs to be well rested and looking her best."

"Why?" I asked. I understood that I had been too tired and my thoughts too scattered last night to have performed the spell, but I didn't understand Mr. Pendergrass's last comment.

He laughed. "My dear, I am a wrinkled old man but you," he waved a hand absently in my direction, "you are a fair damsel in distress. It could make all the difference in their attitude. We are asking a great deal from them and a pretty face can't hurt. I'm hoping that there are some things even death doesn't change in a man," he said with a wink.

I grimaced, my stomach knotting in fear. "I don't think I can do this."

"Oh, come now," he said. "You've flirted your way through every ballroom in the *ton*."

"No, not that. I have no problem with that. I mean the spell. What if I try it and it doesn't work? Or what if it goes all wrong and something terrible happens?" I stomped my foot. "I've trained for this all my life and now that I have to do it, I'm terrified. This is not how it was supposed to be."

"No, it's not, and your fear is part of what's making you so unfocused. Don't worry," he said, patting my hand in what I'm sure was meant to be a reassuring manner. "I'll be there to help you."

Of course, that in itself was one of the things that had me worried. Now I had not only Mrs. Mackenzie and Fiona in the middle of this mess but Archie and Mr. Pendergrass as well. Archie's wife, Kitty, was off visiting her mother; she had no idea that I was leading her husband into danger. I felt ill.

At least with Mr. Pendergrass there, the others stood a fighting chance if the vampires ate me and came after them. I may have relented about the summoning spell, but there was still no way I would allow Mr. Pendergrass or any of the others to be present when the undead arrived. If things went wrong, I wanted them safely locked away in a secure room with every cross in the house and the rather large bottle of holy water I'd pilfered from St.

James' on the way out of town. I wondered if stolen holy water still worked.

We pulled into the drive at four in the afternoon. Ravenworth Hall always took my breath away with the afternoon sun bathing its three stories of gray stone walls in golden light. The manor house was relatively new, having been built at the beginning of the last century by my great-grandfather, who had wanted a country house closer to London than Ravenworth Abbey, somewhere the family could retire to, if they chose, while Parliament was in session. I loved this house with its walls covered in ivy and climbing roses, the gardens and the three hundred acres of parkland and forest, the pond where I had learned how to fish and swim.

My attention went to the front door as we pulled into the circular drive, my stomach quivering in relief as Mrs. Mackenzie and Fiona rushed down the front steps. I had never been so glad to see anyone in my life.

"No trouble last night?" I asked as I hopped down and hugged Mrs. Mackenzie.

"Not here," she said cryptically, and then turned her attention to the gentlemen in the carriage. "Good day to you, Mr. Pendergrass, Mr. Little."

Archie tipped his hat to Mrs. Mackenzie and then looked down at me. "I'll walk the horses down and put them in the stable for the night."

"The lads from the village went home about an hour ago," Mrs. Mackenzie said. "I'm afraid there's no one to help you."

"I'll manage," he replied with a smile.

"I'll lay a protection spell on the stable," Mr. Pendergrass said. "You, young lady, need to have a nice hot bath and get some rest. We have much work ahead of us this night."

"Thank you. Again," I replied, and Archie clucked to the horses and drove them around to the stable.

"You said we had no trouble here," I asked Mrs. Mackenzie as we walked to the door. "Was there trouble elsewhere?" Had Sebastian realized I'd fled and gotten angry?

Mrs. Mackenzie sighed. "Two mornings ago, one of the barmaids from the tavern was found dead, her throat cut. I didn't find out about it until you'd already left. This morning another girl from the village was found dead by the river, killed in exactly the same manner. Lord Lindsey's put a curfew on the whole village. They say that the girls were killed elsewhere and their bodies dumped because they'd lost so much blood, and yet there was none on the ground where they were found."

"The way we figure it," Fiona said, "Lord Montford must have drunk from them and then slit their throats to cover the bite marks."

"Lord and Lady," I moaned. Was that all my fault too? I was the reason Sebastian was here, after all.

No, I thought, shaking my head. No, I was not responsible for what he had become. Someone, some-*thing*, else had done that to him, made him the undead. They would pay. They would all pay for the lives they had stolen. I would work this spell and The Righteous would come and they would hunt these murderers down. The journal had said that that's what they did. And then life would go back to normal. Well, at least as normal as it ever was for a Macgregor witch.

"Maybe if there's no one he can get to in the village, it will mean he'll have to go farther afield to hunt tonight. It'll give us more time, at least, to do what needs to be done," I said, feeling a cold wave of guilt wash through me for speaking so plainly about the innocent life he would take tonight.

"So Mr. Pendergrass has come. Did you find a spell? Or some other way to kill the vampire?" Fiona asked.

"Something like that," I mumbled. I paused in the foyer at the foot of the stairs and looked up. There seemed to be so many more stairs than there had been a few days ago. I sighed. "You're not going to like the idea any more than I do but we really have no other choice. Come, I'll tell you the plan while I get ready."

Chapter Seven

We chose the ballroom to cast the spell. Ideally we should have used my mother's "private workroom," as she'd called it for the benefit of the servants, her sacred space. Instead, we'd chosen the ballroom out of necessity. It was a giant rectangular room with double doors spaced intermittently down three-quarters of each side, opening out onto spacious terraces and the gardens below.

My mother had always taken great pride in those doors because they could be opened during a ball to allow a nice cross ventilation. No one ever complained of stifling heat at a Craven ball. The doors on one end of the room gave way to the house, where guests would enter; the opposite end, where the terrace doors stopped, had solid walls with no windows. During a ball, it was here that the refreshment tables were always set up. High on this far wall was the minstrels' gallery. Mama always had the orchestra play from up there to allow for more room on the dance floor.

Under the gallery was where I would cast my circle. The theory was that the terrace doors would allow the vampires entrance without having them wandering all over the house, and the far end of the ballroom with its three solid sides would allow me to keep my back to the wall and see whatever was coming. I shuddered at the thought of what I was about to do and sank farther into my cloak.

I did look my best tonight. I'd chosen my hooded black velvet cloak with the crimson silk lining. Mama had had the cloak made for me for ceremonies and spell casting, but I'd taken to wearing it more often than that since I'd never quite understood the current fashion of constructing long, warm cloaks and then leaving off the sleeves. My dark copper hair was pulled up on the sides and fell in cascading curls to the center of my back. The pièce de résistance was what was under the cloak, which I was careful not to reveal to Mr. Pendergrass or the others, especially Mrs. Mackenzie.

The dress had been made for the mistress of a duke and surely not with the intention of going out in public. I'd bought it secretly from my modiste using every bit of pin money I'd had saved. I had seen it in the back room and had to have it. Of course, I could never wear it outside the privacy of my own room. It was a Cyprian's dress, a creation for a high-class courtesan. Made of crimson silk, which happily matched the lining of my cloak, it clung to every one of my generous curves. Shockingly sleeveless and scandalously low-cut in a deeply plunging V, its skirt fell from the satin band below my breasts to hug my hips ever so slightly and swirl out in a tiny flare at the floor.

At night when the house was quiet I frequently retrieved it from its hiding place in the bottom of my wardrobe and slid it on. I would put my hair up and dig out the stash of rouge and kohl I had secreted in my dressing table, darkening my lips and applying the kohl to my already-black lashes and around my eyes. I would stand in front of my mirror in my scandalous dress with my face all tarted up and pretend I was one of "those women." I was a viscount's daughter and I would never have the chance to be anything but prim and proper, but for a few hours every so often I would slip on this dress and pretend I was someone else, someone entirely *im*proper. I hoped that wearing the dress tonight would give me the courage to do what I had to do.

"Are you ready?" Mr. Pendergrass asked.

Mrs. Mackenzie, Fiona, and Archie were upstairs, safely locked away in my parents' suite with an arsenal of holy objects and the holy water from St. James'. Mr. Pendergrass would supervise my spell and then join them, keeping them safe while I waited.

I'd already laid out the circle of candles, more than I really needed for doing the spell, but, without lighting the great chandeliers, the ballroom would be dark as a cave in less than half an hour when the sun set. I stepped into the circle and laid the little stone bowl of charged herbs in the center. I also had a jar of sea salt for cleansing the sacred space. I should actually use sea salt and water, but I couldn't bring myself to pour that onto the exquisite hardwood floors; the salt alone would do and be easier to clean up later. Taking the jar, I walked to the edge of the circle facing north. Slowly I poured the salt out as I walked the circle clockwise.

"By the power of the Macgregor witches which dwells inside me, I consecrate this space to the Goddess and banish all negative energies which may reside here. I ask for the blessing of the Goddess that nothing shall enter here unless I allow it and no harm shall come to me inside this circle. Let the sacred circle be cleansed. So mote it be," I said solemnly as I completed the circle.

I looked at Mr. Pendergrass once more.

"Very good," he said gently, leaning on his amber-tipped staff. "Now cast your circle and work your spell. You can do this, Dulcinea. You've cast a circle dozens of times, seen it done thousands of times. Don't worry, I'll help you focus."

I nodded and walked back to the center of the circle and closed my eyes, giving myself up to the magic, not so much letting it in but letting it out. It was already inside me, now I just needed to free it, to let it work for me. I took the image I remembered of the iridescent gold wave in the Winter Garden and focused on it. I imagined it radiating from me and enveloping me, creating not just a circle but a sphere of magic, of protection, around me. I walked to the edge of my circle. Facing north I started to walk clockwise around the perimeter, visualizing the circle of golden energy following me until I'd walked the entire circle and the golden light filled it.

As I walked the circle the second time, I said, "By the power of the Macgregor witches which dwells inside me, I cast this circle to protect me from harm so that I may work in the name of the Goddess. I bless this circle in the name of the Lady and the Lord."

As I walked the third time around and came back to north, I said, "The sacred space is created, the circle is cast. So mote it be!"

I knew the instant the circle had closed; I felt it like a sharp click somewhere deep inside me. The circle was filled with golden light, light that came from me, and it was beautiful. I raised my arms to call the quarters, and with little more than a thought, the candles around the northern edge of the circle flared to life.

"Hail to the Guardians of the Watchtowers of the North, powers of the Earth Mother! I summon, stir and call you to aid my work and protect my circle. I hail and welcome you!"

I moved east and the candles there lit at my unspoken command. "Hail to the Guardians of the Watchtowers of the East, powers of Air and Invention! I summon, stir and call you to aid my work and protect my circle. I hail and welcome you!"

I moved to the south and the candles flared before I'd even thought to light them. I froze, scared. It meant that I was losing focus already. I certainly didn't want to get carried away and burn the house down. My mind reached out for Mr. Pendergrass and I could feel him, feel his energy, his magic, like a cool breeze across my skin, calming and steadying me. I took a deep breath.

"Hail to the Guardians of the Watchtowers of the South, powers of Fire and Passion! I summon, stir and call you to aid my work and protect my circle. I hail and welcome you!"

Turning west, I felt more in control; the candles lit as they were supposed to and I continued, "Hail to the Guardians of the Watchtowers of the West, powers of Water and Intuition! I summon, stir and call you to aid my work and protect my circle. I hail and welcome you!"

I returned to the center of the circle, to my little bowl of charged herbs. Kneeling, I put my hands on the bowl. The herbs inside would help in focusing and summoning. There was cinnamon, frankincense, myrrh, mint, and dragon's blood (which is actually a plant, not the blood of a dragon) crushed and mixed together in the bowl. I concentrated, feeling my palms tingle with warmth as I willed the herbs to a slow burn. Eventually the rather singular scent of the contents of the bowl reached my nostrils. It was time to work the spell.

"I call on you, Morrigan, Great Phantom Queen, Keeper of Death, to aid me as only you can. I call on you to fly far and wide on the wings of a black raven and bring to me those whom I seek. As the Keeper of Death, the guardian of those who have fallen in battle, I ask that you bring to me three of the undead, those whose lives you have taken but who still walk among us. I call The Righteous to me that they may aid me in my battle. Fly, Morrigan! Fly and bring them to me. By your grace, may my will be done. So mote it be."

I felt my power fling out of the circle, felt it flow through the very walls like an iridescent cloud, and move out into the world. It was like a fast-moving mist, rushing along green hills, through the forests. It was seeking, searching, like a hound after a fox. I sat very still and waited. I couldn't see images but I could feel it in my head, as if I were a part of the mist itself. I knew it when the wave of power entered a large concentration of people, because I felt its search slow. They must be in London; anyplace else with a population that large would have taken longer to reach. I felt the mist change shape. Taking the form of Morrigan's raven, it circled and dived through the streets. I was still sightless but I could feel the sensation of flying, the rush of the breeze past my face. And then it stopped.

I'd found them! I could feel two, the female and one of the males. It must have been Devlin, for he was old, older than anything I'd known, and strong. My power pulled at him and he resisted. The resistance was like a psychic slap. He was angry with me.

The spell moved to the female but he held her with

him, lending his strength. Searching, it moved on, finding the other male alone. By the Goddess, this one I would have! Taking a deep breath, I flung every ounce of concentration I possessed into the spell. Just as Sebastian had talked to me, so I talked to the Devil's Archangel.

"Come to me. Come," I whispered. And I felt him stir. I had him.

I felt horribly guilty about using the same sort of compulsion on the vampire that Sebastian had used on me. I knew how frightening it was, but it couldn't be helped. If I'd had time I would have gone into London and found them myself but there wasn't time. If I wanted to live there wasn't time. So I did what was necessary and I'd beg forgiveness later.

I stayed in the circle until I was sure that the vampire was coming and the two older ones hadn't stopped him. Satisfied, I gathered my energy and rose to close the circle. I began by releasing the quarters.

"Guardians of the Watchtowers of the West, I thank you for your aid and protection. I release you and bid you farewell."

I repeated this south, east, and north. I should have extinguished the candles as part of the ritual, but I didn't since I'd only have to light them again later to see by. When I reached north, I walked the circle once counterclockwise, pulling all that lovely golden energy back inside me as I walked.

"I open this circle and send its spell into the world, may it do my bidding. The circle is open but unbroken. So mote it be."

I stood in my circle, blinking a bit like someone who had just woken from a dream. *I'd done it! I'd really done it!* Or rather, *we* had done it. Mr. Pendergrass was leaning heavily on his staff. I had no illusions that I could have performed this spell myself. The magic was all mine, but without Mr. Pendergrass to help me focus, to lend his centering energy to my circle, I wouldn't have gotten past calling the quarters. I looked at him with appreciation and more than a little weariness.

"It worked," I said. "Did you feel it?"

"Yes. You did well tonight, Dulcinea. Your mother would have been proud."

I smiled at that. "So," I said with a heavy sigh, "now we wait."

He looked at me, smiling a tired smile that didn't quite reach his eyes, and nodded. "So now we wait."

Chapter Eight

Somewhere in the depths of the house a clock chimed midnight. I sat in the ballroom, alone, my back against the far wall, and waited. I'd taken off my cloak but the chill in the large, empty room soon prompted me to settle it back over my shoulders. I hooked the clasp, but didn't bother to put my arms through the sleeves. Snuggling deeper into the folds, I shivered. Dear Goddess, what had I done? I'd invited three vampires into my home to save me from the one outside it. I would have laughed if I'd been able.

The wind picked up, beating against the glass on either side of me like some living thing pounding to gain entrance. I picked my head up and looked around, my heart hammering in my chest. He was here; he was close.

One of the terrace doors to my left crashed open and the wind blew a swirl of dried autumn leaves into the ballroom, the leaves twirling around each other in little eddies like fairies waltzing across the floor. They drew my attention for only a moment. What stood in the doorway was far more fascinating.

I had expected him to be bigger somehow, like some great hulking demon, but the fact that he wasn't didn't dampen the frisson of sheer terror that blew through me when I first saw him. Terror, oh yes, and something else. Something that made my blood sing and my stomach tighten just to look at him.

He was several inches shy of six feet and built like some sleek, angry jungle cat. *Michael. The Devil's Archangel.* And indeed that face could have belonged to some fallen god or angel. He was too unearthly, too beautiful, too starkly dangerous to be real. His hair was dark blond and longer than had been fashionable any time in this century. It was tied back at his nape except for several strands that had worked themselves free, as if tousled by the wind or by a lover's hand. His brows were darker, set over eyes that were either blue or green, but what took a face that was merely handsome and catapulted it into the realm of mesmerizing or god-like were his cheekbones. Sharp as a knife's edge, they made my breath catch just to look at him. The candle-light flickered across his face, casting deep shadows in the hollows under those incredible cheekbones, drawing my attention down to his lips. Neither full nor thin, they were incredibly sensual, shaped in such a way as to make me wonder what they'd feel like against mine, what they'd feel like trailing along the bare skin of my throat. The thought made me shiver again but this time not from cold or fear.

In truth, he looked more like a pirate than a vampire. Tall black leather boots encased his legs up to mid-thigh and a simple white linen shirt was tucked haphazardly into his black breeches, as if he'd dressed in a hurry. Perhaps my summons had pulled him from a lover's bed? I didn't much like that thought. His shirt was open at the neck, exposing a smooth expanse of pale chest, its full sleeves gathered at the wrist in a small fall of lace. That lace should have looked feminine but instead drew my gaze to his hands, which gripped either side of the door frame. They were strong, the fingers long and blunted. His knuckles looked as if he'd seen more than his share of brawls, and I wondered briefly whose blood ran in the veins that stood out on the backs of his hands. He was not armed with so much as a dagger, but when his fingers clenched on the door frame and I heard the soft crack of the wood underneath, I realized that those beautiful, lethal hands were weapons in themselves. And even knowing that, all I could think of was what they would feel like on my skin, moving up my arm, drawing my hair aside, moving lower . . .

He made a sound, a growl like that of a jungle cat. A sound unlike any that had ever come from a human mouth.

"Witch," he whispered and pushed away from the door. And then he was moving, crossing the ballroom with such malevolent grace and inhuman speed that it was only two heartbeats before he was nearly upon me.

Driven by fear and an instinct for self-preservation, I raised one hand as he reached for me, and my power flowed out of me, hitting him in the chest and lifting him off his feet. In one fluid movement I spun both of us around and pinned him to the wall. He looked surprised, and quite frankly so was I, but there was no way in hell I was going to let him know that. He was suspended several inches off the floor, my hand on his chest. My fingers fairly itched to slip inside the open V of his shirt, to feel his skin. Would he be warm or cold? Raising my head I looked at him. Up close, his eyes were blue-gray, with a just a hint of green.

"Play nicely, vampire, or I'll stake you where you

stand," I said, my hood falling back as I looked up. "I have no wish to hurt you. I need your help, but I will defend myself if necessary."

He stilled, those haunting eyes slowly moving over every inch of my face, then lower to where my cloak fell open to reveal a generous swell of breast. His gaze lingered there. Tension hummed between us and if he had half as much interest in my body as I had in his, then perhaps I could use that to my advantage. I reached up with my free hand, flicked open the clasp at my throat, and with a shrug dropped the cloak to the floor. The silk lining slithered down my body with a sigh, leaving me clad in only the sleeveless crimson gown. I swayed and caught myself bare inches from pressing against him. The magic it was taking to hold him to the wall was draining. When he made no move to hurt me, I cautiously lowered him and turned him loose, my hand trailing needlessly down his chest. I felt his muscles contract under my fingers and had to force myself to pull away from him.

I reached up and brushed my hair away from my neck, exposing the two puncture wounds still visible there. He frowned, reaching out to touch me, his fingertips slowly tracing the bite, his thumb caressing the pulse at the base of my throat. Those deadly hands were warm and so very, very strong. I wanted to wrap myself up in him, to feel his arms around me, to feel safe again. My breath rushed out in a quivering sigh.

"I see you've met one of my kind," he said softly, his Scots brogue not as thick as it should have been, as if he'd lived a long time among the English. "What is it you want of me, lass? Vengeance? Shall I slay him for daring to lay his mouth on this pretty white flesh?"

There was a strange look on his face, a look of anger, of hunger, perhaps even of jealousy.

"No, I want you to slay him because he's going to kill me."

"Do you now?" he murmured.

"That is what you do, is it not? Protect the innocent?"

"And are you?" he asked, moving closer. His hand moved to my jaw, tilting my face up to his. His lips were so close. "Are you innocent?" he asked softly, and I had the feeling we were not talking about the same thing.

"She'd better be or I'll drain her dry for this," said an impatient voice behind me.

I gasped and whirled around, unconsciously backing up half a step and pressing my back against Michael's chest. I nearly groaned aloud when his hands slid up my bare arms to cup my shoulders.

Devlin, the Dark Lord. Michael had surprised me but the Devil was everything I had expected and more. Well over six feet tall, he was all darkness and menace. Black hair, black eyes, he was incredibly handsome with an arrogant nose and a square jaw. His neck was corded with muscle. A black silk shirt that he hadn't even bothered to tuck in fit his wide shoulders to perfection and skimmed the tops of his rock-hard thighs. His breeches were black and so were the boots that rose just above the knee. In one hand he gripped a sword that looked as if it weighed as much as I did, and yet he stood there, absently tapping it against one booted leg, as if it weighed next to nothing. By the Goddess, if Michael was like a lithe panther, this man resembled nothing short of a brick wall. I could see how he would have been the champion of his day. He leveled that dark gaze at me and inwardly I cringed.

"Do you know who we are, little girl?" he asked. His voice was incredible. Deep and gravelly, it scraped over me like sand against my skin.

"Yes," I answered. "You are The Righteous. You are the defenders of the innocent, the dispensers of justice to those of your kind."

"And *not*," he said with another slap of his sword, "to be dragged around like dogs on a chain by capricious little witches."

Michael chuckled behind me. "Now, Devlin, I'm the one she dragged from a warm bed, you simply followed. If anyone's to do the scolding here, it should be me."

"Ah yes, so sorry, old friend, that I interrupted the tongue lashing you were about to give her," Devlin said with healthy innuendo.

I squirmed and pulled away from Michael. "I apologize for the rudeness of my summons," I said with as much arrogance as Devlin was directing toward me, "but I needed your help and, honestly, what was I to do? Walk into any dockside pub and inquire as to where I might find three vampires? And not just any vampires, mind you, but The Righteous, the walking nightmares of the undead?"

Feminine laughter trilled through the ballroom. "Well, she certainly has you there, *mon amour*."

I had been so engrossed by the men, I hadn't even noticed the woman lounging in the doorway, one shoulder resting on the frame, her arms crossed under her breasts. Her breasts weren't as large as mine but were still more than ample, swelling temptingly above her courtesan's dress.

Justine. The Devil's Justice. She was everything Archie's cousin had written she was. Her hair was a pale silvery blonde, like the full moon on a wheat field, piled high with cascading ringlets. Her eyes were sapphire blue, tilted up at the corners like a cat's and darkened with kohl. Her lips were full and red, and the only thing that kept her face from being classically beautiful was her slightly Roman nose. It did, however, give her a look of strength, of something exotic. There was something indefinable about her that made you imagine her naked in a bed, all that glorious hair tousled around her, her eyes sleepy and heavy-lidded from lovemaking. And I was a woman! I couldn't imagine the effect she had on men. But she knew. Oh, yes. She had power, this one, and she knew well how to use it.

Devlin's eyes softened at the mere sound of her voice. He quietly transferred his sword to his left hand and, without even looking back at her, held out one hand. She stalked across the ballroom, hips swaying seductively, and nestled herself against him. She was tall, all legs under that gown, and she fit against him like she was made to be there. Laying her head on his shoulder, she regarded me with frank curiosity.

"Well, what have we here, *mon ami*?" she asked.

Michael moved up behind me again, reaching out and touching a lock of my hair, twining it around his finger. "I haven't quite figured that out yet."

At least two out of three of them were looking at me like I was perhaps dangerous, probably hysterical, and most likely wasting their time. I had the sudden fear that if what I had to say didn't interest them, and quickly, that I might end up as a midnight snack. One I could have handled, possibly two, but the three of them together were fraying my nerves. I fell back on the one thing I knew how to do with aplomb: be a gracious hostess.

Gesturing to the doors on the far side of the room, I said, "Perhaps we would be more comfortable discussing this matter in the green drawing room? I could offer you some . . ."

Oh, dear. What kind of refreshments did one offer the undead? I was betting tea and cakes wouldn't be their first choice but neither was I going to be so accommodating as to open a vein for any of them. I turned to Michael with a questioning look.

He smiled, and if there were fangs in his mouth, I couldn't see them. "A wee spot of that whiskey you were drinking earlier would do me well."

I jerked back and blushed slightly. Proper English ladies certainly did not drink whiskey and I was embarrassed to be caught at it. "How did you know?"

"Vampires have an excellent sense of smell," he said, retrieving my cloak from the floor and holding it out to me. I slipped into it and he offered me his arm. Leaning down, his face brushed against my hair. "You smell of whiskey and wild honeysuckle."

I took his arm, my fingers curling over his biceps, which flexed in reaction to my touch. My blush deepened as I imagined sinking my fingernails into those muscles, running my hands up to his shoulders, raking my nails softly down the hard wall of his chest. I shook my head to clear it of the wanton thoughts he seemed to evoke in me.

Devlin and Justine followed at a discreet pace. She was humming, and as I turned to look back, I saw him sweep her into a circle as if the wide expanse of the

ballroom was too much of a temptation for both of
them. He was surprisingly graceful for a man of his
size. Justine laughed, a sound low and throaty and full
of promise.

"Tell me, little witch," she called out. "How are you
going to explain our presence to your servants? Your
parents? Or is there a husband?"

I felt Michael stiffen at the mention of a husband.
"My parents were killed in a carriage accident a week
ago, the servants have fled, and no, there is no husband."

"You cannot be all alone in the house?" she asked.

I tensed. Was she merely curious, or was she hunting?

She laughed. "Ah, I see. You have them locked up in
a room somewhere, suitably armed with crosses and
holy water, no?"

I at least had the grace to look embarrassed, though
why I should be, I really didn't know. They were vampires, not country gentry. I had every right to protect
my household, such as it was, and yet somehow I felt
like a bad hostess for not being able to deny it.

"Don't worry so, lass," Michael said, "we wouldn't
touch members of your household. It would be the
height of bad manners to feed without our hostess's
permission, and yon Englishman there," he jerked his
head back at Devlin, "has no patience for bad manners.
At any rate, we've fed well this night already."

Chapter Nine

I opened the doors to the green drawing room and busied myself pouring four generous tumblers of whiskey. The decanter clanked loudly against the glass and I stopped and took a deep breath to steady myself. I had called them here, after all. No point getting cold feet now, especially when so much was at stake. When they each had a drink I sat in my mother's favorite chair, watching Michael swirl the amber liquid in his glass and then take a sip.

"Ah," he said, exhaling, a look of pure pleasure on his face. "God save George Smith."

"Hear, hear," Devlin answered and raised his glass.

Justine took a sip, wrinkled her nose, and settled back into the cushions of the chaise like some reclining empress. Her gaze lingered on the portraits of Charlotte Craven and Rainy Macgregor, which hung on the opposite wall. She grew very still and thoughtful as she stared at them and I wondered what she found so fascinating.

I downed my whiskey in one shot and turned back to the men.

"I didn't realize vampires ate or drank anything but . . . blood," I said.

"We can eat some foods and we can drink liquids other than blood," Michael allowed. "Sparingly, mind you. It doesn't give us sustenance. Still," he said, holding the glass under his nose and inhaling deeply, "a Scot would have to be dead a lot longer than I not to appreciate a good single malt."

I smiled at that and he winked at me in a brazen fashion.

"Now that we have answered your questions, little witch, perhaps you would be so good as to tell me why you summoned us from a very comfortable hotel to race hours through the night over what appears to be the bite of a newly-made vampire?" Justine asked, smoothing a hand over the curve of her hip.

I didn't particularly like the way she called me "little witch," though I could detect no intent to insult on her part and, like it or not, I was hardly in a position to quibble.

"How did you know he is newly-made?" I asked.

Devlin gestured absently with his glass. "Even with the help of a master vampire, an ancient, it still takes time for the body to complete all the changes that come with being one of the undead. The one who bit you cannot be more than two weeks dead or the wound would have closed within an hour of the bite and left no mark on your skin. He is young and has very little power. You, I think, have a great deal. What worries you so about him?"

"He calls to me," I said softly.

Michael and Devlin leaned forward in their seats and even Justine looked at me with new interest.

"What do you mean?" Michael asked intently.

"In my head, he calls to me. He wants me to come to him. I think he intended to kill me two nights ago when he bit me, but I surprised him, the extent of my power surprised him, and I got away. He cannot come into the house, so he calls me out instead. It took all my strength and both my housekeeper and her daughter to keep me from going to him. Tonight two friends of mine, apothecaries from London, have come to stay with me. If you cannot help me, then Mr. Pendergrass means to drug me, because if I'm unconscious I can't hear Sebastian's call."

"You know this vampire?" Michael asked.

"Yes. Sebastian, Lord Montford. He was a suitor of mine, an unwelcome suitor, but a suitor all the same."

"Do you know exactly when he was made?"

"Unless vampires can now walk in the sun, he was human as little as three weeks ago. He took me for a carriage ride through Hyde Park the day before he left London to go to Yorkshire on business. He returned a week ago. Why do you ask?"

Devlin answered. "He should not be able to call you to him. He *cannot* call you to him, not a vampire that young. Since we know for a fact that he is less than three weeks old, it means that the vampire who made him, an ancient, is working through him. It may be Montford's voice that calls to you, but he is only able to do so because his master wills it." Devlin paused and frowned down at his whiskey. "The question is, why?"

"Are you daft, man?" Michael said. "Look at her."

A low laugh sounded from the doorway. I turned to see Mr. Pendergrass shuffle into the room, leaning heavily on his cane. Archie hovered behind him, a dark scowl on his face as he surveyed the occupants of the room. Blast the men, could they not stay where they were told?

"While I applaud your taste, young man," Mr. Pendergrass said as he kissed Justine's outstretched hand, muttering "lovely, lovely" under his breath and then settling himself on the sofa next to Michael, "I think the answer to that question is a little more complicated."

"Mr. Pendergrass," I scolded, "you were supposed to stay upstairs."

"Yes, well, one of the benefits of reaching my advanced age is that I don't have to take orders anymore," he teased.

Archie stood protectively next to my chair, one hand resting on the back. Michael glared at him. Archie glared back. Michael growled low in his throat and Archie quickly removed his hand. Justine had a smile on her face as if she were watching some fascinating play unfold.

"You're a Scot, are you not, my boy?" Mr. Pendergrass asked, gently tapping Michael on the leg with his cane. Michael raised one brow and looked at me as if silently asking me if the old man didn't realize that he was addressing a man who had been on this earth, either living or undead, for a century.

I smiled, shook my head and shrugged.

"Yes, sir," he said respectfully, a hint of amusement in his voice. Mr. Pendergrass didn't seem to notice.

"You know of the Macgregor witches then?"

Michael's gaze jerked sharply to me. "They're nothing more than a highland myth," he replied.

Mr. Pendergrass chuckled. "Like vampires? Allow me to introduce you to Dulcinea Macgregor Craven, a direct descendant of Rainy Macgregor, and a woman who will have more power than even Rainy herself ever thought to possess."

"How do you know that?" Devlin asked.

"My lord, I'm a wizard myself and I've been supplying practitioners of the Craft for nearly as long as this one," he gestured again to Michael with his staff, "has been a vampire. I know witches and I know power when I see it. She hasn't learned to control what she possesses yet, but she will, and when she harnesses her power . . . well," he looked meaningfully at Devlin.

"So," Justine said, "this Montford, he doesn't want her as a woman, his master wants her power."

"Oh, Montford wants her all right," Mr. Pendergrass said, "and my guess is that's why the master chose him."

"If the master wants me so badly why doesn't he come for me himself?" I asked. "Why involve Sebastian at all?"

Devlin got up and paced the room. "To be able to control a vampire you've created requires great power, power that comes only with age. I am four hundred sixty-two years old and nowhere close to being able to do that. The vampire we seek is well over a thousand. It could be that he is simply enjoying the drama."

"So Sebastian died because some crusty old vampire is bored?" I asked incredulously. I didn't care much for Sebastian as a person anymore, but I'd never wished him harm either.

Mr. Pendergrass waved his cane. "Montford is irrelevant. This master vampire, if he managed to turn her, would he be able to control her like he does Montford? To harness her power?"

"Perhaps control was the wrong word," Devlin said. "To my knowledge even an ancient cannot *control* another vampire. We have free will. He could merge with her, get inside her head and use her power, but only if she allowed it. No, my guess is that the master doesn't want to turn her, he wants her alive."

I brightened some at that. "He doesn't want to make me a vampire?"

Devlin shook his head. "I have never heard of a human witch being turned. I'm not even certain that you would retain your magic or if it would die with your human body. I doubt the master is certain either. No, he would keep you alive so that he could be sure of your power and his control over you. Trust me though when I say that death would be preferable to living like that. If you followed Montford's call and they took you, they could feed on you night after night, never killing you, but keeping you in thrall to them. You would be like an opium addict, a shell of yourself and completely in their control. As a human you are weak, but as a vampire you would be strong, and immune to any compulsion the master could create. They would be fools to turn you."

"Will you help me then?" I asked softly.

Devlin looked at Justine and then at Michael.

"You cannot even think to leave her, Devlin," Michael said.

"You've never fought a vampire this old, Michael," he said. "It won't be easy."

Michael threw him a look of contempt.

Devlin turned to Justine. I didn't recognize the look she gave him but apparently he did. He sighed. "So be it."

He leaned down and kissed one of her silk-clad shoulders. "Go and change, my sweet. We hunt tonight."

The entire company stood as she rose.

"Mon amie," she said to me, "perhaps you would be so good as to lend me a change of clothing? This dress, it is pretty, but not much good to fight in."

"Of course," I replied. "If you gentlemen will excuse us?"

Devlin rose. "We have a carriage out front. May we use your stable for the horses?"

"Certainly," I said. "Oh, no. You can't go in there. Mr. Pendergrass laid a protection spell on the stable."

Devlin arched a brow at me.

"I love my horse, my lord. Sebastian knows me well enough to know that."

"I'll go with him," Archie said, "if he promises to keep his teeth to himself."

Devlin laughed. "My solemn oath."

The two departed. Justine stood waiting for me. I wasn't sure about leaving Mr. Pendergrass alone with Michael. It occurred to me that the vampires had just effectively split us all up. Was it a trap? I supposed there wasn't much I could do but trust them and hope it didn't cost us all our lives. It made my head pound just to think of all the ways this could go wrong.

As I walked across the foyer with Justine I asked her what she would require in the way of clothing.

She laughed. "I need only a man's shirt, if you have one to spare." She stopped at the bottom of the stairs, placing one foot on the second step and raising the hem of the deep purple silk skirt. Underneath the skirt and one petticoat she wore boots and breeches similar to Michael's. "So sensible, and yet Devlin will not allow me to wear them in public, only when we hunt."

I had to agree with Devlin. The riot that Justine would create walking around London in breeches and thigh-high boots was difficult to imagine.

"Justine," I said as we climbed the stairs, "Devlin mentioned something about vampire powers, about 'compulsion.' Do all vampires have these powers?"

I was thinking of Michael and the way I reacted to him, the way my body felt when he was near. Surely it was some kind of spell. I'd met many handsome men in my life, well maybe none quite as handsome as the vampire in my drawing room, but I had never reacted to any of them like this. Yes, it was definitely some kind of vampiric power.

"Older vampires, not one as young as this Montford, can bespell you with their eyes. We can make you dazed, almost comatose, so that we can feed and you won't remember it later. Only the true ancients acquire more varied powers, like calling to a human after they have fed from them as this one calls to you."

"But Michael, he's younger than you are. He doesn't have any other kinds of powers?"

She stopped on the landing.

"What is it you are asking, *mon amie*?"

I blushed and looked away. "It's just that he makes me feel . . . *things*." I left it there before I said anything more embarrassing. "I thought it must be some kind of spell or some part of a vampire's power."

She leaned against the wall and laughed.

"Forget it," I muttered and turned away. The throbbing in my head was getting worse by the second. It now felt as if needles were piercing my skull.

She grabbed my arm and it was like a steel band shackling my wrist.

"*Non*, forgive me. It has been so long since I was young and innocent, if I ever was innocent, that I had forgotten." She made a vague motion with her hand. "Our Michael, he is handsome, no?" With her French accent *Michael* came out more like *Meeshell*.

Surely by now my face was as red as my hair. She shrugged in a completely French way.

"It is to be expected. Vampires are generally a race of beautiful creatures," she said, "physically, at least. You see, when you create another vampire, it is usually for companionship, and you would not want to look at an ugly lover for eternity, *n'est-ce pas*? Michael, his beauty was sheer luck. Devlin made him because he admired Michael's skill with the sword, not because of his skill in bed. But to answer your question, no, Michael has no power over you except that of a handsome man. What you feel is not vampire power or a spell," she said with a sly smile, "it is sheer human lust."

Perfect.

I could count only two men in my life to whom I had been physically attracted. There was the footman when I was sixteen, and when I was eighteen there was Lord Beecham. Lord Beecham was a horrible womanizer. I remember my mother actually laughing in my face when I asked her if she thought he could be reformed. Now here was Michael and he wasn't even alive!

I sighed. Well, there you have it. Obviously I am defective in some way.

Come to me. Dulcie . . . come come come . . .

"No," I said, pressing my hands to my head.

"*Mon amie,* it is nothing to be ashamed of," Justine said, confused.

"No, no, no." I dropped to my knees and reached out to her.

"It is him, no? Montford?" she said, grasping me by the shoulders. "Michael! Quickly! *Vite!*"

Come to me, come to me, come to me, he called.

And I screamed.

Chapter Ten

The next thing I knew I was lying on the landing with Michael leaning over me, concern etched on his face. And then all hell broke loose.

"Get away from her!" I heard, and craned my neck to see Mrs. Mackenzie on the stairs, the bottle of holy water in her hand, her arm drawn back as if to fling it on the vampires. Fiona stood behind her with a rather large, ornately wrought gold cross. I had no idea where that had come from. I groaned in frustration. Did none of these people know how to stay put?

"Lassie," Michael said slowly, "tell her we aren't hurting you."

"Oh, no," Mrs. Mac said, coming one step closer. "No mind tricks, vampire. I told her this was a foolish idea."

Mr. Pendergrass thumped his staff on the bottom step. "Mrs. Mackenzie, he's not harming her, I assure you."

She looked skeptically at me. "Then why was she screaming?"

"Sebastian," I said. "He's back. They're only trying to help, Mrs. Mac. Please."

"Oh, baby," she said, thrusting the holy water at Fiona and kneeling down beside me. "Is it the same as last time?"

"Yes," I said. "He's close. Oh, gods! Devlin and Archie, they're out there at the stable all alone. What if he comes?"

Justine snorted. "He would be a fool to tangle with Devlin but I will go warn them just the same. *Mon ami,* take care of her."

She floated down the stairs in a flutter of purple silk. Mrs. Mackenzie's gaze followed her down as if she didn't know whether to disapprove of the former courtesan or admire her.

"Is there a room where we can stay that has no windows?" Michael asked.

"Just the dining room and the cellar," Mrs. Mackenzie answered.

"The dowager's suite," I said. "Grandmother had rheumatism and couldn't abide a draft. Her suite has heavy shutters built inside the windows. They lock very snugly. Will that do?"

"As long as no one comes along and opens them, that should do fine," Michael said. Bending down, he swept me up in his arms as if I weighed no more than thistledown.

"If you would be so kind as to show me the way?" he said to Mrs. Mackenzie.

Mrs. Mackenzie looked at him and then me for a moment. Nodding, she turned and started up the stairs.

"I can walk, you know," I whispered.

"Yes," he said, leaning his head down close to my ear, "but you wouldn't rob me of the chance to play the gallant hero, would you now, lass?"

I giggled and laid my head on his shoulder.

"Oh, Lord," Fiona muttered behind us as we all trooped upstairs to the dowager's suite.

* * *

I sat on the bed, huddled in my cloak. Mrs. Mackenzie, Fiona, Mr. Pendergrass, and Michael were standing around staring at me as if any minute I might conjure a demon to eat their faces off and make a break for the door. That's how Devlin and the others found us.

"What's going on?" he asked, dropping a large leather satchel at his feet.

"We're just waiting for her to turn us all into weasels," Fiona said brightly.

"Fiona!" her mother scolded.

I laughed. "No, she's right. I did accidentally turn Sebastian into a weasel the other night."

The vampires all took a step back from me.

"You can do that?" Michael asked.

"Apparently," I said. "Don't worry, though, it didn't last. The problem is that when he calls to me I feel compelled to come to him." I shrugged. "He makes me want to do anything necessary to get out of this house and go to him."

"He's close then," Devlin said. "We'll hunt him."

I looked at Justine, still in her fine dress. "Fiona, would you take Mademoiselle Justine to my father's wardrobe and let her have whatever clothing she requires?"

Fiona nodded and escorted Justine out the door.

"Do you know where the vampire is staying?" Devlin asked.

"Probably at his estate, which joins our property to the north." I sighed and shook my head. "We used to play there as children. His parents really didn't seem to care what he did until he came of age to go to school. We spent many afternoons together, sailing little boats down the creek or playing in the fields."

"And yet you say he was an unwelcome suitor?" Michael asked.

"He changed after he went off to Eton. I don't know what happened to him there, but when he came home for holidays, he was different."

"Different how?"

I shrugged. "Angry. Mean, belligerent. He kicked my dog once and I punched him in the nose and told him never to come here again. I didn't see him again until years later at social events in London. He pursued me and I spent some time with him, thinking he was grown up now and maybe he'd changed, maybe he could again be the nice boy I'd known."

"But he wasn't," Michael said, not a question but a statement.

I shook my head. "No. Oh, he was gentlemanly and courtly enough. He always said the right thing, was always solicitous of me, but there was still something dark and frightening behind his eyes that scared me. I tried to dissuade him but he just wouldn't give up."

"What exactly did he say to you the night he bit you?" Devlin asked.

I explained how Sebastian had come after dark to pay his respects, and what had transpired afterward, including my narrow escape.

Michael arched a brow. "You outran a vampire?"

"With a little magical help."

The bedroom door opened and Justine stalked in, there was no other word for it. The white blouse reached the tops of her thighs, the black pants clung invitingly and her long legs were encased in leather boots. Archie actually tripped over the leg of a table. Devlin rolled his eyes at the man.

"Did Sebastian say anything else?" Michael asked.

"Threats. 'You can't stay in here forever,' 'There's no escape for you' . . . et cetera, et cetera. Oh, and he said, 'We need you,' whatever that means."

Devlin just nodded. The humans in the room stared in fascination as he opened the leather satchel and started pulling out weapons. He handed several items to Justine and I watched as she strapped on a belt with knife sheaths attached at each hip. The sheaths were then buckled around each thigh so that she had two very wicked-looking daggers ready at hand level. Each dagger was set with a sapphire the size of my thumbnail in the hilt. She added a spine sheath with a short sword, which ran down her back. Devlin had one also and added two daggers himself, one in the top of each boot. He threw a sheathed sword and a dagger to Michael.

As they walked to the door, Justine paused in front of Archie. "I just realized why she knew to call for us," she said, cocking her head to one side. "Was he your brother?"

"Who?" Archie asked, confused.

"The slayer who was killed in London a few weeks ago. You have the look of him."

"He was my cousin."

Justine nodded. "If it brings you any comfort, I took the head of the one who killed him."

Archie opened his mouth and then closed it again, not knowing what to say. Justine smiled sadly and turned away. Devlin put his hand on Michael's shoulder when he moved to follow her.

"Justine and I will hunt," he said. "You stay here and watch the girl."

"I should be at your back."

"Someone strong enough to control her must stay here."

Michael paused, then glanced at me and nodded. "Good hunting, old friend."

Chapter Eleven

Dulcinea, you've been a naughty girl. What have you done? Come out, come out! You must be punished.

"Let me go!" I yelled as Michael grabbed me around the waist and hauled me back from the door.

A book and a vase flew past his head to smash into the opposite wall.

"Pendergrass!" he yelled. "Can't you do something about this flying debris?"

"I can give her laudanum so she'll sleep, but that's the best I can do."

"No," I said. "Please, not yet. I don't want to be helpless."

"We could tie you up again?" Fiona suggested.

"Oh, gods," I said, and sat down, my head in my hands. It felt like my head was a pumpkin that someone was carving out, this constant dull scraping inside.

"Did it work?" Michael asked.

"Mostly," I replied.

"Until she broke the chair to pieces and I had to knock her unconscious."

"Which we will not be doing again," I said, leveling my gaze at her. "I think you enjoyed that far too much."

"Did not," she muttered. "But we should probably tie you to something sturdier than a chair this time."

I caught Michael's gaze straying to the large, carved

oak bed. A small smile played on his lips and then he turned his attention back to me. I cocked my head, beckoning him closer.

"As much as I hate the idea, we should probably do as Fiona suggests," I whispered. "It won't keep things from flying around the room, but it'll keep me from running. One less thing to worry about. It's just that, well, I really don't want to be tied up with everyone standing around staring at me. Do you understand?"

He looked at me with those blue-gray eyes and his lips curved up in a small smile. "I'll take care of it."

He went over and spoke quietly with the others. Fiona slipped an arm around my shoulders and laid her head on mine.

"I love you, you know," I whispered.

"I love you too," she said. "Don't worry, we'll fix this. If anyone can, I think it's these three. He's quite handsome, is he not?" she said, nodding toward Michael.

I didn't answer. What could I say? Yes, he was the most sensual, attractive man I'd ever met. He was also dead. I could not be interested in him. A girl should have some standards, after all.

Mr. Pendergrass and Archie left the room. Mrs. Mackenzie came over to me.

"I'll go down and fix some tea and sandwiches for Mr. Pendergrass and Mr. Little. I'll leave Fiona to help you get settled and keep you company," she said, glancing at Michael. *Company,* as in chaperone. "You let me know if you need anything."

"The dawn would be good. Could you manage that?" I said with a smile.

"Impertinent baggage," she said with a hug, and left.

Fiona immediately took charge. She waved a hand in Michael's direction. "Shutter the windows and pull the drapes, and then bring two cords."

I groaned. "When this is over I'm going to burn every bloody drapery cord in this house."

"And I'll be more than happy to help you," Fiona said as she pulled off my cloak. "Jesus, Mary, and Joseph! Dulcinea Craven, wherever did you get that dress?"

Damn. I'd forgotten the dress. "Not a word to your mother, Fiona Mackenzie," I said. "And keep her out of here until dawn."

Fiona narrowed her eyes at me. "On one condition."

"What?" I asked skeptically.

"You let me try it on tomorrow!"

"Agreed."

Michael returned with the dreaded drapery cords. I sighed and sat down on the bed. It was the only thing in the room that was too heavy for me to break if things went badly.

"No," Fiona said. "Best get under the covers, that way if anyone comes in we can pull the spread up over that dress."

I pulled the sheets down. Michael stood across from me and we stared at each other over the empty bed. How easy it would be to crawl across that bed, kneel before him, run my hands up his chest.

"Fi, why don't you go get some rest?" I said, my eyes never leaving his.

"Because I'm supposed to be the chaperone," she said loftily.

"And you can chaperone just as well from the wonderfully comfortable settee in the next room."

She looked at me and then at Michael, and then smiled a wicked smile. "I can, can't I?" she said, humming as she left.

I lay down on the bed and watched as Michael tied one of the braided silk drapery cords to the bedpost. He stopped and looked down at me. I offered up my right wrist.

"I'll leave some slack in it," he said. "No sense in you not being able to move a bit. You'll break the bedpost before you ever break these cords."

He tied my wrist. I could move my arm down until my elbow nearly touched my side. He walked around to the other side.

Dulcinea! Stake him and be done with it. I grow tired of these games.

"Hurry," I whispered. He tied the cord tight.

You think these two can stop me? My master and I will kill them both and then I will come for you. Come to me now and save the lives of those you love.

"No," I moaned.

"What is it?"

"He knows they're there. He's hunting them."

"Do not worry for Devlin and Justine," Michael said, but there was something in his eyes that hadn't been there a minute ago. Not worry exactly, but concern, restlessness. He wanted to be out there hunting and I didn't blame him. I watched him pace the room.

"Talk to me," I said. "Distract me. It might help."

He stopped pacing and ran a hand through his dark blond hair. "What do you want to talk about?"

"Legend has it that you died at Culloden. Is that true?"

He sat at the foot of the bed. "No, I didn't make it that far. 'Twas Falkirk."

"They say you're an excellent swordsman. Were you always a soldier?"

He sat there and looked at his hands as if seeing them for the first time. At first I wasn't sure he was going to answer me. Then he said softly, "No. I was a gardener, actually."

My eyes flew to his face. I hadn't expected that. The Devil's Archangel had been a gardener? Surely not.

"I'd wanted to be an apprentice to the blacksmith, but he wouldn't take me because I wasn't big enough or strong enough. My father was dead, and there wasn't enough food to feed my mother and sisters and my little brother. The head gardener at the big estate down past the village had known my father. He took pity on me and gave me a job. It didn't pay well but it kept us from starving, mostly."

"How old were you?" I asked.

"Eight," he said. "The laird's son was my age. He used to practice fencing in the gardens. He caught me watching him one day and asked if I'd like to try it. Before long we were practicing every day. I don't think he'd have had any use for me if he'd had anyone else to practice with, but I didn't mind. The gardeners were more than happy to turn a blind eye, because if the wee devil was fencing with me, then he wasn't attacking the roses. Eventually his instructor even allowed me to take part in their lessons.

"I was good at it and I learned everything I could. When I was sixteen I went to Edinburgh. I trained with all the best swordsmen—known masters, street toughs, anyone who would teach me. At night I would work at the pubs, the docks, anyplace I could earn some money to send home."

"And your goal was?"

"My goal was to learn enough, to become good enough, that rich aristocrats would pay me my weight in gold to teach their sons."

"Did it work?"

"I'll never know. The war came. I signed on to fight for the Jacobites. I figured with my skill I could make a name for myself." He laughed bitterly.

"And Falkirk?"

"The battle started late in the afternoon. It was raining and so dark and gray, you know how it gets in Scotland in January?"

I nodded.

"We won the battle, didn't last more than half an hour, I expect, but there was such a mass of confusion, some saying we won, some saying we lost. By dark there were still stragglers. I was one of them. In my youth and arrogance I thought to take a few prisoners back with me. I had it in mind to be a war hero, if you can believe that." He shook his head ruefully and sat quietly for a minute.

I waited patiently, afraid if I said anything, he wouldn't continue.

"There were three of them, English, alone, turned around in the dark just like me. I engaged them. The rush of battle, the feel of the sword in my hand, it was better than whiskey. I would have taken all three of them. It was nearly over when a fourth redcoat came out of nowhere.

"I never heard him, never saw him. I had disabled two of the Englishmen in front of me and was making quick work of the third when all of a sudden," he looked down like he was seeing it, "there was a sharp pain, not really anything like I would have expected, shock I guess, and I looked down and there was this sword sticking out of my stomach. Bloody coward crept up behind me and stabbed me in the back. It still amazes me that no matter how many battles you fight, no matter how many men you see die, knowing that you could be next, it still comes as a surprise when it's you. I almost wish I could have seen the look on my face when it happened."

"What happened then?" I asked. Sebastian was being strangely quiet, and I wanted to hear the end before he started up again.

"I lay there on the ground, curled on my side with my hands over the wound as if I could somehow stop the blood from flowing out onto the ground. The English soldier was laughing and helping his mates to their feet. Then I heard a growl and this giant of a man came out of the darkness. He was more terrifying than anything I'd ever seen. In a matter of seconds he massacred the four Englishmen and then he knelt by me. I'd heard him speak; I knew he was no Scot. I thought he was going to kill me," he laughed. "I guess you could say he did. He said something to me about fighting well, but I was too weak and too near unconsciousness to understand. I remember him lifting me in his arms like I weighed nothing. And when I woke, I was healed and I was strong, and yet I was still very, very dead."

Dulcinea, avoiding your assassins is getting tiresome. Come out, my dear, because if I have to make you, you will be a very sorry girl.

"You can't make me and you know it!" I shouted.

Michael cocked a brow at me.

"Not you," I said, my breath coming quickly from the pain in my head. "Sebastian keeps interrupting."

"Devlin will find him soon," he said, and laid a hand on my knee. "Is there anything I can do to help? To distract you from it?"

I looked at that hand, only a scrap of silk between it and my bare flesh. "Yes," I breathed. "Hit me or kiss me."

He looked up sharply. "Kiss you?" he asked.

And yet he didn't move. He just sat there staring at me, me staring at him, tied to the bed, wishing I could take back my words. And then he shifted. Bringing his other leg up onto the bed, he crawled toward me on hands and knees. Muscles that I'd never imagined existed moved under his clothing. He hung there, hovering over me, a lock of hair falling across his face. I reached up a hand to brush it back but the cord wasn't long enough. He tucked it behind his ear and then ran his fingers down my face to cup my chin.

"My God," he whispered, "you're the most beautiful thing I've ever seen. Are you sure?"

I stared at that sensual mouth, his lower lip slightly fuller, slightly parted. Waiting for my answer. He wouldn't take advantage of the fact that I was tied to the bed, helpless. No, he was going to make me ask for it.

"Please," I begged. I'd never wanted anything more.

His mouth swooped down and my eyes drifted closed, all thought of anything but Michael fled from my mind. His lips were like the silk cords that bound my wrists, smooth and strong. His tongue ran across my lower lip. I moaned and he moved inside.

I'd been kissed before but nothing could have prepared me for this. It was as if we were both dying of thirst, drinking of each other and never getting enough.

One hand ran down the side of my breast, past my waist and over the swell of my hip. He grabbed the fabric of my skirt and pulled it up past my knees. I was shaking but I didn't stop him, couldn't have even if I'd wanted to. He settled between my thighs, his hand moving up to cup the back of my head. Something innately female inside of me understood what he wanted. I raised my legs and wrapped them around his waist. He groaned and pressed into me. I could feel him against me, nothing between us but the fabric of his breeches. I pulled at the cords binding my wrists. Lord and Lady, I wanted my hands free. I wanted to feel every inch of him. I was quivering when he finally pulled free of my mouth and ran his tongue down the side of my neck. I stiffened when I felt the sharp brush of teeth against my pulse.

I'd forgotten. For a few brief, shining moments I'd forgotten what he was. He laid his head on my chest, breathing heavily, shaking.

"Don't worry," he said, his voice so hoarse it was almost unrecognizable. "I won't do it. God help me, I want to, but I won't."

He sounded like he was in so much pain that for an instant I nearly offered myself to him, let him taste me. Would I have done it? I don't know. At that moment pain ripped through my chest. I arched my back and screamed. Michael jerked back, staring down at me in confusion. I looked down myself, half expecting to see my chest ripped open, the pain was so real. I screamed and twisted, trying to break free, to claw at whatever was ripping at my chest.

The door to the bedroom flung open. "What the devil do you think you're doing?" Fiona shrieked.

"Come here," Michael yelled. "Something's wrong."

Fiona's worried face bobbed into view. They both gasped and Michael, still kneeling between my legs, moved back, his hands brushing the skirt of my dress down as he moved.

"What is that?" he asked, his voice hoarse with fear now. "What's happening?"

What indeed? They were both staring at me in such horror that I pushed down the pain and turned my face toward my hand, trying to feel what they were staring at. My hair was in the way.

Ah. I knew then.

"The glamour," Fiona said in awe.

"What do you mean, lass? What's happening?"

Fiona shook herself. "It's the glamour, the first spell she ever learned. Aunt Lora, er, her mother, said her hair color was unnatural, said people would talk, so she taught her to hold the glamour and hide the color. It's as natural as breathing to her. When we were young I once saw her fall from a tree and break her arm, and she never dropped her glamour. I can't imagine the pain she's in to be unable to hold the spell. I haven't seen her true hair color since we were small children." She looked into my eyes, saw my ragged breathing. "I'd better get the laudanum."

She ran from the room. Michael reached out and took a lock of my hair in his hand, staring at it in wonder. Gone was the natural, coppery color I'd seen every day of my life. In its place was my true color, a deep scarlet red like fine rubies. Michael cocked his head as if listening, and then moved off me, pulling the bedspread up to my chin. I thrashed and moaned. He pinned my shoulders down with his palms.

"Easy, darling, we'll get you something to take the pain away and make you sleep. Devlin's found your vampire and that's probably what you feel."

"Did you know?" I choked out.

"That you would feel Montford's pain? No, lass, I swear it. I'd have given you the laudanum first thing if I'd even suspected. I'd never intentionally cause you pain. If you believe nothing else of me, believe that."

There was a clamor in the antechamber and Mrs. Mackenzie and Fiona rushed in, followed closely by Archie and Mr. Pendergrass. They all stopped and stared. Mrs. Mackenzie recovered first, pouring out a spoonful of the drug and putting it to my lips.

"Sleep now, baby," she said, "where he can't hurt you."

My head was getting fuzzy. I saw Michael spin around as if in slow motion.

"They come," he said. He inhaled sharply. "Something's wrong."

He moved swiftly to the door and everyone cleared a path. A moment later Devlin came striding in carrying Justine. Her white blouse was soaked with blood, but she was conscious, clinging to his neck. Like some avenging demon, he stalked to the side of the bed and drew the big sword from its sheath along his spine. In one fluid movement he sliced through the drapery cords that bound me. A collective sigh of relief washed over the room. Maybe it was the influence of the drug, but I hadn't thought for a second that he meant to harm me. I pulled my arms under the covers, rubbing my wrists, and used every last ounce of strength to scoot to one side of the bed so he could lay Justine down.

She turned her head to look at me and smiled weakly. Devlin grabbed her face in both his huge hands and, with his nose inches from hers, shouted, "You willful little bitch! When I tell you to run, you run! Do you understand?"

"We . . . do not . . . run," she said defiantly.

"We bloody well do when I tell you to. You have no idea what you were fighting. It's sheer luck and stupidity that you're not dust and bone right now," he yelled, shaking her as he did so.

"Devlin," I whispered, "is this really productive right now?"

His head snapped around and the pure menace in his glare would have made me jerk back if I'd thought I could move. The room was starting to spin. Devlin turned back to Justine with a growl, kissed her hard on the mouth, and pushed away from her in a swift, angry movement.

"She needs blood," he said, glancing at the clock on the mantel and then at Michael. "We have just enough time to make it to the tavern in the village and back again."

"You won't find anyone there," Mrs. Mackenzie said. "Sebastian has been leaving bodies scattered about the countryside and the magistrate's ordered a curfew for the entire village."

"Dammit!" Devlin roared.

"She can drink from me," I said weakly. "The laudanum already in my blood might even help her rest."

"No," Michael said.

"It's fine, Michael. She risked her life for me. It's the least I can do. Please."

"You're too weak," he said.

"I am not weak," I said fiercely. "I'm drugged, there's a difference."

"How much blood does she need?" Archie asked, stepping forward, his gaze on the blonde beauty lying next to me.

"You'll feel lightheaded when it's over but that's the worst of it," Michael said. "She can't take enough in one feeding to kill you."

Archie nodded. "I owe her for avenging my cousin. I'll do it."

"You . . . do not owe me . . . anything, *mon ami*," Justine said.

"It would be an honor," Archie replied, loosening his cravat.

Devlin looked at him, jealousy etched across his handsome features for a brief moment, and then he nodded.

I closed my eyes. It was too much trouble to keep them open anymore. So, what did you do when the cavalry retreated, broken and bloody?

Damned if I knew.

Chapter Twelve

I woke to Fiona slapping me lightly, and then a bit harder, on the cheek. How long had I slept? Not long, not nearly long enough. I could barely open my eyes to focus on her face.

"Wake up," she said, her voice sounding as if she were speaking to me from down a long, dark tunnel. "We don't have much time before the others return. I've brought a nightgown and I'll hide this dress if you'll just help me get it off."

For a minute I couldn't remember where I was or why. Then I turned my head and saw Justine lying on the bed next to me, her face pale and lifeless. Was she dead? They'd removed the bloody shirt and, I assumed, her breeches and slipped her into one of my nightgowns.

"She's fine," Fiona said impatiently. "Can you sit up?"

I nodded; it was too much trouble to try to speak.

"Do you need help?" came a deep, masculine voice from across the room, rough and gravelly. Devlin.

"What I need," Fiona said, "is for you to keep your back turned as you promised."

He grunted.

Fiona unbuttoned the dress with ease. It had taken me half an hour of twisting and turning to get those buttons latched without help. I was still almost certain I'd missed several of them, but my long hair hid those that were hardest to reach. Fiona slid my legs over the side of the bed. For some reason I couldn't get them to work properly.

"All right, up with you now." With that she grabbed my arms and pulled me to my feet. My knees buckled and I fell into her. I tried to reach out to the nightstand to steady us but only succeeded in clipping Fiona in the jaw with my elbow. She grunted and we tumbled into the nightstand with a heavy thud.

"Oh, bloody hell, woman," Devlin growled and moved across the room. "All this fuss over a silly dress. She's a grown woman, isn't she? She should be able to wear what she wishes."

"You tell that to my mother," Fiona grumbled. She was trying to push me up and I was trying to help, truly, but my body felt like lead.

Devlin grabbed me from behind, pulling me off her. "I'd rather just get this over with," he said, taking hold of my wrists and pulling me up like a marionette.

Fiona giggled. "Coward."

He growled at her.

Fiona reached down and grabbed the hem of the skirt. "Look at the ceiling."

"You've got to be joking," he said.

"Help if you want to, but avert your eyes."

"Little girl, I am four hundred ninety years old. I've seen plenty of naked women."

"Not this one you haven't. Now, avert your eyes."

He snorted but must have done so, for Fiona pulled the dress up and shoved it over my head.

"You have absolutely no fear of me, do you?" Devlin asked.

"No," she said with a smile as she unlaced the short

corset, "but remind me later and I'll try to work some up for you."

"Impudent wench."

Between the two of them, they managed to get the dress, petticoat, corset, and chemise off and slide the flannel nightgown over my head. Devlin lifted me in his arms and laid me on the bed, gently pulling the covers over me.

"Sleep, little witch," he said. "We have many problems to sort through when you wake."

Many problems. Lovely.

I succumbed to the sucking void and slept.

Six hours later I was sitting up in bed, propped up on pillows, staring at three vampires and four humans, a forgotten cup of tea raised halfway to my lips.

"She's a what?" I asked slowly. Oh, this just kept getting worse and worse. Maybe I was still groggy from the drug and I'd misheard.

"A demon," Devlin said. "Montford's master is an ancient, very powerful demon."

Justine was pacing, my dark blue dressing gown swirling around her bare feet. Whatever her wounds last night, she seemed to be healed now. "Looked like a vampire to me," she muttered.

"Well, she wasn't, not exactly. I knew it and that's why I told you to run. The next time you will obey a direct command or there will be no more hunts for you."

She stomped over to the chair next to the bed and flung herself into it with a petulant flourish.

"So, let me get this straight," I said. "Sebastian's master, the one who wants me so badly, is a woman and a demon and not *exactly* a vampire? Explain please."

A muscle ticced in Devlin's cheek as he regarded me for a moment and then said, "She is Kali, the Destroyer."

Mr. Pendergrass stood. "She's a Hindu goddess?"

"No, no," Devlin said, waving a hand, "she just liked the name. Whatever her true name was, it is long lost to the mortal world. She has been the Destroyer since before Jesus walked the earth."

"She's that old?" I asked.

"She's older than anything you can even imagine."

"And a demon?"

"Yes. Finding a true demon is rare. For one to exist in this reality, it has to take a shape that is natural to our world. Demons find the human body too limiting. You could live five hundred years and never see one."

"So there are other . . . realities, other worlds, if you will, where demons reside?"

"Yes."

"And they can just hop into our world at will?"

"Well, it's a bit more difficult than that and takes very powerful magic to accomplish, but essentially that is correct."

"So if demons don't like our world, then why is she still here? Why hasn't she gone home? Two thousand or more years is a long time to stay in one place, especially if you don't like the body you're wearing."

"She can't go home. She's bound here," Devlin sighed, raking his hands through his black hair. "Let me start at the beginning. When Kali entered this world, this plane of existence, she took the body of a newly-dead East Indian princess. Her subjects, who had gathered to mourn the passing of their young princess, worshipped her as a goddess when she rose from the dead. Being an immortal demon trapped in the mortal body of a human, she came to realize that eventually her body would age and it would die."

"Let me guess," I said, "she liked her human body and she liked being worshipped as a goddess and so she found a vampire to make her immortal."

He nodded. "She killed many of her people, bathed in their blood. The peasants worshipped her in fear but the holy men knew her for what she was. The temple priests laid a powerful spell on her, attempting to send her back to her reality and bind her there. It worked only in part. They failed to send her back but succeeded in binding her. Instead of sending her home, they chained her to this world. It could be that she wants you because she thinks you can break the spell."

"It's impossible. Only the one who laid the binding spell can undo it. Surely she knows that by now."

"I don't know," Devlin said, shrugging his shoulders.

"Mr. Pendergrass," I asked, "I am right about this, aren't I? Only the one who laid the spell can break it, right?"

"That is my belief. However, if she is this determined, maybe she's gained some knowledge over the centuries that we have lost."

"You mean it might be possible to break the binding? That she might possess a spell that would do it, and for some reason she thinks that I can work it?"

He nodded once, slowly. "It is possible."

"If the binding spell were broken she could again travel between worlds," I thought aloud, to no one in particular.

"Thousands would die," Devlin said softly. "Coming to this world, becoming a vampire, it wasn't a plan for the future, it was a pleasant diversion. Now she's trapped here and she is not happy about it. If she could again move between worlds, without the limitations of the undead, she would be unstoppable."

"You don't think she would just go home?" I asked.

"I think she would wreak bloody vengeance."

"But she is stoppable now," I said slowly. "As a vampire bound to this realm she is, in theory, killable. Right?"

He nodded slowly. "We aren't truly immortal. We can be killed."

"So," Michael said, moving to stand next to me. "When do we kill her?"

"We don't," Devlin said grimly. "We run."

"What?" This from me, Michael, and Justine in unison.

"What are you talking about?" Michael said. "We don't run from a battle. You taught me that."

Devlin pointed at Justine. "She didn't run either and she got a sword through the chest for it."

Justine pulled herself up straight in the chair and said haughtily, "But not before I gave the same to her pet, Sebastian."

I rubbed the spot in the middle of my chest, right above my heart, where the pain had nearly eaten me alive last night. Michael saw and pulled my hand away, giving it a small squeeze.

"Devlin, what's going on?" Michael asked. "We are the protectors of the innocent. We do not run from vampires. There must be something we can—"

"God *damn* it!" Devlin roared, and Mrs. Mackenzie, Fiona, Archie, and Mr. Pendergrass moved back against the wall. "I have fought wars on four continents. I have led men to their deaths in battle. I have killed thousands who stood against me over the centuries. I have never failed in any mission I have undertaken. Do you think it pleases me to have to say that this is a fight we cannot win? Do you?"

He snatched up a porcelain figurine of a shepherdess and sent it crashing into the far wall. Bracing his hands on the table, he hung his head and reined in his temper before saying slowly and calmly, "The Destroyer has not lived for millennia by being weak or stupid. Trust me, I know her. I had the misfortune of *enjoying* her hospitality once. She's stuck in this world and the only joy she knows is death and pain, and she has perfected the art of both. We run or we all die. Take your pick."

The silence in the room stretched from seconds to minutes.

"If I were to run . . ." I said softly.

Everyone looked at me.

"I have plenty of money. I can run as far as I need to. But she'll come for me, won't she? She'll follow me. For the rest of my life I'll be running and looking over my shoulder until she finally catches me. Won't I?"

"Yes," Devlin said, his voice full of regret.

"Or, option two, I do what she wants, which, as far as I can see, will result in one of two things: If I *can't* break the binding spell, then she's going to kill me, and I'm going to assume it won't be quick or easy. If I *can* break the binding, then thousands of innocent people will die, and she'll probably still kill me anyway. I'm dead if I do and dead if I don't."

No one answered. They didn't need to. I took a deep breath, feeling a strange sense of calm wash over me.

"There's only one answer then," I said, looking at Devlin and then Justine, my gaze coming to rest on Michael's beautiful face. "One of you is going to have to kill me."

Chapter Thirteen

"No!" Fiona cried, as she flew at Devlin, beating at him with her fists. "You were supposed to help! You were supposed to fix this! What good are you then? What good?"

Devlin stood there like a statue and allowed her to hit him, a look of shock and puzzlement on his face as if he didn't quite know what to do with her. I got up and ran to her, grabbing her hands and enfolding her in my arms. Mrs. Mackenzie looked equally stricken. I stared at her over Fiona's head. She swallowed hard and started picking up dishes and stacking them on the tea tray. I understood. It was something familiar to do, something to keep herself occupied so she wouldn't have to think.

"No," Michael said. "No, I won't allow it. There has to be another way."

He crossed the room and I turned from Fiona's weeping form. He grabbed my face in both his hands.

"We'll run if that's what we need to do. I'll stay with you. I'll protect you."

"Even when I'm old and wrinkled and you still look like a god?" I laughed harshly.

He smiled. "Even when you're old and wrinkled and don't remember my name or your own. I'll keep you safe."

"You know, *mes amies*," Justine said. "There may be another way."

We all turned to her, hoping.

"If she must die, she does not have to *stay* dead, now does she?"

Michael was already shaking his head.

"*Non*, listen." Justine turned to Mr. Pendergrass. "You say she will be a great witch one day, no?"

He nodded.

"If she were a vampire she would be young and strong forever. She will have none of her human weaknesses. *Mon amour* says we cannot fight the Destroyer, that she is too strong. This I have seen. She has magic of her own to call. It is not like human magic. It is the power of a demon. Who is to say, though, that given enough years, *mademoiselle's* magic will not be stronger than the Destroyer's? She could kill the demon with our help."

"But Mr. Pendergrass said that I may not even keep my magic, that it might die with my human body."

Devlin shrugged. "Then without your magic you are of no use to her."

I swung on Mr. Pendergrass. "The magic. It's what she wants. Can you take it away? A binding spell or a ritual?"

He shook his head sadly. "I can bind you from certain acts, say from performing particular spells or from doing harm, but I cannot take the magic away. It is a gift from the Goddess and only she can take it from you."

I walked to the window and put my hand on the closed shutters. I wanted to feel the sun, to feel something good and pure in all this darkness.

"I need to be alone," I said and shoved my way through the crowd, snatching up my dressing gown as I fled.

I was kneeling in the Winter Garden, staring down at a small patch of evening primrose, rubbing the velvet petals between my fingers, when I heard the drawing room door open and close. I looked up and saw Michael standing in the shadows, the morning sun not yet flooding the room with light. I stood up and brushed the dirt from my nightgown. Giving the happy little flowers one last look, I walked into the drawing room.

"The sun is up. Shouldn't you be sleeping?"

He shrugged. "I don't have to sleep during the day any more than you have to sleep at night. I can even stand here and look out at the sun on the garden, as long as I don't walk outside. They shouldn't be blooming, you know," he said, nodding at the yellow flowers.

"I know, it's the magic. They'll die in a few more days I'm sure." I laughed bitterly, thinking that in a few more days I would probably be dead too. "It's so useless."

"What is?"

"This magic. I can feel it inside me, filling me up, and I can't control it enough to use it."

"I don't understand," he said.

"Turning Sebastian into a weasel, I didn't mean to do it. I thought he was a weasel and there he was . . . weaseled. I shouldn't be able to do that, Michael, not with a mere thought. The dress I wore to my parents' funeral? I was upset and I simply *thought* about burning it and the thing went up in flames. I do well enough in a structured setting, like when I worked the spell to summon you, but when my emotions are running wild, it's anyone's guess what might happen. You've seen the books and chairs flying all over the room. I don't mean to do that, it just happens. I have no control over it and I don't know *how* to get control over it."

"But you've trained, I heard Pendergrass say so."

"Yes," I said, hugging myself. "Since I was eight years old, and even before that. I don't know how to explain it to you." I paced the room, thinking. "All right, say you're a child and you're going to be a swordsman when you grow up. You spend your life watching other swordsmen, reading everything you can get your hands on about the art, and then one day when you're twenty-two, someone puts a sword in your hand for the very first time. You know all there is to know in here," I said, tapping one finger to my head, "but you've never actually held a sword before. Now do you understand?"

He nodded. "It must be extremely frustrating."

"That," I said, "is an understatement."

Michael moved in front of me and grasped my shoulders. "We can fight her, and we will. Devlin may not have been able to beat her before, but there are three of us now. The Destroyer is dangerous, she's a killer, but this is what we do."

"But you heard what he said. She's too strong. You'll die."

He shrugged. "I've already lived far longer than I have a right to. I will die in battle one day, I've done it before. I'm a vampire, Dulcie. I won't die asleep in my bed. If I fall against the Destroyer, then at least it would have been for a good cause."

I leaned into him and laid my head on his shoulder. "Don't be stupid," I said. "I won't have you all die, not when I can save you. The world needs you . . . and I'm just a girl."

He stiffened and whispered, "Why do you care so much?"

I looked up into his eyes. "Why do you?"

He brushed the side of my face with his hand and then ran his fingers through my hair, looking at it as if it were something precious. "I've been content with who I am for many years. I've enjoyed what I do, and up until last night, I wouldn't have traded it for any other existence."

"And now?"

"You make me wish I were human," he said softly.

I laid my head back on his shoulder, slipping my arms around him, my fingers splaying over the hard muscles of his back. "That's funny," I said with a sigh. "You make me wish I weren't."

Chapter Fourteen

I rode Missy into the stable yard two hours before sunset. Dismounting, I tossed the reins to one of the village boys and walked into the stable. Devlin's giant coach was pulled in alongside our older town coach. The vampire's coach had been specially made, I was sure, to fit his large frame, the velvet seats inside easily accommodating three people across. There was a coat of arms emblazoned on the door: a black falcon with its wings outspread; under the right wing was a golden fleur-de-lis and under the left a white Jacobite rose. The motto inscribed around it was in Latin. I memorized the phrase, intending to look it up in the library later. Latin had never been one of my better subjects. One of the village boys was just bringing the first of Devlin's four matching grays in from the paddocks.

"Charlie Harper, correct?" I asked. He and his two younger brothers were the tavern keeper's sons.

"Yes, miss," he said, pulling his forelock. He put the gray into one of the empty stalls and then came back to stand before me.

"You've done a fine job here," I said. "When you're through today, go up to the house to Mrs. Mackenzie. I'll ask her to pay your wages, you and your brothers, for the month."

"For a month, Miss Craven?"

"I may be traveling soon. I want you to look after the house and the barn until Tim and the regular boys return. Come up every morning and, weather permitting, turn the horses out in the paddocks. Clean the stalls and put out fresh hay and water. Bring them in and give them grain in the late afternoon but mind you're home by sunset. Can you do that for me? I'll pay you all handsomely."

"Yes, Miss Craven, certainly. I don't mind telling you that the extra money will come in handy, what with the killings in the village and everyone afraid to leave their houses at night. Papa's fair worried about feedin' us all through the winter if the magistrate don't find the killer and lift the curfew soon."

I was distracted from replying by a small, long-haired white and gray kitten rubbing itself against my black riding habit. I reached down and picked her up and she purred to me.

"Well, aren't you just the prettiest thing? You're entirely too lovely to be a barn kitty. Wherever did you come from? Well, no matter. Why don't you come up to the house with me and tell me all about it?"

I scratched her behind her ears and her purr grew louder. "What's your name, puss?" Leaning down, I put my ear next her whiskers and pretended to listen to her. "Priscilla K. Pussycat? That's a fine name indeed."

I called to Charlie Harper, "I'll give you a bit extra to bring some supper to the barn cats on occasion," I said, rubbing my nose against the kitten's. One furry foot reached up and touched my face.

Charlie smiled. "Yes, miss. Be happy to."

I walked into the kitchen and scrounged up a bit of

chicken for the kitten. She sat purring happily and eating. I wasn't aware one could purr and eat at the same time, but there it was.

Mrs. Mackenzie walked into the kitchen as I was leaning against the counter, contemplating purrs.

"I told Charlie Harper to come up and get a month's wages from you."

She stilled. "Dulcinea, what are you going to do?"

"I don't know," I said with a sigh, "but if I pay them their wages in advance, it's one less thing I have to worry about."

She crossed the room and pulled me into her arms. I felt like I had as a child when I'd cut myself or fallen and skinned my knee, and Mrs. Mackenzie had been there to comfort me.

"What am I to do?" I asked, burying my face in her shoulder, my voice quivering on the edge of tears. I'd ridden for an hour and still had no answer. In fact I hadn't even been able to form a coherent thought the entire ride. Feelings, images, fragments of thoughts, they all just chased around like kittens inside my head.

"I can't tell you what to do, Dulcie."

"If it were you, what would you do?"

She was quiet for a moment and then she said softly, "I would survive. Whatever it took, I would survive."

And so she had, once. She'd left her family and everything she'd ever known, took her destiny in her hands, and made a new life for herself. It was a good life, but not, I'm sure, the one she'd envisioned as a little girl. Could I do the same? If it came to it, could I be brave and live?

"Where is Devlin?" I asked, pulling away.

"I think he's in the library."

I walked to the door.

"You're not going to leave this kitten in my kitchen, are you?" Mrs. Mackenzie called after me.

"If you don't want her in, then put her back outside when she's finished her chicken."

Mrs. Mackenzie snorted, but as I walked down the hall I could hear her cooing to the little ball of fur, something about her "pretty, tufty ears."

Kittens are good for the soul.

Chapter Fifteen

I found Devlin in the library. The heavy velvet curtains were shut against the afternoon sun, and he was sprawled on the red leather sofa, a snifter of brandy resting on the hard plane of his massive chest.

"I owe you an apology," he said without even looking up.

"You don't," I replied. "I'm the one who dragged you all into this."

He sat up. "And if it were any other beast who stalked you, you would be free now. Last night, Kali, she came out of nowhere. I have trained for centuries to be prepared for anything in battle but I wasn't prepared to see her. I told Justine to run. I thought she was with me. I was twenty yards away from her when Kali lent her power to Montford and Justine was wounded." He smiled. "Though my girl did get the bastard before she fell."

"Then what happened?"

He shrugged. "We both gathered our wounded and retreated. Kali could have killed us both. I don't know why she didn't. Perhaps it suits her temper to play with us awhile longer."

"How is Justine?"

"She's weak. She needs to feed. We'll have to go out after sunset and hunt."

I narrowed my eyes. "May I ask that you don't feed in my village?"

He stood. "I can feed from a human and they would never know it. We don't harm humans, Miss Craven."

"Tell that to the families of the dead girls in my village."

"The human body holds too much blood to drink in one feeding. It takes three feedings in a short space of time to kill someone. If a vampire kills a human, it isn't an accident, it's a plan. And if we leave bodies in our wake, the humans begin to notice and we are hunted. That is why killing humans is forbidden by the Dark Council. I am their instrument of justice. I am judge and executioner."

"Except you can't kill this one," I said sadly.

A dark storm raged across his face and he turned and braced his hands on the mahogany desk. I could see the tension in his massive shoulders.

"Devlin, I'm sorry."

"No, you're right. I should be able to keep you safe and I can't."

"You said earlier that you knew this demon, that you'd been her . . . guest. Tell me what happened."

He turned. "That is very personal."

"I have an impossible decision to make, Devlin. I think I have a right to know everything."

"I suppose you do at that," he said, waving a hand toward the sofa. "Sit."

I did, smoothing the black wool folds of my riding habit around me.

"The year was 1359. I was not much older than you are now. I was a knight, the son of an earl, and a wealthy man for I had the favor of the king and the king's son. I had won my spurs on the field of battle at Crécy alongside Edward the Black Prince. I was young, arrogant, and thought myself invincible. I was wrong."

I waited while he stared into the distance, remembering.

"I was in a brothel celebrating a recent victory at a tournament. That's where she found me."

"Kali?" I said, blushing.

"No, Yasmeen, Kali's lieutenant. She was a beautiful woman, all dark hair and dusky skin and eyes like melted chocolate. I took her upstairs to one of the bedchambers. I was dead drunk, and when she bit me, I passed out from liquor, shock, and blood loss," he laughed, a harsh, grating sound like broken glass. "What the entire French army couldn't accomplish in years, she did in minutes. I awoke in Kali's harem."

"In her *what*?"

"It's the only way I can describe it. She liked to drink from young, strong men. There were perhaps thirty of us bound in chains in one large, well-appointed room in the cellar of some great house. We were fed and clothed well and every night Yasmeen would come and choose two of us to make love to her while Kali watched."

My face flamed. I had to ask though. "Kali didn't—?"

"No, never. She prefers women."

I looked at him blankly.

"In her bed. She prefers women in her bed, not men."

"Oh," I said, but it took a minute before understanding truly dawned on me. "Oh," I said again.

"Yasmeen was Kali's lover as well as her lieutenant

but Yasmeen was not so . . . particular about whom she took to her bed. Afterward they would feed from us, damned near kill us."

"Did you ever try to escape?"

"Yes, many times. There was no escape though and the punishment for trying . . ." His voice trailed off. "My only hope was that the next time, one of them would kill me. They often did that with those they tired of. We were expendable. Yasmeen could always procure more of us, the same way she had taken me."

"How long were you there?" I asked softly.

"Three years, six months, and twenty-three days."

I sucked in a breath. Lord and Lady!

"One morning Yasmeen came to the cellar. She took me into one of the bedrooms and told me that Kali had decided to slaughter all the men, to bathe in our blood, literally. She said to me, 'If you will make love to me as you would to one of your pale English ladies, not because you fear me or because I command it, but of your own free will, I will risk my mistress's displeasure and free you. If you do this, you will see another moonrise, you have my word on it.' I asked her why, and she said simply, 'Because you please me, knight.'"

"And so you did it."

"Yes. I should have asked her to be more specific about her intentions though. I should have known the only way out of that house was death. She freed me by making me what she was: a vampire. When Kali found out what Yasmeen had done, she went insane. I've not seen such jealousy before or since. They fought and she killed Yasmeen before my eyes. I don't think she meant to do it. When she realized what she'd done, her grief and rage knew no bounds. She slaughtered the rest of the men, slaughtered them and reveled in it. I have seen many battles over the years, bloodshed you could not even begin to comprehend, but nothing could compare to the horror of that night. I tell you, she cannot be fought because I have seen what she is capable of."

He shuddered.

"What did she do to you?"

"She left me there. She locked me in with the dead. It took me a full day to break the door down. Twenty-four hours locked in a room with pieces of dead men everywhere I turned, and Yasmeen's headless corpse, haunting me. It took me several more nights to bury all the bodies. I traveled back to my estate, slipped into my own house like a thief in the night, took everything of value that I could carry, and fled the country."

"And that's why you do what you do? Protect the innocent, the ones like you were?"

"I don't think I was ever innocent," he said harshly, "but yes, that is one of the reasons why, but yes, that is one of the reasons why we work for the High King and the Dark Council."

"What is the Dark Council?"

"A council of ancients, only the oldest and wisest among us. They make the laws we must all abide by. Those who break the laws have to answer to me, or others like me."

I nodded silently.

"Dulcinea, I know the Destroyer. I lived under her tender mercies for years and I have seen her wrath. The demon inside her gives her power that a normal vampire wouldn't have. She has some magic but nothing like you can call up, I'm sure. When I tell you she can't be fought, it's not because of that, it's because she's stronger and faster than any creature I've ever faced. She's simply better, Dulcinea, as much as it galls me to admit it. I have waged war in one form or another for nearly five hundred years. I am a soldier, a general, and I know that one of the virtues of a good general is to know when a battle is unwinnable. If we had months to plan or to seek the protection of the Council, then maybe." He shook his head. "But I don't think we have that kind of time. Kali likes to play her games but she will grow impatient soon."

"So what do I do, Devlin? Tell me."

"I cannot advise you," he said regretfully.

I threw my hands up. "Not this again. Everyone says, 'Decide, Dulcie, live or die,' but no one can *advise* me."

He held up his hand. "I didn't say *no one* could advise you. I said *I* cannot. You have questions. Ask Justine."

"Justine? Why?"

He turned his back to me, pouring another brandy. "Trust me. She can help you as no one else can."

When he didn't turn back around, I got the distinct impression his lordship had just dismissed me.

Chapter Sixteen

I was on my way up to the dowager's room to see Justine when I heard the high coloratura trills of *The Magic Flute's* "*Der Hölle Rache*" coming from my dining room. Her voice was incredible, each note coming so effortlessly, so clearly, and her pitch was perfection. Quietly peering inside, I saw her, clad in her breeches and boots and another of my father's shirts, gracefully moving down the length of the dining room, slashing at the air with one of my father's fencing foils. Each move, each thrust of the sword, seemed choreographed to the aria she sang. The massive table had been moved against one wall to give her room to maneuver. I didn't know how she'd done it; I'd seen six strong footmen struggle to move that table. She stopped in mid-thrust and turned to walk back to the far end of the room.

"Come or go," she called, "but do not hover in the doorway."

I flushed as if I were a child who'd been caught spying and slipped into the room, closing the door behind me.

"I would have thought you would prefer the role of Pamina," I said.

Justine smiled. "Pamina may be the lead but the Queen of the Night is much more difficult to sing. Herr Mozart wrote it for me when I told him that I hadn't been given anything truly challenging in a hundred years."

"Have you ever performed it?"

"Not publicly," she said, and then effectively changed the subject. "So tell me, do you fence?"

"I know the rudiments," I said. Sebastian and I had played at being knights when we were children, and my father had thought it a lark one summer to teach me a few of the basics.

Justine hooked her toe under a second foil lying on the floor and flipped it into the air. Catching it deftly in one hand, she threw it to me.

I took off my jacket and folded it neatly across the back of one of the chairs. Gathering up my skirt in one hand and the foil in my other, I faced her. She tipped her sword to me and began.

She was toying with me, I knew. I was less than a novice and she'd had centuries of practice. She could have disarmed me in a stroke, but she didn't. When she'd gently backed me against the far wall, she stepped back and said, "Again."

Walking back to the end of the room she winced a bit and put a hand to her chest.

"You're still injured," I said. "You should be resting."

"We are women," she said, engaging me again, her voice rising to be heard over the clashing of steel. "Even with the strength of the vampire, the men are still bigger and stronger."

The sharp staccato of metal against metal echoed in the room as we moved in a deadly ballet across the polished wood floor. She hooked my sword and drew up, pinning it to my body with the press of her own. "They have an advantage over us in brute strength so we must be quicker and smarter and better. Again."

As we circled each other, lunging and parrying, I asked, "What does it feel like? To be a vampire?"

"I can see as well as the hawk, can hear like the wolf. I can run as fast as a deer for miles without tiring. To be a vampire is to know strength and power . . . and great sadness." She stopped in the middle of the room. "But that is not what you came to ask me."

"It's not?"

"You want to know how you could possibly make such a decision. You want to know if your soul will be damned for all eternity. You want to know what will become of you if you give up your life."

My eyes widened. She was right. Those were the questions, even if I hadn't yet formed them in my own mind. Those were the things that had been swimming in my head as I was out riding. "How did you know?" I asked.

She laughed, sliding up to sit on the edge of the dining table, her long legs dangling. "Because I was once where you are now."

I stepped back in surprise. "You were a slayer. You hunted them. I just assumed—"

"That I was made as Devlin and Michael were, against my will? *Non*, the choice was mine to make." She looked at me for a long moment as if deciding whether or not I was worthy of the story, or possibly she was wondering if I could be trusted with it. "My parents died of smallpox when I was sixteen. I had a younger sister to look after. Solange was only six, and we were all alone. We nearly starved to death that first winter. I vowed we would not spend another month on the streets. One night I broke into the shop of the most fashionable modiste in Paris and stole a gown. The next morning I presented myself at court to audition for Jean-Baptiste Lully. He gave me a position with the *Académie Royale de Musique* and a room at the court of King Louis XIV.

"Soon I had gained the lead roles in Lully's operas and in the ballets and plays at court. I also gained the attentions of wealthy men. At seventeen I was the mistress of the Sun King himself. At eighteen I was sent to the English court of Charles II to spy for Louis from the comforts of Charles's bed. To keep Solange from the debaucheries of court life, I enrolled her in the best convent school, keeping her far away from my less-than-proper lifestyle. I vowed that we would never be poor again. I sang and I danced and I collected a string of wealthy men who paid me handsomely for my favors. I loved my life. And then one night all of that changed."

"A vampire?"

"Yes, five of them caught me one night in the gardens of the Tuileries Palace. They nearly killed me. I must have had twenty bite wounds from neck to knee. I spent every waking moment after that learning to fight. I learned swordplay from my wealthy protectors and then one night at a Cyprian's ball a duke introduced me to a Chinese antiquities merchant. We became friends and he knew fighting styles I'd never even seen. I paid him well to teach me. I would not be helpless again, not ever. In a year's time I went hunting the ones who had attacked me."

"Did you find them?"

"Oh, *oui*. They died screaming, begging me to spare them," she said with a cold smile.

"But you didn't stop there." It was a statement, not a question.

"*Non*, why should I? I was young and strong. I knew which vampires I could take and which ones, the old ones, were better left alone. Within two years I was feared among the undead in Paris, so much so that the Regent hired an assassin to kill me." She laughed, twirling a lock of pale hair around one finger. "It did not turn out as he expected."

I was confused for a moment. "Devlin?"

"*Oui*. He was not always as he is now. When I met him he was a mercenary. The fights we had across the length and breadth of Paris were incredible," she said with a wistful sigh. "And despite what he said this morning, there was one mission that he failed to accomplish."

"So you became a vampire to be with him?"

"As much as I wanted him, I could have given him up. Then. *Non*, it was his coming to kill me that made my decision for me. I was young and I had thought myself invincible. I did not consider that I may grow old, weak. That when I did, the vampires would come for those I loved. Devlin's assassination attempt would have been the first of many. I was too good at what I did. Maybe it was because I was a woman and the undead didn't expect me to be anything but a helpless victim." She shook her head and shrugged.

"I had a taste of my own mortality and it was like ashes in my mouth. What would become of my sister when I went out hunting one night and failed, as I'd come to realize that I must, eventually? I had thought to protect her and my city but I hadn't thought, not really. It was arrogant and foolish of me. I should have left well enough alone. I should have been grateful to have survived."

"You were afraid that when you died, the vampires would take their vengeance out on your sister?"

"*Oui*. She was going to take the Holy Orders. Do you understand what it would have been like if they'd gotten her? The evil undead defiling a Bride of Christ?"

"Did you tell her? Did she know what you were?"

She shook her head, and her hair spilled over one shoulder and obscured her face from my view. "I did not see Solange after her fourteenth birthday. The good sisters, they knew I was a courtesan, and they were happy to take my money, but they did not think the way I lived my life was a good influence on one so young. They turned her against me and I suppose that was as it should be. Every immoral thing I had done had been so that she would never have to do it herself. When I came to visit her on her birthday, she . . ." Justine looked down, swinging one long leg back and forth. "She asked that I not come back. I suppose it was an embarrassment for her sister the whore to set foot inside those sacred walls."

"Oh, Justine," I said, seeing the pain etched on her face.

She shrugged, as if she wished me to believe it was of little consequence, and pushed back her hair. "She was young. She did not yet understand. But even though she had turned her back on me, I could not leave her alone in the world, defenseless. When Devlin offered me eternity, I took it, because I loved him and because it would make me young and strong forever. It is ironic, isn't it," she laughed in a tone that held little humor, "that to protect my sister and my city I had to become the thing I had hunted for so many years?"

"That's what you meant when you said you'd been where I am now."

She looked at me with fire in her eyes. "Devlin and Michael are good men but they cannot possibly understand. They weren't given a choice. Devlin became a vampire because he walked into the wrong whorehouse, Michael because Devlin liked his way with the sword. The decision wasn't theirs to make. They can sympathize all day but they have no idea the strength and courage it takes to stand where you are now, where I have been."

I nodded. Devlin had been right when he'd said he couldn't advise me. He had understood that, at least.

"To become a vampire you must have strength, Dulcinea. You will know much more sorrow as a vampire than you ever would as a human. It is tempting to be young and beautiful forever, to be strong and flush with power, but you must understand what you sacrifice."

"I am strong," I said, with more bravado than I felt.

"Yes, you are, but are you strong enough? Are you strong enough to watch all of those you love grow old and die, as I watched my sister, while you will never look a day older than you do now? You will see Mr. Pendergrass, Mrs. Mackenzie, young Archie, and *petite* Fiona grow old and wrinkled, and they will die. You will live forever while their children and grandchildren and great-grandchildren's lives pass before you, so very quickly. You will grieve over deaths that would never have touched you if you were human. Remember that."

"And my soul?" I asked. "Do vampires have souls? Is your soul lost, Justine?"

"Can you feel a soul? I feel no different than I did when I was alive. The good sisters would have called me a suicide. They would say my soul was damned for eternity. I hope that God understands that I did what I did for the greater good. As a vampire I can save so many human lives. If I had stayed human, I would be just one more body in the ground. Even so, we are not truly immortal. One day, maybe soon, I will fall in battle. I hope that when God judges me, he will weigh the lives I have saved against the decision I made."

"But the vampires you fight, the ones like Sebastian, how can they do what they do and still have a soul? Perhaps the three of you are just different than all the others?"

She laughed, a high beautiful sound. "I have been on this earth for over one hundred fifty years. Trust me when I tell you that you don't have to be a vampire to be evil. I have seen evil in mankind the likes of which you cannot imagine. If evil is inside you, then becoming a vampire will only bring it out.

"If it is inside you to hurt others, to steal, to rape, to kill, and suddenly you are a vampire, you are strong and no one can stop you. Those weak of character are especially vulnerable because any weakness will be magnified by the power they now wield. *Non*, vampires are not all like Sebastian, but an evil human will make an evil vampire, and those are the ones we fight."

"The vicar would say that no one is wholly evil. That there is some good in everyone."

She snorted. "Ignorance. The vicar has not lived as long as I have, or seen what I have seen." She raised a brow at me. "Are you a Christian, little witch? You worry that God will damn your soul?"

"I was raised between two faiths, the Church of England and the Old Religion of my mother's people."

"But when you pray in your heart, to whom do you pray?"

I was quiet for a moment. That was not a question I would answer to most people. "The Goddess, the Earth Mother. When I was a child, I used to be scared of my father's God. The vicar would say that I'm a heretic because I'm a child of the Old Religion. It isn't a choice, though; it's how I was made. I was born a witch and I'm proud of what I am. As I've gotten older, it no longer frightens me. I think I've come to believe that there can only be one Higher Power, one Creator. There can't be as many gods in heaven as there are religions of men. I think that we just find our own ways to worship, we find what speaks to our own souls."

She regarded me silently, and then nodded. "Very wise for one so young." She hopped down from the table in one liquid movement.

"Now," she said, picking up her foil and slashing the air with a deft flick of the wrist, "ask me your last question."

I paused for a long moment. "If I do this, what will become of me?"

She smiled. "For the answer to that, you must ask young Michael, no?"

Chapter Seventeen

I walked down the hall to my bedroom. I wasn't sure if I could face Michael yet. How do you tell someone you've just met: *I feel a certain attraction to you. If I were to become a vampire, would you care to court me?* It was ridiculous. I just couldn't do it. I closed the door behind me and leaned against it, closing my eyes.

There was just the barest whisper of rustling fabric and a finger fell over my lips. I gave a little shriek.

"Shhh. I mean you no harm."

"Michael," I whispered, my heart pounding frantically in my chest. Was it from the fright he'd given me or simply from the closeness of his body?

"You've been talking to Devlin and Justine."

"Yes," I said, puzzled.

"Don't let them sway you, Dulcie. We'll figure a way out of this. You *will* live," he said fiercely, as if by saying it, he could make it so.

"I don't think I will," I replied in a small voice.

"I won't let them have you. I won't allow you to become what I am because you have no other choice."

"You don't think I'm strong enough to be one of you."

"Oh, God," he said and pulled me into his arms. I stiffened and then sank into the hard wall of his chest. "I think you're the bravest creature I've ever met."

He pulled back and took my face in his hands. "I

want you to have a life, Dulcie. The life you were meant to have. You were born to fine things and fancy houses. You should die a very old lady surrounded by your grandchildren," he said, but there was pain and perhaps a bit of jealousy in his voice as he said it.

I laughed and laid my head on his shoulder. "I don't know that grandchildren are in my future at any rate. I'm a willful old maid who hasn't been attracted to a man in more years than I care to count."

He tipped my chin up with one finger. "No?" he breathed.

I opened my mouth but nothing came out. Good Lord, I was acting like a green debutante! I was widely known throughout the *ton* for my sophisticated banter and yet now I couldn't even seem to form a sentence. Instead I did what I'd longed to do last night and this morning. I reached up and ran my fingers along the edge of one sharp cheekbone, down the side of his face, softly skimming his lips. He groaned and pressed my back against the door before his lips fell on mine.

He was wild and hungry, his tongue tangling with mine. My knees nearly buckled and I grabbed handfuls of his shirt to steady myself.

"Michael," I said between kisses, "if I were to become like you, do you think . . . that is, we seem to have this . . . thing."

We seem to have this thing? Gods, what was wrong with me? He looked at me in confusion for a moment and I knew I'd bungled it. Then something inscrutable passed over his face.

"I could never have dreamed to have such a lady for my own," he said, his voice husky with some unnamed emotion.

It wasn't truly an answer, but at the moment I didn't care. That wonderful body was so near mine and oh so very touchable. I pulled his head back down to me, running my fingers through his hair. I moved my hands over his shoulders and down to the buttons of his shirt. He pulled back and looked down at me as I flicked open one button after another until I'd opened them all and pushed the shirt down over his shoulders.

He was breathing heavily but I didn't dare look at his face or I'd lose my nerve. I'd never seen a man's naked chest before. Well, my father's a few times but I'd been only a small child then. I ran my palms over the hard plane of his chest, down over his nipples, along the rigid muscles of his stomach. Those tight squares fascinated my fingers. He growled low in his throat and reached down, grabbing me by the thighs and lifting me to straddle his hips.

"Let me see your hair," he said against my temple, "its true color."

I dropped my glamour and my hair bled to ruby.

"So beautiful," he whispered.

I clung to him, kissing him and running my hands over every inch of him that I could reach. My body felt as if it were made of hot quicksilver.

A loud knock on the door behind my head made me pull back with a small squeak. I braced my hands against the door, my eyes wild. We'd been caught. By whom? Dear Goddess, please don't let it be Mrs. Mackenzie!

"Michael," Devlin's deep voice growled from the other side. "The sun is set. Come."

I could hear his footsteps move down the hall. I had never heard Devlin move before. He was quiet as a wraith. The loud footsteps had been for my benefit. I flushed a dozen colors of crimson.

Michael lowered me to my feet and we stood, leaning against each other and catching our breath. Did vampires really breathe? I wouldn't have thought so. I'd have to ask him about it later.

"You need to go," I said against his chest.

"Yes," he replied, but made no move to leave.

"Don't hurt anyone," I said.

"Dulcie, we do not—"

"I know. I've already gotten the 'We do not harm humans' speech from Devlin. I simply had to say it again."

He smiled and moved away.

"Please be careful," I said.

He picked up his sheathed claymore from where it rested against my dressing table.

"Don't worry," he said with a grin, patting the huge sword. "Ophelia has yet to fail me."

"Ophelia? You named your sword?"

"All men name their swords," he said, laughing. I had the feeling I was missing something there but I let it go.

"Why 'Ophelia'?" Had he named it after a former lover?

"Have you never read *Hamlet*?" he asked.

"Oh. Of course. But why choose a name from *Hamlet*?"

He shrugged. "It seemed like an appropriate play."

I laughed, bemused. "Why?"

"Well, because," he said, looking at the sword with pride and affection, "everyone dies in the end."

Chapter Eighteen

A door slammed somewhere in the house. I jerked awake, nearly dropping the large book of Latin that had lain across my lap as I slept. I looked around the library. Mrs. Mackenzie was sitting up on the red leather sofa, her head tilted at an angle that was likely to hurt when she woke up. Fiona lay curled on her side, her feet tucked under her skirt and her head on her mother's lap. Mr. Pendergrass had nodded off in one of the wing chairs next to the fire, his chin resting on his chest, the book that he'd been reading lying open and forgotten on his lap. Archie stood in the doorway of the library. When he saw that I'd awakened, he beckoned me over. Closing my book of Latin, I moved silently through the room to his side.

"They've just returned," he whispered. "How are you feeling?"

I shrugged. "Fine. The only person in my head is me tonight. What time is it?"

"Five."

I nodded. "Well, whatever Sebastian was doing tonight, it's too late for him to start up with me now. If he were going to be a nuisance, he'd have been here by now. I'm going on up to bed. Will you wake them?" I asked, motioning toward my sleeping guardians.

"Certainly," he said. "And I'll help keep watch until sunrise."

"Thank you, Archie," I replied, and hugged him briefly, pulling away before it became too awkward.

I met Devlin and Justine coming down the hall. She was dressed in her deep purple courtesan's gown again, her arm entwined with Devlin's, and a look of promise in her eyes as he guided her toward the stairs.

"Has all been well tonight?" Devlin asked. "You look rested."

"Nary a peep," I replied. "We all fell asleep in the library. Well, except for Archie. He stood watch."

Devlin nodded. "Montford's probably nursing his wound this night. He'll likely be back tomorrow. We'll go out and hunt again then."

I frowned. "I don't want you to get yourselves killed over me. I couldn't bear it."

"My dear," he said with a smile, "we're already dead."

"Yes, so Michael keeps reminding me. Don't get yourselves hurt, is what I'm asking. If she's too strong to fight, then come back and we'll think of something else."

"Like what?" Justine asked, a faintly condescending smile on her face.

"I don't know. Look, I know this is what you do, and you must be good at it if you've survived this long. But the three of you, you're a family. You two are so much in love, you fairly glow with it. If anything happened to any of you because of me . . ."

"Don't worry so much," Justine chided.

"If all goes badly we'll fall back to the house," Devlin said, "and Pendergrass and his boy can take you

somewhere safe as soon as the sun rises. Our options
are fight or flight and, as I have been reminded recently, we are fighters first and foremost."

"Where is Michael?" I asked.

Justine waved one hand airily. "He said he had
something to do. I don't know."

"Oh," I said, not liking the wash of disappointment
that swept through me at the thought that I wasn't going to get to see him tonight. "Well, I'm off to bed,
then. Good night, and thank you again for everything."

I climbed the stairs and walked down the hall to my
room. Pausing at my door, I shifted the large Latin tome
to one side and put my hand on the knob. A frisson of
anticipation ran through me, and before I even opened
the door I knew that my room was not empty.

"What are you doing in here?" I asked, closing the
door behind me.

Michael whirled around and backed up into the
nightstand. I looked at what he held, at the expression
on his face, and my heart melted. In his hands was the
priceless blue and white Ming bowl from the foyer
table. He'd filled it with dirt and planted the bright yellow evening primrose in it. Obviously as a poor crofter's
son, a gardener, and then a soldier, he didn't realize the
value of that bowl, and that it was not something to be
used to plant flowers in.

I smiled at that and my heart gave a little flutter. He
stood there, clutching the bowl of flowers with a look of
vulnerability and uncertainty on his face. It was the look
that most of my would-be suitors had when they were
presented in my mother's drawing room, flowers in hand,
the morning after a ball. It made my breath catch in my

throat to see that look on someone so deadly, so dangerous, and to know that I was the cause of it.

"I, um, you liked looking at the primrose this morning. I thought maybe they'd last longer if they were in the house where it's warm."

"They're lovely, thank you," I said, setting my book aside and taking the bowl carefully from his hands. I placed it gently on my dressing table. "There. That way they'll get the afternoon sun through the balcony windows."

"So, Sebastian's gone to ground to lick his wounds?"

"Yes, it was a refreshingly quiet evening."

"Good. We'll go out tomorrow night and hunt them again."

"Michael," I said, clutching his arm, "promise me you won't do anything foolish."

"Of course, lass," he said softly.

"Promise me you'll all come back in one piece."

"I can't promise that and you know it. This is a fight to the death. Someone will die and hopefully it won't be us."

I wrapped my arms around myself. "I've never had to fight for anything," I whispered.

He was quiet for a moment and then said, "I know. And I've had to fight all my life."

His eyes were distant; I couldn't read anything in them. It was as if he'd retreated somewhere deep inside himself that I couldn't touch.

"I must go," he said, his voice thick with some emotion I couldn't name.

What had just happened?

"Michael, don't go."

He looked at me and shook his head. "Sometimes, lass, I forget what you are."

Icy fingers seemed to squeeze at my heart. "What I am? What does that mean?"

"You're a viscount's daughter and I'm nothing but—"

"I know very well what you are."

He shook his head. "You don't understand. Even when I was human, I was nothing more than a servant. Last night and earlier this evening, I shouldn't have kissed you, and tonight I shouldn't have brought you flowers as if I were a man able to court you. You have my apologies; it won't happen again."

"Oh, really?" I asked, arching a brow at him.

He raked one hand through his hair. "When I was alive, you would have been so far above me, as untouchable as the moon, but now . . . I'm dead, Dulcie, can't you understand that?"

"And you think I'm not? No matter what you think, Devlin says that this beast can't be killed. If that's so, then I'm a walking dead woman, Michael. Do you think I like that thought? Do you think it brings me joy? I don't want to die, Michael. I want to live. I want to walk along the Seine in Paris. I want to float in a gondola on the canals of Venice. I want to shop in the markets of Morocco. I want to dance at the Winter Palace in St. Petersburg," I said, hating myself for the catch in my voice and the tears I felt welling up in my eyes. "I don't want to die, but I will. I can feel it coming like a black cloud hanging over me."

I walked up to him and ran my hands up the front of his shirt, feeling silk and muscle under my fingertips. "Right now, the only thing that brings me joy is you. What I feel, it's not something I take lightly. I've been attracted to all of three men in my entire life, Michael. You make me burn, and if I'm going to die, don't let me die a virgin. Stay with me tonight," I whispered against the sharp plane of his cheek.

A shudder ran through him. His hands moved up my arms to rest on my shoulders and I thought he would give in. And then his fingers tightened and he pushed away from me.

"You are not going to die. You're going to live, and one day when you find the right man and get married, you'll look back on this night and be thankful I walked away."

"I very seriously doubt that," I commented.

He looked at me for a long time, not speaking. It was as if he lacked the will to turn and leave. I was fairly certain that if I tried again, I could melt his reservations, but in the end I decided against it. My pride wouldn't allow me to be rejected twice in one night. So I let him walk away. When he got to the door, I called out to him.

"Michael?" He turned. I propped one hip on the footboard of the bed and crossed my arms under my breasts, making them swell invitingly over the neckline of my gown. "You were right about one thing. I am a viscount's spoiled daughter and I'm used to getting exactly what I want. You'd do well to remember that."

He smiled and inclined his head and then shut the door behind him as he left.

Chapter Nineteen

I stood in the shadows in the doorway of the kitchen the next evening and watched Fiona. She was humming and moving efficiently around the kitchen, preparing supper. She was so young and full of life. If it came down to it and I had to make the choice, could I do it? Could I watch her age, watch her die? And even if I could, what was to become of me then? Would I go with The Righteous? Travel the world fighting evil? I nearly sat down and laughed, or cried.

I was no warrior. I was a debutante, a viscount's daughter, as Michael was so fond of reminding me. From the cradle I had been expected to do nothing braver than marry well and bear children. I was not meant for the life they led. Wouldn't it be easier to end it now? If I became one of them, there would be no easy death. A stake through the heart, beheading, fire.

I could end it all right now with a simple sip of a potion. Why didn't I do it? If I let the opportunity pass, I would never get it back. It would be so easy to walk past Fiona and down into the stillroom. I knew herbs; I knew what to take, what would make me simply fall asleep and never wake up. They would lay me out at Ravenworth Abbey next to Mama and Papa. I could be with them. I could rest. So why didn't I take that walk down into the cool dark of the stillroom?

Because I was a Craven and I was a Macgregor witch, I thought to myself with a weary sigh. I was no warrior, true, but neither could I face my parents in the world beyond and say that I'd laid down my life without so much as a fight.

So I would fight. And I would die. So be it.

"Dulcie!" Fiona called, spotting me in the doorway. "Come in and give me a hand. Mother thinks I can manage pork chops and gravy but I'm not so sure. Does this taste right?"

I took the spoon from her and bravely tasted the gravy. "A little more salt and flour, I think."

"Hmm," she said, looking down with narrowed eyes as if one good glare would whip the gravy into shape. "Mr. Pendergrass and Mr. Little are helping Mother move all the heavy drapes into the rooms that our friends are likely to frequent during the day. Mother and the gentlemen seem confident in my heretofore untried culinary abilities." She looked at me with her delicate features, her glossy chestnut hair pulled back in a chignon, flour up to her elbows and smeared on her cheek. "I don't think I was meant for kitchen help though."

Kitchen help, indeed. She looked like a fairy princess who'd been dumped in a vat of flour. Poor Fiona. Hers was not an easy road. Neither servant nor gentry but caught somewhere in the middle. I smiled at her and patted her on the hip as I passed.

Devlin, Justine, and Michael had gone out an hour ago to hunt. My stomach was in knots and I didn't think I could eat, but I could certainly help Fiona with supper.

"I'll cut up the last of the hothouse strawberries. That way if you bollocks up the pork chops, we'll still have something to eat."

She giggled. "Dulcie! Language!" she said in a perfect imitation of her mother.

I was halfway through with the strawberries when I heard a scratching at the kitchen window. I looked up, my pulse racing just a bit, only to see the little white and gray barn kitten sitting on the sill, looking inside.

"Who is this?" Fiona asked, tapping her finger against the glass.

"That's Priscilla, one of the barn kittens," I said. "I made the mistake of bringing her in the last two afternoons and giving her a bit of chicken. She probably thinks she's a house cat now."

"As well she should be," Fiona said. "Look at all that long hair! She's much too pretty to be a plain barn cat."

Fiona opened the kitchen door and called to the kitten. Prissy hopped down off the sill and ran over to the door. I looked back down at my strawberries. The kitten growled.

"Well, what's the matter with you? Come on in now," I heard Fiona say and looked up to see her lean over and try to pick the kitten up. The kitten wasn't looking at her, but somewhere to its right, and every long hair on its back was standing on end.

"Fi, no!" I yelled as her head and shoulders cleared the doorway, bending down to pick up the kitten.

It was too late. One pale long-fingered hand snaked out of the dark and grabbed her wrist. By the time I'd run around the table, knife in hand, tripping over the terrified kitten who'd bolted inside, Sebastian held Fiona. With one arm wrapped around her waist, pressing her back to his chest, he jammed a pistol against her temple.

"I am tired of playing games with you, Dulcinea," he said coldly. "Come out or she dies."

I clutched the knife tightly in my hand. "I come out there and you'll kill her anyway."

"Perhaps," he said, a slow, evil grin marring his otherwise handsome features, "but really, my dear, you have nothing to bargain with."

"Don't I?" I said and pressed the knife under my breasts. "Pull that trigger and I'll plunge this knife into my heart. Your master won't be too pleased with you if I die, will she?"

His eyes narrowed and something like fear flickered behind them.

"Let her go and I'll come with you willingly."

"No, Dulcie! Don't!" Fiona cried.

Sebastian regarded me for a heartbeat and said, "Walk halfway to me and I'll release the girl."

I did as he asked, and to my surprise, he let Fiona go, shoving her toward me. She ran to my arms and clung to me.

"Now," Sebastian said, the pistol pointed at Fiona and me, "she goes inside and you come to me. A bargain is a bargain. And Dulcinea, if you make a move toward that door, I'll shoot her in the head."

"Go inside," I told Fiona.

She shook her head, tears streaking her pretty face. "Dulcie," she whispered. "I didn't mean it. It's all my fault. I'm so sorry."

"It's not your fault. It would have happened sooner or later, you know that," I said. "Go inside and bar the door, Fi, and stay away from the windows. Live to see another dawn. For me."

She looked at me as if she were memorizing my face. "I love you," she said.

"I love you too. And tell the others . . ." I couldn't finish, couldn't say it.

She nodded and ran to the house. As she closed the door, a movement behind her caught my eye. That wee fiend of a kitten was on the kitchen counter, a panicked look on her face and a stolen pork chop clamped tightly in her mouth. I couldn't help it; I laughed.

"I wouldn't be so quick to laugh if I were you, young lady," Sebastian said from behind me. "Your magic won't save you tonight and your protectors have gone hunting and left you all alone."

There was no sense in trying to explain a kitten to Sebastian, so I let it go. "What do you mean about my magic?" I asked.

"Put down the knife and I'll tell you," he said, an unsettling look of triumph on his face.

I threw the knife at his feet. Its blade sunk deep in the earth with a satisfying thud. We both started at it. Sebastian's eyes were a little wide when they met mine. It was dumb luck. I couldn't have duplicated that throw if I'd done it a hundred more times. But he didn't need to know that.

Sebastian seemed to collect himself. He tucked the pistol in the waistband of his pants. For the first time I noticed that he was not dressed in his usual impeccable style. His boots were unpolished, his jacket unbuttoned. He wore no vest or cravat and his shirt lay open at the neck. I looked him up and down in my best condescending manner.

"Rough day, Sebastian?"

"I ate my valet," he said with a shrug, "and it's so hard to find good help these days."

He watched me as if waiting for my reaction. He wanted to shock and horrify me. I pushed down my revulsion and gave him a bland stare. "You said something about my magic?"

He opened his shirt at the throat. Around his neck hung a gold chain and suspended from it was an intricately wrought gold disc. The designs around the disc appeared to be runes of some sort but I was too far away to tell. In the center was a large ruby. For all its size it seemed to be a feminine piece. It also reeked of magic.

"My mistress has given me her talisman. Your magic cannot harm me," he said with triumph in his voice.

Damn. He could be lying but I doubted it. I could feel the magic in the thing. Would it harm me if I tried to use magic against him or would my magic simply not work? I thought it best not to find out at this juncture. If Sebastian had the talisman, that meant that Kali didn't. Perhaps I could use that to my advantage. I tried to look bored and shrugged.

"I want this over with, Sebastian, one way or another."

"Happy to oblige you at last, my dear," he said and took the pistol from his waistband again. Motioning toward the woods with a flick of his wrist, he said harshly, "Now move."

Chapter Twenty

Sebastian followed me through the woods, giving directions here and there, but resisting my attempts to draw him into any kind of conversation. All he would tell me was that his mistress would reveal everything in time. Twenty minutes later my white muslin dress with the lavender trim was soaked with dew, clinging to my legs in what I was sure must be an obscene manner. My wet slippers made squishing noises with each step, and finally I stopped, rubbing my hands up and down my bare arms in an attempt to warm myself.

"Scared?" Sebastian mocked from behind me.

I turned, "No, Sebastian, it's cold out here, and I have no coat. At one time you were a gentleman and would have noticed such things."

He shoved the pistol into his waistband again and shrugged out of his jacket. He held it out to me and I paused, reluctant to take anything from a man who was trying to kill me, or at the very least enslave me.

"My apologies," he muttered, and I decided my pride wasn't worth freezing to death. I slipped into the jacket and Sebastian motioned me forward again.

It didn't take long to figure out where we were headed. Sebastian and I, and even Fiona, had come this way many times as children. I thought of those happier times as I walked along, rolling up the sleeves of the jacket as I went.

At the southwest corner of the Montford estate sat an old, ruined thirteenth-century Cistercian abbey. The monastery had gradually fallen prey to the ravages of time after Henry VIII's Dissolution of the Monasteries in 1536. Now the church was just a shell, the ceiling having fallen in centuries ago, the stained-glass windows removed when the rest of the building was sacked for its riches. All that remained were the four outside walls of the church, heavily covered in red and green ivy.

We entered through the yawning arches which had once been the front doors. Large stones lay scattered where they had fallen among the grass that grew inside the ruins. Torches were lit at intervals along the walls of the nave, the light illuminating the arched windows of the clerestory and fading away into the dark sky above. The far corner still retained a portion of its stone floor, the scorched walls behind it indicating that it had been used as a hearth by squatters over the centuries. A large fire burned there now.

Pale, shadowy shapes, perhaps ten of them, stood around the perimeter of the nave. Sebastian nudged me and I walked on. As I passed one of the shapes, I stopped and looked at it. It was Peterson, Sebastian's butler.

"Peterson?" I asked.

The figure didn't move, didn't so much as blink. He was dirty, his clothing unkempt and foul. The smell of rotten flesh permeated the air around him. I shrank back.

"Is he a vampire?" I asked.

"No," Sebastian said. "We do not share that gift with just anyone. He is the walking dead, no more, no less."

It was wrong. It was unnatural. "How did you do it, Sebastian?"

He laughed. "My mistress's powers are great, Dulcinea. Come, see for yourself."

He led me toward the far wall but I saw nothing in the dim shadows that flickered and danced by the firelight. I moved closer to the fire. I don't know if it was that age-old human instinct to draw closer to the light in the threatening darkness or the sheer fact that my lightweight muslin dress was soaked with mist and dew, but I desperately needed its warmth. I put my back to the blaze and looked expectantly at Sebastian. The ruby talisman at his throat gleamed in the firelight. My fingers itched to rip it from his neck. I put my hands behind my back and clenched my fists.

"Well," I said with more bravado than I felt, "here I am. Does she intend to make me wait all night?"

A low, throaty laughter filled the air and the hair on the back of my neck stood up. Kali the Destroyer appeared from the shadows, seeming to take shape from nothing but fog and darkness. One look at her and I understood why she'd become a vampire, why she liked the human body she had chosen when she entered this world. She was exquisite.

Her hair was parted down the middle and hung in a straight veil of jet-black to her waist. The muscles of her arms and shoulders were well defined, her breasts high and full as if millennia of gravity had taken no toll on them. Her waist was narrow, her stomach flat, the muscles toned. Her hips swelled lushly, her legs were long and shapely. Her eyes, black and glittering, were darkened with kohl, her lips a dark blood-red.

She wore hammered gold bands on her upper arms and wrists, and small golden chains ran from the bracelets to connect to her ringed fingers. She wore nothing above the waist but a curtain of gold necklaces of graduating lengths. Tiny rubies were interspersed throughout, looking like small drops of glittering blood on her dark skin. Rubies had always been my favorite gemstone but I wasn't sure I'd ever look at them the same way again. With every graceful step, the chains would sway, exposing a dusky nipple, and then fall back to cover it. Something like a large diamond winked from her navel. Her skirt of golden silk rode low on her hips and shined with an iridescent red glow as she moved. It was slit up both sides to mid-thigh, flashing a glimpse of her shapely legs with each step. Her feet were bare except for gold anklets on each ankle and a gold ring on one toe.

"Humans," she said in heavily accented English as she walked around me, looking me up and down as if I were a mare for purchase or possibly a side of beef at the butcher's. "You are so impatient. But then, I suppose that is to be forgiven. Your lives are so very short."

"What do you want from me?" I asked.

Her hand shot out and she grabbed my chin, fingernails digging into my flesh. "I am Kali. I am the Destroyer. I ask the questions, witch, not you."

"Fine," I said between gritted teeth. "I've got all night. Have you?"

She laughed and released me. "I like your spirit. It will be such fun to break you." She ran her fingertips along the pale purple bruises of Sebastian's bite on my neck. "And you humans break so easily."

I shuddered. *Well done, Dulcie,* I thought, *antagonize the evil houri.*

"What do I want from you? I will get to the point, then. I want you to open a portal for me."

"What?"

"A portal, a mystical door between worlds. I want you to open one for me and call something forth from my world."

"I wouldn't even begin to know how to work magics like that," I said truthfully.

"I have the spell," she said. "I just need the witch to work it."

"Why me? There are other witches, more powerful witches."

"Others, perhaps, but I think none more powerful. Before I ripped his throat out, the foolish priest who laid this binding spell on me told me that only the Red Witch could deliver me from this realm." She grabbed a fistful of my hair, which I hadn't bothered to hide with my glamour, and held it up to the firelight. "And that, my dear, is you."

I shook my head. "He lied to you. Only the one who laid the spell can remove it."

Her hand cracked across my cheek with such force that I found myself sprawled on the ground looking up at her face, which was dark with fury.

"Do you not think I know that?" she yelled. "I did not ask you to remove the spell. Haven't you been listening? I want you to open a portal and call forth the Crown of the Goddess Inkhara. I want my crown, witch, do you understand?"

I frowned, not understanding at all, but nodded anyway. Kali whirled around, her arms raised heavenward, and said, "With my crown I can fold back the fabric of time. I can correct all of my mistakes. I will kill that knight and get Yasmeen back. I will kill those meddlesome monks before they can work their dark magic on me. I will call forth the warriors of my people, and my army will spread forth over this world, sucking the human race dry and picking our teeth with their bones."

She crouched down in front of me on the balls of her feet, her elbows resting on her knees. "I will go home in triumph, Yasmeen at my side forever, and be worshipped again as a goddess among my people. And you will make it happen."

I looked into her eyes. There was madness there but there was also desperation and pain. I saw it whenever she said Yasmeen's name. Whatever she had felt for the woman, it was clearly as close to love as a creature like Kali could feel. I understood her grief well. I knew what it felt like to want to turn back the hand of time and regain what was lost. In that moment, if it had just been Yasmeen she was after, I might have been tempted to agree. But it wouldn't stop with saving Yasmeen. If I worked this spell for her, Devlin would die, Michael and Justine would never have been turned, and Kali would have the power to destroy the world.

I scrambled to my feet, shaking my head violently. "No, I won't do it. There's nothing you can do to make me do it."

"Oh, I think you're very, very wrong about that," she said with a low growl.

I backed up, putting her between me and the fire.

"Do you think you and your three erstwhile protectors are the only ones in all these long centuries who have tried to stop me, tried to kill me? They have come one by one, sometimes army by army, to their deaths. I have killed more people than famine and flood combined. You will do as I wish," she said, her figure outlined by the red glow of the fire behind her, making her look truly like the demon she was. "I am the Destroyer, child. I have broken thousands much stronger than you. I have brought emperors, warriors, and holy men to their knees before me, and every one betrayed their families, their countries, even their gods to bend to my will," she spat, her eyes glowing red from the fire, and her entire body vibrating with evil. Power rolled off of her in waves, every word slapping at me like a mystical hand. "What makes you think you can possibly stand against me, little girl?"

Nothing. Dear Goddess, she was right. There was no way to stop her. She was powerful and so very old. I could feel the weight of centuries pressing against me like warm bodies. I couldn't stand against her and live, no one could. We were all going to die.

I stumbled back, shaking my head. No, this wasn't right. It was true that I was frightened, but this overwhelming sense of hopelessness and doom wasn't mine. I raised my eyes to hers and saw smug satisfaction there. She was in my head, feeding my fear, making me more afraid than I really was. I gathered my courage and took a calming breath, pushing everything down deep inside until nothing showed in my eyes. I would not give her the pleasure of letting her see my fear.

Kali laughed and came toward me, moving like a predator stalking its prey. "Do you really think this show of bravery wins you any ground? I am inside you now. I can feel your fear no matter how much you try to hide it."

She raised a hand to me and I resisted the urge to pull back from her touch. All she did was put one finger on my chin and turn my face to hers.

"Tell me, little girl," she whispered, "what frightens you? Spiders?"

The hand that was touching my face turned, palm up, and she spread her fingers open. I looked down as the biggest spider I'd ever seen crawled across her fingers. I batted it away as its long, hairy legs reached for my cheek.

"Parlor tricks," I spat, stumbling backward until I was out of her reach.

"Perhaps," she said, smiling.

She was more pleased with herself than she ought to be and that worried me. Clasping her hands in front of her, she looked skyward as if she was expecting something to appear. I looked up as well but saw nothing. After a moment she cocked her head to one side, as if listening, and then a slow smile spread across her face.

"Oh, this should be fun," she said.

I looked up again. Oh, dear Goddess, she wasn't somehow conjuring my fears, was she? As I heard the first high-pitched squeaks, I knew she was. Bats. Creepy little flying rodents. I glared at her but stood my ground. I would not run. I would not show fear. The squeaks were getting louder now, accompanied by the sound of wings beating the air. Leathery wings, furry little bodies. I shifted my weight. I really hated bats.

When the first one flew past me, clipping the side of my head, I broke and ran. I heard Kali laughing as I ran past her, my arms flailing madly at the swarm of bodies that flew around me, their wings beating at my face, their bodies slamming against me, making my skin

crawl. I swatted at them as I ran, trying to get them out
of my hair and away from my face. Panic welled up inside me and I screamed over and over. I tripped and my
hands and forearms hit the ground, breaking my fall.
The bats flew low over my huddled form and then disappeared into the night. I sobbed in relief and laid my
forehead against the cool, damp ground.

The jingle of Kali's chains swaying as she walked
drew my attention. I pushed myself up and looked
behind me. She moved purposefully toward me and
everything in my entire being screamed for me to run,
to do anything I had to do to keep her from touching
me. She was right. I couldn't stand against her. It was
bad enough that she was physically stronger than I
was. It was worse that she had her own magic to call
and centuries more experience in doing so than I had.
What made her unstoppable, though, was the fact that
she could get inside my head and use my own fears
against me. She could break me without ever laying a
hand on me.

I swung my head around and judged the distance to
the doors of the abbey. Running was futile. With Sebastian and the walking dead in front of me and Kali
behind me, I wouldn't get ten feet. I gasped in pain as
Kali grabbed my arm, jerking me to my feet in one
swift movement.

"Now, perhaps we will try this again," she said.

I was saved from having to respond because something in the darkness beyond the abbey doors drew her
attention. A look of extreme irritation crossed her face
and then the tension seemed to ebb from her body and
she smiled. She grabbed my shoulders gently and turned
me to face the open doorway.

Leaning down, she whispered in my ear, "Tell me what you see out there, what you feel."

"I can't see anything but shadow and torchlight," I said, not bothering to add that I couldn't hear anything either over the pounding of my own heart.

She chuckled against the side of my neck. "I have always wondered how you humans survived as a species. Your senses are almost nonexistent."

"Dumb luck?" I said in a small, choked voice.

"Undoubtedly. Let me tell you what I feel," she said, her hand grazing over my hip, up and down, up and down. "Your friends are close. They are quiet. They think to rescue you. Isn't that sweet?"

I could see Sebastian from the corner of my eye. His head snapped up and his nostrils flared, one hand moving to rest on the gun tucked in his waistband. So much for us stupid humans; her vampire protégé hadn't heard them either.

"Why don't we give them a little show?" she purred, her lips trailing over the spot where my blood pounded so close to the surface.

I panicked. I tore free of her and ran. She grabbed the back of my dress and I pitched forward, once again ending up on my hands and knees on the sodden ground. Before I could even catch my breath, I was on my back, Kali lying fully against me, pinning me to the ground. With a loud ripping of cloth she tore the bodice of my gown down the middle. I beat and clawed at her but her fingers deftly grabbed my wrists, shackling them like steel manacles.

"Oh, I will enjoy tasting you," she said as she ran her tongue slowly across the top of my breast, her body pressing intimately into mine. She rolled her eyes up and looked at me as her canines lengthened. Sharp teeth pierced my breast, drawing blood from the shadowy blue veins. I screamed and cried, unable to move, her hips grinding into mine as she moaned with pleasure.

A hoarse, masculine shout of denial sounded from somewhere behind me. I craned my neck and turned my head to see that Devlin, Justine, and Michael had entered the ruins. The pain on Michael's face tore through me. His sword was drawn and only Devlin's restraining hand on him kept him from rushing forward to his death.

Kali sat back on her heels. She put her hands to her head, eyes closed, and moaned softly. Her face was a mask of erotic pleasure.

"Oh, witch," she breathed, as if the word were a lover's endearment. "The power of your blood makes everything shimmer and sparkle."

"Get off of me, bitch," I growled, my fear having quickly turned to anger at the sight of my blood on her lips. That Michael had seen it too only added to my fury. Pulling my feet out from under her, I kicked with all my might, hitting her square in the sternum.

I took her by surprise and she fell back in the grass. Scrambling to my feet, I ran for Michael, but before I could reach him, an icy wind blew out of nowhere, pushing me back. Michael tried to reach me, but a jagged bolt of lightning hit the ground at his feet and ran across the grass, seeming to chase him backward. I turned slowly.

Kali was sitting cross-legged in the grass, her palms resting on her bare knees, a smile that could only be called sweet on her full lips.

She can call the elements, I thought.

"Yes," she said, her smile widening, "I can."

I froze. I think my heart even skipped a beat. Oh no. Did taking my blood mean that she could now not only sense my fears but hear my thoughts as well? Was she truly that powerful?

She clapped her hands. "Very good. We usually have to go through the tiring ordeal of denial. How very considerate of you to skip that part."

Baobh, I thought in Gaelic. Bitch.

She cocked her head to one side. "Interesting. I don't know the language, what is it?" she asked, her tone light and interested, as if we were sitting down to tea together and discussing the latest style in bonnets.

"It's Gaelic," I replied, "the language of my mother's people."

She stood in one graceful movement as if pulled up by hidden strings.

"You will have to teach it to me later. Now, the night wanes and there is much to be done." She snapped her fingers and the dark, silent sentinels stirred to life. The ten or so dead men had been so still and unmoving, I'd forgotten they were there. "Kill them all except for the red-haired witch. She is mine."

The dead moved toward Michael, Devlin, and Justine. Their faces were blank; they had no thoughts, no motivation, but to fulfill their mistress's command. Still, they were nothing more than walking corpses. I wondered if Kali really thought they would succeed against The Righteous.

"It matters little to me," she said, easily reading me. "They are an expendable distraction and I have no wish to fight tonight." She looked me up and down in a way that made my skin crawl. "There are so many more pleasurable things to pursue."

Whether or not the dead men would give them a good fight was a moot point. They took my rescuers' attention from the Destroyer, the three of them standing back to back, swords drawn as the enemy moved in. I turned back to Kali, keeping all my thoughts in Gaelic.

"You don't actually believe I'm going to let you take me out of this place, do you?" I asked.

"You don't actually believe you have a choice, do you?" she mocked me.

"Lady, I've had just about all of you I can take for one night. You're not the only one who can call the elements. And you don't have your talisman."

Her hand fluttered to her throat and there was a moment of uneasiness in her eyes. She pushed it down, her face becoming a mask of serenity. She raised her arms away from her sides, palms up.

"Do your worst," she said.

I purposely thought about lightning in English and the instant her eyes turned heavenward to face the challenge, I gathered my power and forced it out into the night.

"Teine!" Fire, I called out in Gaelic. "Come to me!"

I don't know what she saw or heard in my mind, but she turned her head at the last second as the blazing hearth fire exploded outward like the fiery breath of some angry dragon. It caught the hem of her skirt, sending the silk up in flames and catching her long hair on fire in the process. She shrieked and Sebastian ran to her, throwing her to the ground and trying to beat the fire out. The minute he came in contact with her, the flames leaped to him as well. They were both writhing on the ground, screaming, burning. I darted forward, grabbed the chain around Sebastian's neck and jerked the talisman free with an audible snap. It was a stupid chance to take but somehow I felt that it was important.

I turned to run to Michael and recoiled in horror. Body parts littered the ground, body parts that were still writhing and moving. A decapitated corpse got up and started for Michael, its arms grasping for him.

"These things don't die, Devlin!" Michael shouted as two of the dead men charged him at once. Devlin and Justine were overwhelmed by five others.

I pulled one of the torches up out the ground and ran forward. I touched the fire to the back of one's shirt and the thing started to burn. And it still didn't stop.

"Michael, what do I do?" I shouted.

"Run!" he said. "Get back to the house where you're safe."

"I won't leave you."

"Woman, do as you're told!" he snapped, his sword severing an arm.

I lit the rest of the body on fire.

"Don't you take that tone with me," I snapped back. "I'm trying to help."

The first body was consumed in flames. It faltered, then fell to its knees. I watched in horror and fascination as it fell forward and lay there smoldering and, most important, not moving. As quickly as I could, I lit the others. Their orders were to kill the vampires and not one of them even turned to look at me. When they were all still and silent and in charred pieces on the ground, the four of us stood and stared at each other, the smell of burned flesh strong in our nostrils. Michael was the first to recover.

"We must take their heads," he said, nodding to the dark pile where Kali and Sebastian lay unmoving.

They were no longer burning. I didn't know if that was a good sign or a bad one. Michael started forward, his sword clamped tightly in his hand. I looked at the bodies. One of Kali's outstretched hands twitched and a tremor ran through the earth. Michael paused and looked back at me. My eyes widened in fear.

"Run," I whispered.

He clenched his jaw, a muscle ticing in his cheek. His knuckles were white where they gripped the sword. I looked back at Kali, watching in horror as she planted both blackened hands firmly on the ground and started to push herself up. The ground trembled beneath my feet. She may be burned but she was alive. And she was angry.

"You'll never get close enough," I yelled. "Run!"

The wind picked up, howling through the clearing like a legion of angry demons. It chased us all the way to the tree line before it caught us, branches flying, leaves blowing up in our faces. The rain started next, pelting us like thousands of tiny razors as we raced through the forest. A branch as thick as my wrist hit Devlin in the temple. He stumbled and we ran on. It was as if the forest was throwing everything it had in our faces: rocks, acorns, dirt, leaves, bark, and branches. Lightning split a tree in front of us, showering us with sparks, and the earth shook with thunder. The wind wrapped around us, a swirling vortex of debris. I tried to push forward, even though I could no longer see where I was going, but the wind held me back. It would hold us here, helpless, until Kali came to kill us. I fell to my knees.

"Enough!" I yelled, my lungs burning. I was shaking with exhaustion and fear. Blood was running down my chest. Again. I'd had enough.

"Dulcie, come on!" Michael yelled and bent down as if to pick me up. I put up a hand and stopped him, shaking my head. The three of them stood staring down at me as if my mind had finally snapped and they didn't know whether to humor me or fight me.

I gathered my power around me like a shield—what little of it I could still feel, as exhausted as I was—focused, and yelled out into the fury, "Hearken well, ye elements, unto me! Earth and wind, fire, and sea! Calm be the night, finished be the fight! By my words and by my will, go in peace, the night be still!"

Everything stopped in an instant. Branches fell from midair as if dropped by invisible hands, leaves floated back to earth, acorns hit the ground with a scattering of soft plops. The forest was deathly, unnaturally still.

I breathed a sigh of profound relief and fell face first into the leaves.

Chapter Twenty-one

I became aware of two things at once. First, that I was lying on some soft surface, covered with a blanket, and second, that someone near me was in pain. I kept my eyes closed, thinking that if we'd been captured, then it might be best if they didn't know that I was awake yet. I could hear a low humming noise and intermittent masculine grunts of pain. It then occurred to me that if Kali had taken us, she could hear my thoughts anyway and would know by now that I was awake. I cracked one eye open.

That was my ceiling! I turned my head to see Michael lying next to me on top of the covers, arms folded behind his head, and the small white and gray kitten sitting on his chest, kneading him furiously with her big, hairy paws. I giggled and rolled onto my side, watching them. She had a very loud purr for such a little kitty.

"Your wee cat has no sense," he said. "I think God asked her if she'd like to be smart or beautiful and she chose beautiful."

I laughed. "Why do you say that? It seems to me that you're the one with no sense, allowing her to torture you like that."

He laughed. "No, I mean that animals sense vampires and they don't like to be around us. They sense that something is wrong about us. Your kitten here doesn't seem to have enough brains to know when she's facing something dangerous."

"Well, maybe so. I suppose she's a housecat now. She doesn't seem to be fit for the stables and it certainly appears that she's made herself quite at home here."

"What's her name?"

"Priscilla K. Pussycat."

"Quite a big name for such a wee little thing."

I shrugged. "She can be Prissy for short."

"Prissy," he said softly and stroked her fur. There was a look of contentment on his face, as if this was something he enjoyed and hadn't been able to do in a very long time.

"I think that maybe she's not so dumb," I said. "Maybe she knows you for what you are and likes you anyway. I do," I added softly.

I looked up at him and there was so much sadness in his eyes. Sadness and something else.

"Why do you look at me with distrust?" I asked.

He sighed. "I don't mean to, lass. I promise. It's just . . ."

I was quiet while he gathered his thoughts.

"After Devlin turned me I stayed with him and Justine for a few months. I learned to deal with what I'd become. Then came Culloden. Bonnie Prince Charlie's army fell and the redcoats swarmed over the country, using any excuse they could find to slaughter the innocent and the not-so-innocent. I worried for my family and so I went home to protect them. Devlin told me not to. He warned me but I wouldn't listen.

"Oh, they were glad to see me at first. My mum cried. My sisters had grown into bonny lassies since I'd seen them last. My wee brother had just had his tenth birthday. We stayed up all night talking about what would happen now that the war was lost. There was talk of going to America but they were so poor they would have had to indenture themselves for passage. I wouldn't allow them to sell themselves into bondage. I told them I'd find another way. Just before dawn, my mum gave me her room so that I could sleep after my long journey. I pulled the curtains closed tightly and slept. She came in to wake me near sunset, clattering on about how I'd slept the day away as she pulled the curtains open."

"And she figured it out, what had happened to you, what you were?"

He took a deep breath. "Yes," he said softly. "My own mother cursed me for a devil and drove me from my home."

"Oh, Michael, how could she?" I couldn't imagine my own mother ever doing that to me. Then again, I'm sure Michael hadn't imagined it either.

He shrugged. "Her son was dead. She thought I was a demon. Devlin found me and I had to listen to his 'I told you so' speech about a dozen times. I was eaten up with grief and anger. I felt betrayed by them on some level but I still wouldn't leave them all alone, unprotected."

"What did you do?"

"Devlin wanted to leave, Justine was tired of war and Scotland in general, but I wouldn't go. It didn't matter that they'd turned their backs on me, they were my family. So Devlin marched down to the croft one night doing his best impression of a fourteenth-century lord and gave my mum enough money for her and the children to go to America, buy a fancy house, and live like aristocrats for the rest of their lives. My mother was a stubborn woman and she told him that it was blood money and she'd not be taking it."

"She refused?"

He nodded. "I don't know what Devlin said to her to change her mind, but I'm sure it's probably something I'd have to punch him in the jaw for. Two weeks later I stood in the shadows of a dockside inn and watched them board a passenger ship out of Inverness bound for North Carolina. They looked well."

"And you went away with Devlin and Justine?"

"Yes."

We were silent for several minutes, each of us thinking our own thoughts. No wonder he didn't trust lightly if his own mother had turned her back on him. I could work with this, though, now that I knew. I just needed some time. I decided to turn the conversation elsewhere for the moment.

"When Devlin was human, who was he? What was his title?" I asked. It was something I'd been wondering since I'd seen the falcon crest on his carriage.

"I don't know. I wonder sometimes if he even remembers his own name."

"His own name?"

"Devlin is probably the name he took when he became a vampire. It's commonly done among our kind. You'll never get back the life you once had, the person you once were, so you start over fresh with a new existence and a new name."

"And what was yours?"

"Michael," he said with a sheepish grin. "Devlin took a fancy to it, said I fought like the Archangel Michael."

I laid my head on his shoulder. "I should really get up now. What are the others doing?"

"Looking at some book. Pendergrass was all aflutter over that bauble you stole from Montford."

"Really?" I asked with a yawn. "I should go help."

He put his hand on my head, smoothing my hair. "You'll stay right here and rest. You scared me to death when you fainted in the forest."

"You're already dead," I murmured.

"You know my meaning. You were magnificent tonight, so brave."

"I was terrified."

"You were still brave."

"I made you run. It felt cowardly but I can't be sorry about it. She was injured but I could still feel her power. If you'd gone for the kill, she would have destroyed you."

He stroked my hair. "In every situation you have two choices: You can run, or you can stay and fight. Running doesn't always mean you're a coward any more than fighting always means you're brave. Sometimes the braver thing is to run and live to fight another day; any fool can make a stand and die. You understood the danger better than I did and you made the right decision. Because of you, we lived to fight another day. Now, your wee beastie here has curled up and fallen asleep and I want you to do the same. I'll wake you in a few hours."

I opened my eyes and looked at Prissy, sound asleep on his chest. She was curled into a little ball with her nose buried in her fluffy tail.

"You know, Michael, it seems that I'm not any

smarter than my kitten. I didn't drive you from my home, I summoned you into it."

He stiffened. "Lass, we've had this discussion. You're a viscount's daughter and I'm a vampire who grew up dirt poor in a two-room crofter's hut."

"Hmm. And as you can see, I'm horribly repulsed by the idea," I said and snuggled closer. "Now, don't argue with me anymore, just hold me while I sleep."

"Yes, milady," he mumbled, and kissed the top of my head.

Chapter Twenty-two

"Who died?" I asked as I walked into the dining room a few hours later, freshly gowned in a dark green evening dress. The faces that greeted me were grim.

"Dulcie, oh dear God," Fiona cried and launched herself at me, nearly knocking Michael down in the process. "I'm so sorry. I'm so sorry."

"Hush now," I said, patting her back as I held her to me. "I'm fine, Fi. It's not your fault."

"Yes, it was. I was so stupid."

"That's enough," I said, giving her a small shake. "I'm fine and we have more information than we did before, so don't worry yourself about it."

I looked at Mr. Pendergrass, who was seated at the table, Kali's talisman before him. His face held concern but not despair.

"What can you tell me about that?" I asked, nodding my head at the large ruby.

Clearing his throat, he picked up the pendant. "Well, I can't tell you what the runes mean, they're unfamiliar to me. Did Sebastian tell you what it was for?"

"He said it was Kali's and that it would protect him from my magic."

"Did it?" he asked.

I shrugged. "I didn't test it but it didn't keep him from catching fire, no."

"Hmm. Well, I have good news and bad news."

"Good news first," I said. "I haven't heard any of that in a while."

"The good news is that we now have some leverage. This stone looks like a ruby but it's not. It's a conjured stone made from Kali's own blood, and, if its purpose is to protect her against magics, then it's probably from the blood of a powerful witch as well."

He looked at me and smiled. I shook my head.

"I don't understand."

"It's a personal effect, and what's more, it's made from her own blood. It can be used to bind her."

"A binding spell? You mean we could bind her from doing harm?"

"Better yet, you could bind her to one place, say, one house. Or even better, with a little remix of ingredients, we could bind her into a stone or a tree or some other immovable object."

"That's . . . that's not exactly white magic, Mr. Pendergrass," I said.

"It's not exactly black, either . . . more of a light gray, I'd say."

I arched a brow at him and pursed my lips.

"Don't be squeamish, Dulcinea," Mr. Pendergrass said in a practical tone. "I think exceptions can be made for this situation. Or would you rather allow her to kill us all?"

I flinched at that. "No, I suppose you're right. It's just that the thought of casting a spell that traps her for eternity . . . it's rather cruel and horrifying. Is there no way to work a spell which could immobilize her long enough to stake her?"

"She's not an ordinary vampire, Dulcie," Devlin

interrupted. "I'm not sure that staking her would work. I'm not entirely certain that she can be killed at all. At the very least you'll simply free her demon form and it will find another body to occupy. I know what we're asking of you is awful but I don't see any other choice."

"All right." I nodded. "What does the spell require?"

Mr. Pendergrass frowned. "That's the problem. I don't remember exactly and we can't find the book. I know your mother had it; I sold it to her two years ago, but," he gestured to the table piled with books, "this is everything, and it's not here."

"She probably left it in the townhouse in London," I said. "We hadn't yet moved everything out after the Little Season. Before we get too excited about this spell though, what's the bad news?"

Mr. Pendergrass grimaced. "The bad news is that you have to get close enough to her to work it."

"How close?"

"Several feet."

"Impossible," I said. "Even if I could get that close to her, the probability of failure is staggering. Besides the fact that she's the most terrifying thing I've ever encountered, we have the little problem that now that she's tasted my blood, she can read my mind at will." Unconsciously, my hand moved to the spot on my breast where she'd fed from me. After only a few hours the wound was now healed, the skin as flawless as it had ever been. "You don't think she can read my mind right now, do you?"

"No," Devlin said. "She would have to be close to you to do it, the same as Sebastian had to be close to call to you. Vampire . . . magic, for lack of a better word, doesn't work well at a distance. Besides, I'm not certain she was actually reading your thoughts. I've heard tales of the old ones being able to do that but I always believed it to be nothing more than a parlor trick. Are you sure she really—"

"Very, very sure," I replied. "The only way I managed to call the fire without her figuring it out was by thinking in Gaelic. Thankfully she doesn't understand Gaelic but I don't think she'll be fooled by that again." I thought about it for a minute and then asked, "Devlin, when I was with her, I was terrified but I remember feeling more scared than I think I should have been. I remember feeling despair, feeling that she was so powerful, and I should just give in to her. I don't think they were entirely my own thoughts. Do you think that's possible?"

He nodded. "If she really can enter your mind, then I would say it's also possible that she could be magnifying your fears and feelings of hopelessness."

"Did you feel it too?" I asked.

"No. Vampire tricks do not work on other vampires."

"So," Archie said, slumping in his chair, "we're back where we began."

Yes, I thought, *I suppose we are*. As a human, I had little to no recourse. If I fought her and failed, millions of people would die. The noble thing to do would be to kill myself, I supposed, but I didn't want to die. There were so many places I wanted to go, so many things I wanted to do. If I became a vampire . . . I laughed to myself. I was still thinking *if*. Justine was right; it would be the hardest, bravest thing I'd ever done. I felt a deep kinship with her in that moment. I looked at her, as serene and coolly beautiful as ever, and I knew that she knew what I was thinking. She'd thought it once too.

I couldn't take the easy way out and leave my friends and family unprotected. If I killed myself and thwarted Kali's plans, her vengeance would know no bounds. I would be consigning them all to a fate worse than death.

No, I would be brave. I would stay and fight because I had no other choice.

I stood. "Mr. Pendergrass, I think it's worth a try and I'd like to take a look at that book. I think you and Archie should leave in the morning, take Mrs. Mackenzie and Fiona with you, and go to London. The rest of us will follow at nightfall."

Mrs. Mackenzie protested. "I don't want to leave you here, Dulcie."

"I need you more in London, Mrs. Mac. Do you think my cousins are going to let Archie or Mr. Pendergrass in the house to search through my mother's things?"

"Oh," she said. "Of course."

"This way you can get the book and have it for me when I get there tomorrow night. Mind you're back to Mr. Pendergrass's well before sunset though. I think that Kali and Sebastian will be lying low for a few days while they heal their wounds, but we can't be too careful."

"I was very proud of you for that bit of magic, Dulcinea," Mr. Pendergrass said. "Your control is improving."

"Calling and releasing the elements isn't exactly difficult magic, Mr. Pendergrass."

"Yes, but you managed to do exactly as you willed with no mishaps. It's progress; you should be very proud."

"I am." I sighed. "Let's just hope that I'll be able to

work this binding spell. Because if I ever had doubts, I now know that we'll never beat her with brute force. If we're going to win, it will be through trickery and cunning. If we fight her head-on, we'll lose. Our only hope is that her arrogance and her own belief in her strength and immortality will keep her from noticing what we're up to until it's too late."

"Dulcinea," Mr. Pendergrass said, "you never said, did Kali tell you what she wanted from you?"

"Yes," I said softly.

"What?"

Seven pairs of eyes turned expectantly toward me.

"She wants me to help her destroy the world."

Chapter Twenty-three

I sat on the kitchen steps with Priscilla in my lap, watching the sun rise in the morning sky. The world was a dozen shades of pink and gold and blue. Archie was down at the stable with the Harper lads, hitching up the carriage. Fiona was humming in the kitchen, packing anything that wouldn't keep for a few days into a picnic basket.

I rested my chin on top of Prissy's head and bathed in the cool golden glow of my last sunrise. I had never been an early riser. If I ever saw the sun rise, it was usually as I was slipping out of a ball gown and falling into bed. Now that I would never stand under another dawn, I suddenly wished I hadn't wasted so many of them.

"You've made your decision, haven't you?"

I shielded my eyes and looked up at Mrs. Mackenzie. She sat down on the step next to me.

"It's the only way. You understand that, don't you?" I said softly.

She swallowed hard and nodded. "I feel like I've let your mother down," she said. "I was supposed to keep you safe."

I put my arm around her waist and laid my head on her shoulder. "No one could have protected me from this. Mama would have understood that. You've been like a second mother to me all my life, Mrs. Mac. I love you and nothing is ever going to change that, not for me, anyway."

We sat like that for a few moments, watching the sunrise, and then I found that I had to ask, had to know.

"Mrs. Mac, when Michael went home to his family after he was made a vampire, his mother didn't take it so well. When she realized what he was, she called him a demon and ordered him from his home."

"Poor lad," she said, shaking her head.

"Well, I was just wondering, when this is done . . ."

"Dulcinea Macgregor Craven!" she hissed. "That you would ever think such a thing of me! Gracious, child, I've been caring for you since before you were even born. How can you think that I would ever stop loving you? You're about to sacrifice yourself to save the rest of us, and possibly the entire world, and you think I'll bar you from your own home?"

I looked away, ashamed I'd even thought it. Mrs. Mackenzie grabbed my face in her hands and forced me to look into her lovely green eyes.

"Ravenworth is your home and it will always be your home. Do you not think that I'd much rather have you walking and talking and flirting with your young man than lying cold and dead in a grave?"

I shrugged. "You are a vicar's daughter."

She snorted. "If God counts this a suicide, then I'll have a word or two to say to Him when I get to heaven, I can guarantee you that."

I smiled. "I'm glad you're on our side, Mrs. Mac. And he's not my young man, not really."

She laughed. "You can't fool me, missy. I'm not quite in my dotage yet. I remember what it's like to look at a man the way you look at him."

"He has a problem with the fact that we're of different social standings."

"He's a vampire, Dulcie. He doesn't have a social standing."

"You know what I mean. When he was alive, he was a poor gardener. He's being a terrible snob about the whole thing."

"Your father would have liked him," Mrs. Mackenzie said.

"Really? Do you think so?"

She nodded. "You should have seen the look of pain on his face when he came in last night, carrying you in his arms, all pale and still as death, him barking orders left and right. Your father would have approved. Why, after Fiona and I had gotten you out of your wet gown, which is completely ruined by the way, he actually had the gall to order me out of your room! Me! Can you believe that?"

"I'm surprised you let him."

"Well," she said, "sometimes it's expedient to let men think they're really in charge, but never for extended periods of time, mind you. Besides," she said with a wink, "I left the kitten in there. No man can make love with a kitten in the middle."

I laughed and blushed furiously.

"Dulcie, do we need to talk about, well, *things* before I go?"

"Things?"

"Yes, you know, the kinds of things that happen between a man and woman. In bed," she blushed. "Or elsewhere."

"Oh. No. I mean, I've lived in the country most of my life. I think I know the rudiments."

"Oh, good," she said. "You realize, of course, that you won't be able to be married in a church, but I fully expect at least a handfasting before you go anywhere with that rascal."

"Marriage?" I squeaked. "Mrs. Mac, no one's said anything about marriage."

"Well, then he'd better get off his bum and do so. I realize that when you're going to live forever that certain social customs may no longer be relevant, but right is still right. Your father, God rest his soul, would expect me to see to it."

"I'll, uh, mention it," I said, "but we're getting way ahead of ourselves. We still have evil to fight and I'm not sure if we can win. Handfasting may be a moot point."

"Have some faith, Dulcie," Mrs. Mackenzie said, looking up into the eastern sky. "Kali may be strong but she doesn't have a heaven full of angels looking down on her. You do."

I looked up. I certainly hoped she was right. We needed all the help we could get.

Chapter Twenty-four

I rode Missy out through sun-filled glades and past sparkling streams. If this was to be my last day in the sun, I intended to enjoy it fully. The day was warm for October and there wasn't a cloud in the sky. I kept Missy out of the shaded woods, where the air had a bite of autumn chill to it, and steered her toward the wide-open expanse of grass leading down to the small lake at the center of our property. When I reached the pond, I slipped off Missy's back and ran my hands over her white blaze, scratching her ears as I slid the bridle off, and let her graze.

Michael had been adamant that I not go out today. He'd reasoned that although Kali and Sebastian couldn't walk in the sun, that didn't mean that she didn't have control of a human, or one of her walking dead, who could take me as I rode out alone. Devlin had argued that if Kali and Sebastian had made it to shelter before sunrise, they were wounded and healing, and I was probably safe enough. I think he understood that I'd made my decision and wanted to say good-bye to the sun.

I walked to the edge of the lake and looked out over the calm water. With a thrill of wicked excitement I slipped out of my boots and stockings, my riding habit and chemise, and stood naked on the shore. I'd always wanted to swim naked. I could have chosen a better time of year, I supposed, but there was no help for it. If I ever wanted to swim naked under the sun this would be my last chance.

Taking a deep breath, I waded out into the chilly water. It was glorious. And freezing. I gritted my teeth and swam to the center of the lake, where I floated under the pure golden light of the afternoon until I couldn't stand the cold water anymore. By the time I climbed back onto the shore my teeth were chattering and my toes were quite a lovely shade of purplish blue.

I sat in the sun until my skin dried and then I slipped my riding habit back on. When my hair was nearly dry I caught Missy and slid her bridle back on. Finding a fallen log, I managed to climb back up into the saddle. We walked at a leisurely pace back to the house, stopping occasionally to enjoy the view or to let Missy nibble some choice greenery. Michael had said that animals had a sixth sense about vampires, and I wondered if she would ever let me on her back again after tonight.

When we reached the stable I waved Charlie Harper away and unsaddled and brushed Missy myself. Laying my head against her silky neck, I stood there for a long time, breathing in the scent of her.

"I'm leaving tonight for London for a few days," I told Charlie. "Take good care of her."

"Aye, miss, I sure will," he said, patting her as he came into the stall with an armful of hay. "She's a good girl."

"You'd best be getting home," I said. "The sun will be setting soon. Has there been any more trouble in the village?"

"Naw, miss, but the magistrate still ain't caught the murdering devil, so everyone's still making sure they're all locked up tight in their homes after dark."

"Probably wise," I replied.

"I'll bring some table scraps for the cats until you get home, miss, but I ain't seen the little gray and white kitten around," he said worriedly.

"She's apparently moved herself into the big house," I laughed. "Actually, she's gone to London in a posh little basket with Fiona this morning, but I appreciate you looking after the others. Take care of yourself, Charlie."

"Aye, miss, you do the same."

There was no one about in the house when I walked in. It seemed so unnaturally quiet without the bustle of servants, or at least without Fiona humming and singing in the halls. I went to the dining room and opened the door a crack. Justine had moved the table again and was practicing, this time with the short sword she wore sheathed down her spine.

"Where is everyone?" I asked.

"Devlin and Michael closeted themselves in the library shortly after you left and I haven't seen them since," she replied, never breaking stride.

"When you're through here, will you ask Michael to come up and see me?"

She stopped and looked at me, a combination of pride and worry in her eyes. "You're going to go through with it?"

"What choice do I have?"

She shook her head sadly. "None. You know that Michael still thinks he can find a way to save you."

I smiled but there was no joy in it. "This is the way."

"And if he won't do it?"

I laughed harshly. "Do you really think I can't persuade him?"

She smiled. "You may have a bit of the courtesan in you after all, *mon amie*. I'll give you an hour to prepare yourself."

I nodded and closed the door.

Chapter Twenty-five

When I reached my room, I pulled off my riding habit and the damp chemise. With Fiona not there to help me dress this morning, I'd left off my stays and only managed half the buttons at the back of the habit, but the jacket hid the fact adequately enough. There was a slight bulge, which didn't exactly make me look like a hunchback, but if anyone other than Charlie or my houseguests had seen me, I'd have been mortified.

I sponged off with clean water from the basin and then opened the jar of my favorite honeysuckle-scented cream, slowly working it into every inch of my skin. I dropped my glamour and watched my hair bleed from copper to crimson, and then brushed it until it shone in thick waves down my back. Slipping into my dressing gown, I pulled my valise from the top of the wardrobe and packed what I would need. I wondered if Justine would take me to buy some of those wonderful breeches and boots like she wore when we got to London.

The sun was low on the horizon as I pulled the heavy drapes closed over the windows and then walked out onto the little balcony off my bedroom. There was a knot in the pit of my stomach. Could I really do this? Could I give up everything I was, everything I was meant to be?

I looked down over the Winter Garden. I used to love

the smell of the roses but the roses were gone. The scent of honeysuckle and jasmine filled the air now. I gripped the stone rail of the balcony and looked out over the new shrubs and flowers that my magic had sown. My eyes traveled from one to another as I leaned farther over the railing.

Night bloomers, every one of them. My magic had created a vampire's garden.

My knees nearly buckled under me.

"Lord and Lady," I breathed.

Whether the magic had chosen my path for me or whether this was a sign, a blessing, from my mother, I didn't know. Maybe I wasn't giving up what I was meant to be after all; maybe this *was* the person I was meant to be. I looked up at the sky.

"Thank you, Mama," I sighed, and I fancied the gentle breeze carrying my words to her in the next world.

The western sky was pink with fluffy golden clouds hanging lazily above the horizon. It was one of those sunsets where everything—the grass, the trees, even Ravenworth itself—seemed to be rose colored. All my life I'd had hats and sun bonnets shoved on my red head so that I wouldn't freckle in the sun. Until this afternoon I'd never sat outside without a wide-brimmed hat on my head and gloves on my hands. Now I embraced my last opportunity. After tonight freckles would no longer be an issue.

I opened the dressing gown and let it slide to the floor. Standing in the pink twilight, gloriously naked and alive, I raised my hands to the sky and exalted in the glow of the sun, the hum of the earth around me, the beating of my own heart. The sun warmed my skin and I threw back my head and closed my eyes, opening myself to the world around me. I don't know how long I stood there, not nearly long enough, when I heard the bedroom door close softly behind me. I turned, clad in pink sunset and nothing else, and watched Michael walk across the room. If I live a thousand years, I will never forget the look on his face in that moment.

Lust, desire, tenderness, a fierce masculine need to possess, all passed across that angel's face. And, yes, perhaps even love. His blue-gray eyes raked over me and made me shiver with expectation. Would he be gentle or fierce? Did I care as long as I could feel him next to me? The setting sun bathed the balcony and splashed a pool of light across the floor of my bedroom. He stopped a few feet from the deadly sun and held his hand out to me.

Such a simple gesture, but it meant everything. If I went to him, I would lose myself, everything I'd ever known I was. If I lay down on that bed with him, it wouldn't be me who got up again, but someone new, someone different. I would never again be exactly who I was at this moment. He would take my innocence, and my life.

I looked at that chiseled face, at that strong, battle-scarred hand reaching out to me, and I walked forward. Stopping at the edge of the light, I stared at his hand. He was so still I wasn't even sure he was breathing. Did he expect me to turn and run? I reached my hand out, placed it in his, and he pulled me out of the sun and into the shadows.

"Are you sure, lass?" he asked, his voice harsh with emotion.

I pressed myself against him and felt him shudder. "Don't I feel sure?" I purred.

He grabbed my hips and lifted me, my legs wrapping around his waist. I leaned down and pressed my mouth to his. His tongue plunged in, and then he was walking toward the bed, every step moving me against him in delicious ways, and we fell to the sheets in a tangle of limbs.

As he kissed me again and again, my fingers moved to unbutton his shirt. I pulled the material from the waistband of his breeches and pushed it down over his shoulders, needing to feel his bare skin against mine. His lips slid like silk to my jaw and my neck as I arched my back and pressed myself against him, running my hands over the tight muscles in his back. His lips paused briefly at my neck and then trailed lower. I sucked in my breath as his tongue slid over one nipple. Arching under him, silently begging him, I fisted one hand in his hair. His mouth closed over me, pulling, the gentlest hint of teeth, and my legs came up around him. I could feel the hard length of him against me, and I shuddered, my limbs shaking.

His mouth traveled the valley between my breasts; he kissed me there as one calloused hand moved slowly up my leg, over my hip. His lips closed over my other nipple, drawing tightly and then releasing, his tongue making a single pass over the tight crest before he drew it roughly into his mouth again. I threw back my head as his weight shifted and his hand moved over the most intimate part of me, fingers tangling in my curls. Pressing myself against him, I cried out for his touch, but his fingers lightly circled me, teasing me.

"Michael," I begged. "Please."

"What do you want, lass?"

"I don't know," I said, my head thrashing back and forth on the pillows, "but you do. Give it to me!"

His finger slid inside me and my hips jerked, a small scream tore from my throat.

"Oh, God, you're so hot," he moaned against my lips.

He moved me onto my side and curled his body behind mine, his finger constantly moving in and out in a delicious rhythm that sent my blood flowing like molten quicksilver in my veins. His other arm came around me, cradling my neck against his shoulder as his free hand reached out to stroke my breasts, to roll the rigid peaks between his fingers. Moaning, I laid my hand over his, feeling his finger pressing inside me, and rocked against him as he slowly slid another finger inside. I sank my teeth into his bicep to keep from screaming, and fiercely rode the waves of pleasure, reaching, always reaching to something that was not quite attainable.

"No, not yet," he groaned and slid his fingers from me, their wetness trailing across my stomach. I felt the bed move and, trembling, I turned to watch him undress.

He was magnificent. He was all long, lean muscles and rigid planes and angles. His manhood stood out proud and terrifying. I sucked in my breath and stared. He had to be joking; there was no way this was going to work. I reached out one hand to touch him, my fingers skimming the length of his manhood before I closed my hand over it. I reached my other hand up and placed it next to the first, and I still couldn't encompass him completely. He was hard as marble and throbbing in my hands. I looked into his eyes with grave uncertainty.

"Oh ye of little faith," he muttered, and tossed me back on the bed. Stalking around the bed, he stopped at the foot of it and stared down at me.

My hair spilled over the pillows in a pool of ruby waves, my skin nearly the same color as the cream sheets. I raised one leg and trailed my long fingers over my knee and down the inside of my thigh in what I hoped was a provocative manner. He growled and came down on the bed on all fours. Stalking me like the predator he was, he moved with liquid grace to rest between my thighs, his eyes never once leaving my face. His breath was warm on my moist curls and I screamed his name as his mouth covered me, hot and wet and urgent.

"Michael," I moaned. Surely proper people didn't do this but I couldn't quite bring myself to ask him to stop. It simply felt too good.

"Dulcie," he whispered against me.

I stiffened.

"What is it?" he asked, looking up at me in confusion.

"My mother called me Dulcie. It doesn't seem right somehow to hear it from you as you're doing . . . that."

"What should I call you?" he murmured, and licked my cleft in one long stroke.

I shivered. "Give me my new name, Michael. I've chosen you. You choose my name."

"Dulcinea," he whispered and kissed my thigh. He looked up at me and I watched him as he rose over me, his hands moving over my generous hips. "Cin," he said, "for God knows you've a body made for it."

"Cin," I repeated as he pressed himself against me. "Yes, I like it."

"My sweet Cin, I haven't even begun," he said wickedly.

The head of his shaft rested against me and I was hot and wet and willing. I opened my thighs and he pushed forward, pulled back, pushed forward, filling

and stretching me. Then he gripped my thighs and slid
home in one deep stroke. Pain lanced through me and I
shoved at him, but he held me still.

"Shh, shh," he muttered against my lips and began
to move again.

Long slow strokes in and out, and soon the pain was
forgotten; a haze of lust filled me instead. He nearly
pulled out of me and then moved back in, just enough
that I felt the marble tip of him at my entrance, teasing,
entering and retreating, but never going farther than an
inch or two. I was insane with wanting, with needing,
but I knew not what. I raked my nails across every inch
of skin I could find.

"How do you want it, Cin?"

"Harder," I moaned, and he drove forward.

He drove into me again and again. There was nothing
gentle about him; he was every inch the hard, dominant
male. And I loved it. His fists tangled in my hair, his
breathing as hard and fast as my own. I dug my nails into
his back as I felt the world spiral out of control and burst
over me in wave after wave of scalding hot pleasure. He
yelled and sank his teeth deeply into the frantic heartbeat that pulsed in my neck. I screamed, not knowing
whether in pleasure or pain, as my body spasmed and
my legs quivered around him. The very earth seemed to
shake beneath us.

As he drank from me, it was almost as if, in those
few shining moments, I was inside him. I could feel my
blood flowing into him. I could smell my perfume and
feel my hair against his skin. Even as I felt him inside
me I could feel myself surrounding him, hot and puls-
ing with need. I screamed again as pleasure washed
over me for the second time, leaving bright white lights

dancing behind my closed eyelids. He was still throbbing deep inside me when he picked his head up, ran his tongue over the punctures in my neck, and in one quick movement rolled us both over so that I lay sprawled on top of him.

Chapter Twenty-six

"What was that?" I asked, knowing instinctively that what had happened at the end was not in the normal course of things.

He laughed softly. "I think that is our compensation for never being able to walk in the sun again."

"It was like I was seeing what you were seeing and feeling what you felt," I said with wonder.

"Yes," he said and shivered, running his hands over my back. "It's always there to a certain extent when you drink from someone but it's more . . . intense when you do it while making love."

"Will it be the same after I've turned? Or does it only work with humans?"

"Oh, it'll be even better afterward. But always remember, between two vampires, blood is like a drug or an aphrodisiac. Only take a little and only for pleasure. If you take more than a few swallows of blood from another vampire's body, it'll make you horribly ill."

"I suppose you've done this quite a lot," I whispered, not liking the feeling of raging jealousy that swept through me.

He stilled and then said carefully, "What do you want me to say to you, Cin? I've been undead for seventy years and I haven't been a monk."

I buried my face in his neck. "Of course not," I replied, feeling virginal and ridiculous.

"Look at me," he said and wiggled around until he was nose to nose with me. "As long as you'll have me, there will be no one else. I swear that to you. My God, woman, as if I could even think of any other female with you by my side and in my bed."

I smiled a smile of pure feminine pleasure and laid my head on his chest.

"Am I too heavy for you?" I asked.

He grunted. "Move and I'll bite you."

"Promises, promises," I purred and kissed his collarbone. "Michael?"

"Hmmm?"

"I can't feel my toes," I said in a sleepy and unconcerned voice.

His rumbling laughter answered me. "Were you planning on leaving?"

"No," I said. "I just thought you should know."

"So," he said, wrapping his arms around me, "what did you do this afternoon?"

"I rode Missy and I . . . I swam naked in the lake."

"Did you now? Is that something you do often?" he teased.

"No, never, you wretch. I just thought that since it was something I'd always secretly longed to do and since I only had one more afternoon in the sun, then I should do it, is all."

He went very still. "Are you determined to do this, then?"

I sighed. Bless him for still wanting to save me, but he was going to have to give up the idea and do what needed to be done.

"You know there's no other way," I said, running my fingers across his chest, lightly grazing his nipple. "If you won't do it, then I'll get Devlin to."

He grabbed my hair and forced me to look at him. "No other man will lay finger or fang on you, do you understand?"

A thrill of pleasure coursed through me at his ferocity but there were still doubts clouding my thoughts. There were questions about the future that he and I needed to resolve.

"Do you keep fighting this because you don't want me with you? I know the three of you are like a family and I don't want to intrude where I'm not wanted. I mean, I could always go—"

His laughter stopped me in mid-sentence.

"Good God, lass, for seventy years I've traveled with Devlin and Justine, envying them for what they have together and wanting it for my own. I just never thought when I found it that it would be with someone as fine as you. It's a hard life we live. I just want you to be sure it's *me* that you want."

I breathed a sigh of relief and pleasure. He did want me. I laid my head back down. "My father would approve of you."

He snorted. "I very much doubt that."

Putting my hands on his chest, I pushed up so that I was straddling him and glared. "He would. Mrs. Mackenzie said so just this morning."

"Did she now?" he asked with a smile. "Lord, I'd love to paint you just like that."

"Naked?" I asked, arching a brow.

"No, it's that haughty look on your face I'm after."

"But not naked?"

He shook his head. "No, not for this portrait. I'm thinking I'd like to see you looking like that, clad in something red and silken and scandalous. That dress you were wearing when we first met, perhaps."

I smiled and stretched out on top of him, reveling in the perfect fit of our bodies. "You paint?"

"Given enough years to practice, you can become good at anything."

"Hmm, maybe I'll finally master the piano, then."

He quirked a brow at me. "Don't all young ladies of quality play?"

I grimaced and hid my face behind the fall of my hair. "Apparently not. I can't seem to get my left hand and my right to work independently of each other. It's a flaw."

"Hmm, I may have to change my mind about this, you know. I mean, a vampire who can't play the piano . . . what good is that?"

I giggled and he clasped me tightly to him and rolled us over until he was staring down at me.

"Wait here while I light some candles. I want to see you."

"Let me do it," I said, not wanting to lose the feel of him over me, inside me.

I closed my eyes and called to that place deep inside me where my magic goes to rest. It welled up in me, making me feel alive and flushed with power. I imagined the candles lit, and an instant later every wick in the room burst forth into flame and then settled to a soft glow.

"You amaze me," he said softly and kissed me high on my cheekbone. "I love this little freckle."

"It's not a freckle, it's a beauty mark."

"It's a freckle and it's precious."

"Are you going to argue with me all night?"

He groaned. "What would you rather do?"

I moved my hips against him.

"Again, my little wanton?" he asked.

"Can we?"

I felt him stir and harden inside me. He leaned down to kiss me.

"Michael, wait," I said, my hand on his chest. "First tell me what will happen—when you turn me, that is."

"I have to drink from you one more time tonight, soon, and then you must drink from me. You will simply feel as if you're falling asleep but your body will die and be reborn."

"And then we'll see if I still have my magic or not."

"Yes."

"You've done this before? Turned someone, I mean."

"No, but Devlin gave me very specific instructions."

"I don't want to end up actually dead, Michael."

"Don't worry so. Make love to me, Cin, and let me take care of you."

He pulled out of me almost entirely and then thrust forward, and I was lost in the rapture. Some time later when the world split and fell into shimmering stars, he bit the other side of my neck, exactly where Sebastian had marked me. This time I didn't feel pain, only white-hot pleasure. The room spun lazily and I realized dimly that I was weak and dizzy from blood loss. I seemed to see everything as if I were standing outside my body, looking down on a tableau.

Michael pushed my hair from my pale face and got up, rummaging through the discarded pile of clothes until he found his *sgian dubh*. The *sgian dubh* is a

Scottish dagger worn tucked into the boot or the top of a man's knee sock. Michael's had some kind of large golden stone—topaz or amber I would guess—cut and set at the tip of the hilt. It was old and battered, the leather sheath scarred and well worn. He had probably been wearing it when he'd fallen at Falkirk.

He gathered me into his arms, unsheathed the blade, and sliced across the big vein in his neck. Blood welled up, so red on his pale skin.

"Drink," he said, and pressed my lips to the wound.

Blood, hot and salty, ran into my mouth. I swallowed and gagged and tried to pull away.

"No," he said, pressing my face to his skin. "If you don't drink, you will die in truth, Cin. Stay with me. Drink."

Blood washed over my tongue and I swallowed again. The more I consumed, the better it tasted, until I was clinging to him, my mouth fused over the wound. *Feeding,* and it felt good.

I pulled away, repulsed by what I'd just done. I knelt on my hands and knees on the bed, my head hanging down, the room spinning uncontrollably, and I moaned. Michael eased me onto my back and brushed my hair from my face.

"Easy, love, I'll stay with you. I promise I'll guard you while you rest. Sleep well, my darling."

He stroked my hair and spoke, low and soothingly. It was like I was hearing his voice down a long dark tunnel, softer and softer, until sleep, or death, claimed me and I heard no more. I lay there cold and pale and unmoving, with Michael bending over my naked and bloody body.

Chapter Twenty-seven

What really surprised me was that I woke up at all. On some level I really hadn't thought it would work. But I did wake up and I knew I was different. I lay there with my eyes closed, feeling my body. I didn't feel my heartbeat. I wasn't breathing and yet I didn't feel as if I had to. It was strange and frightening. My mind and body felt rather fuzzy and disoriented, but I could hear snatches of conversation around me.

". . . any time now . . ."

"What do you think the chances are of her retaining her magic?"

". . . no way to tell . . ."

I lay there like a child holding its breath underwater, waiting until my lungs burned before I finally gave in and surfaced. I waited but the sensation never came. I was truly as still as death. Oh, dear Goddess, was I really dead? Was I not in my body at all? Panicking, I sat up, pleased that I could do so, and dragged in great heaving gasps of air. No, I wasn't dead. I wasn't dead, I thought over and over again, and the panic eased until I could finally see what was around me.

I was in some large, dimly lit room. There were no windows. Long tables filled with jars and books lined the walls, and herbs hung from the ceiling in drying clumps. The bed I was lying on was tucked neatly into one corner. I shoved myself back into that corner and stared at the people surrounding me.

"Dulcinea. Cin, listen to me," said a beautiful blond man. "You're fine, do you hear me? You need blood and then the confusion will go away."

Michael. Yes, Michael. I remembered him. He did this to me. Blood. Yes, I needed blood. I looked around, my eyes scanning the people who stood staring at me. Vampire, vampire, old man, an older woman who looked at me with pain in her eyes, a young girl. Yes, she would do. I held my hand out to the girl.

"Come," I said and thrust my power out. My body was coursing with it, burning with untapped magic.

The girl flew through the air to me, landing in a limp pile on the mattress next to me. The woman screamed and the vampires rushed me. I flung one hand toward them and the magic pushed them back against the wall. Grabbing the girl, I turned her face up to me, exposing her neck. She looked at me with pain and disbelief clouding her large, liquid green eyes.

"Dulcie?" she choked on a sob.

Fiona. I remembered now. Dear Goddess, what was I doing? I shoved her away from me and huddled in the corner, curled into a tight ball, the hunger gnawing at me. What had I become that I'd nearly hurt Fiona? I couldn't even bring myself to look at her mother. I was supposed to be strong but I felt weak; I felt like a monster.

"Well," the old man, Mr. Pendergrass, said, "at least we know she's kept her magic."

Fiona cried, "What's happened to her?"

Michael came to me and stretched out his hand. Such a familiar gesture. "Come, Cin, you must have some blood."

"Yes," I said in a small, rather frightened voice, and took his hand. He led me away from the bed, one hand holding mine, the other arm wrapped around my shoulders. I looked down as I heard the rustle of fabric around me. They had dressed me in my good funeral dress, the black lace covering the dove-gray silk. The irony was not lost on me.

Michael stopped at the far end of the long, rectangular-shaped room. A small figure sat in a ladder-backed chair. It was a boy. I took a step back. Someone put their hand in the small of my back and gave me a little push.

"Go on," said a deep, gravelly voice behind me. "He's been bespelled. He won't feel a thing. Take just a bit to get you oriented, and then we'll go out."

"I don't like this," came Mrs. Mackenzie's disapproving voice.

"Hush, woman," said the voice behind me, Devlin, and he pushed me gently forward again.

I took a few steps and the child turned his empty eyes to me. It was the street urchin who had held Missy for me the first day I had come to Mr. Pendergrass for help. I stumbled backward.

"No," I said, shaking my head.

"You must feed," Devlin said and grabbed my arm.

"No!" I shouted and shoved at him. He had forgotten, in that small moment, that I wasn't human anymore, and my new strength caught him off guard. He stumbled and I ran for the door. Michael reached for me but I sidestepped him and plunged through the open doorway. I slammed the door as I passed through it, and then stopped and turned.

"Lock," I said, pushing my will into the heavy door.

I could hear them pounding on it as I fled down the stairs. It wouldn't hold them for long.

I realized when I reached the landing that I had been upstairs above Mr. Pendergrass's shop. I pushed open the rear door of the shop, ran into the alley, and kept running, blind to where I was going, blind to everything except the need to get away. It felt as if a stranger had taken over my body, as if the skin I was in wasn't my own anymore. I needed some space to think and breathe and feel again.

I expected to tire soon but I didn't. It felt as if I could run forever. After a while I realized that nothing looked familiar anymore. I was on a small, dark street, taverns and bawdy houses lining the avenue. *And somewhere near the docks, by the smell of it,* I thought, wrinkling my nose. I stopped and put my hands against the nearest wall, letting my head hang down as I stood there and breathed.

What had I done? What had I become? Who were they to offer up some poor, defenseless child as a captive snack for me? I shook my head. Turning, I leaned my back against the wall and looked at the sky. There were no stars, there rarely ever were in London.

"Hey now, wot we got 'ere?" said a disembodied voice.

A man walked out of the shadows, his clothing dirty and tattered over his pot belly. His head was bald and a full, rather impressive red beard covered his face.

"Wot's a foine lady like you doin' out 'ere? Slummin'?" he said, grabbing his crotch and adjusting himself obscenely. "Want a taste of ol' Ned?"

"You have got to be joking," I said, more to myself than to him.

My first instinct was to scream and run, but I didn't. If I knew nothing else about myself anymore, I did know that I had no reason to fear this man. Let him come. He staggered up to me and I could smell cheap gin on him from ten paces. He reached out a hand and I batted it away.

"Don't touch me," I snapped.

"Ow, like it rough, do you? Wot you say we take us a walk 'round the corner there an' you let ol' Ned have a taste?"

Hunger welled up inside me again, beating against me like some dark, winged thing. I could hear his heartbeat; I could feel his blood moving in his veins.

"No," I said with a smile, "why don't we take a walk around the corner and you let *me* have a taste?"

His eyes widened. I turned and walked around the corner of the building into a narrow, grimy alley. I listened to Ned's stumbling footsteps following me. I sensed a small movement behind me and turned. Grabbing his hand as he reached for me again, I flung him against the wall.

"Don't ever touch me," I said. "Now, you want to know what it's like to be with a woman like me?" I said, laughing. A part of me heard the nearly hysterical edge to my laughter but the rest of me didn't care.

There was excitement and a bit of fear in his eyes. "You ain't the first fancy piece come down 'ere for a bit of a tumble."

"Oh, trust me when I tell you that you've never met anyone quite like me. Now, close your eyes."

"So you can stick a knife in me gullet and take me purse? I don't think so, fancy piece."

I shrugged. "Fine, have it your way. You have only one thing that's worth stealing anyway."

"Wot's that?" he said, eyeing me suspiciously.

I leaned in toward him. He stank but I could smell his blood just under the skin. Hunger gripped me and I felt my teeth lengthen and sharpen. I ran my tongue over them, learning the feel of them in my mouth. I looked up at Ned.

"Your blood," I said simply.

He jerked back. "Wot the bloody 'ell?" he cried and tried to push past me.

I grabbed his shoulders and pinned him to the wall. The strength I had was amazing. I felt strong and powerful. I leaned close, Ned screamed, and I sank my teeth into his neck.

Blood poured into my mouth with each frantic beat of his heart. I gagged at first, my mind rebelling at the thought of blood in my mouth, but then instinct took over, and I drank deeply of the coppery liquid. Life, his life, poured into me. The blood, I realized, fed whatever magic created a vampire, whatever animated its dead body, and that magic mingled with my own. I could feel both of them inside me, rolling around like two sleek otters playing in a river. I could feel Ned's fear and, somewhere deep inside, a bit of excitement as well. I stumbled back and he slumped to the ground before me.

Michael had said that a vampire couldn't kill with one bite, but I reached down to check the man's pulse anyway. He was unconscious but definitely still alive. I rolled him onto his side and, fishing in his pockets, came up with a dirty handkerchief. I wrapped it around his neck and knotted it over the bite wound.

"There," I said, frowning down at him, "maybe that'll teach you to accost young women on the street." I leaned against the opposite wall. "Good Lord, man, you must have pure gin running through your veins!"

Except for feeling a bit drunk, I felt strong now. My thoughts were no longer fragmented and I was no longer scared. I tipped my head back, took a deep breath . . . and smelled blood. I looked down at the sleeping man on the ground. No, it wasn't his. I inhaled again. It was farther away and there was a lot of it.

Slowly I walked down the alley. The brick wall of the tavern to my left led to another small alley littered with refuse. A large warehouse, one of many to be found near the docks, loomed before me, its windows black with grime. I walked on silent feet to the window nearest the door and quietly reached out to rub a spot clean. When the grime didn't lessen, I realized that it wasn't dirt; the windows were painted black. There was no light in the alley, and yet I could see as clearly as if the moon were full. I moved quietly to the door and gently grasped the knob. It opened on well-oiled hinges, just an inch or two, and the smell of fresh blood wafted from the interior, assaulting my nostrils.

The warehouse was a large, open building two stories high and well lit inside with many lanterns. Nine male vampires were lounging around on various tattered and mismatched pieces of furniture. Another vampire, apparently their master, sat farther away from the others on what looked like a throne, one leg slung over the heavily carved wooden arm of the chair. He was small and dark, his face rather common but strong and arrogant. He reminded me a bit of Napoleon, actually. Wooden shipping crates lined the walls except for one blank spot opposite the door. There a man slumped to his knees, his arms pulled taut by chains that were bolted into the wall, his shackled wrists raw and bloody. His head was hanging down and his face was obscured by shadows, but he had to be an older man for his black hair was liberally streaked with gray. I saw the faint rise and fall of his breathing. Whatever shape he was in, at least he was still alive.

My gaze traveled back across the room and it was then that I saw the girls, and I finally saw what my brain had refused to see while I took in every other detail. Girls, perhaps half a dozen of them, scattered across the floor like forgotten toys in a child's nursery. Dead girls with their throats ripped out, their open eyes staring blankly. I gagged and spun around, running. At the end of the alley, past the still-sleeping Ned, I ran into someone. Strong hands curled around my shoulders.

Chapter Twenty-eight

"Cin! Cin!" he yelled as I struggled against him.

Michael, I realized and collapsed against him.

"Michael," I said, trying to catch my breath, the images of the dead girls filling my head.

"God, Cin, I'm so sorry. We really buggered this up. I swear to you we do not feed from children, but Devlin couldn't bespell an adult for as long as he could a child. You needed fresh blood and we had no idea when you'd wake up. It was supposed to be just a little blood, Cin, just enough to calm you so that we could take you out and teach you to hunt. I swear to you the child wasn't in any distress, and he wouldn't have felt a thing or even remember it happening. You've got to believe me. It was not supposed to happen this way, I promise you, and I'm sorry as hell about it."

"Thank you, Michael, I believe you and I'm sorry too, but now you must be quiet and listen to me for a moment."

He looked at me and his brow creased. "You've fed." He glanced over my shoulder at Ned. "Is he all right?"

"He's fine. Michael, listen to me," I said, shaking him gently. "Dead girls, Michael, so many dead girls."

Michael's eyes widened. "What have you done?" he whispered.

I smacked him on the shoulder. "Not me," I snapped.

"Vampires. Down the alley in the warehouse on the left."

He stood very still and inhaled. I knew he could smell it too, the blood. "Stay here," he said.

I grabbed his shirt. "Michael, don't go alone. There are too many of them."

"I'm just going to have a look. Devlin and Justine are behind me. Stay here and wait for them."

He walked off down the alley, his stride lethal and dangerous. Memories of him naked in my bed flooded my mind. I sighed. Barring the debacle that followed my awakening as a vampire, I thought that perhaps this had been the best night of my life. No, that wasn't right. If I was in London, it must be the next night. Had I been "dead" all day? Lying like a corpse in Mr. Pendergrass's attic?

Good Lord, poor Mrs. Mackenzie and Fiona. That must have been torture for them. And then I'd all but attacked poor Fiona. I sighed again. I'd have to beg on bended knee for forgiveness. Would she forgive me, or from now on would she look at me and see a monster?

Footsteps sounded on the cobblestones outside the alley. I looked up to see Devlin and Justine approaching. Justine's long cloak swirled around her black silk shirt, fawn-colored breeches, and thigh-high boots. She reached out to me and grabbed my shoulders, speaking in a torrent of rapid French and petting my hair like a child. She produced a handkerchief from the depths of her cloak and dabbed at something, probably blood, on my chin.

"Justine. Justine, I'm fine," I said, grabbing her hand. "I stumbled across a nest of vampires. Dead girls, one man chained to a wall. Michael's gone to look."

Devlin looked past me down the alley. Michael raised his hand and motioned to him.

"Come, love," he said grimly. "Time to go to work."

Justine nodded. *"Pauvre petite,"* she said to me. "We will make all of this up to you, I promise."

I nodded, hoping it would make her feel better and stop fussing over me, and turned to follow them down the alley.

Devlin stopped and turned to look at me. "Stay here," he said.

"I will not," I replied. "I'm not some helpless human anymore. I want to come and help."

Devlin glanced from me to Ned, still unconscious in the alley. "No, you are no longer human. You're feeling strong and flush with power, but the things we're going in there to kill aren't human either, Cin. They're just as strong as you are and you haven't yet learned to fight."

I stuck out my chin. "They're my vampires, I found them, and I'm going with you."

"Fine, but stay out of the way and don't get yourself killed."

We joined Michael at the end of the block. There was another argument about me staying behind, followed quickly by the same "stay out of the way and don't get yourself killed" speech.

"Six dead prostitutes, one chained man, ten vampires. The vamps are all blood-drunk and conveniently unsuspecting," Michael said with a wink.

Devlin smiled, pushed the door open, and strode inside with all the arrogance of a lord. Michael and Justine flanked him and I stayed near the door, my back to the wall, and watched.

"Tsk, tsk, tsk," he said, kneeling down and closing the eyes of one of the dead girls.

The man who reminded me of Napoleon stood, his hand reaching around to the sword propped against the side of his throne-like chair. "Who the hell are you?"

"You do know, don't you," Devlin drawled, "that the Dark Council has forbidden the killing of humans?"

The master shrugged. "What are a few dead whores? And now I ask you again, mate, who the hell are you?"

Devlin stood slowly and stepped around the girl's body.

Dripping with barely leashed fury, his deep voice rang through the warehouse. "We are The Righteous. We are the defenders of the innocent."

Justine stepped forward. "We are the hand of justice."

Michael pulled his claymore from its scabbard. "We are the sword of vengeance."

The master's eyes widened in recognition. He snapped his fingers at the other vampires. "Kill them," he said, but I saw the fear in his eyes, and I noticed that he made no move toward them himself.

The nine other vampires stepped forward on their leader's order, each picking up a weapon as they came. I watched in fascinated horror as Devlin and Justine dispatched two of their attackers, the vampires' heads rolling to the floor at the first stroke of their swords. The other vampires seemed to be more skilled than the first two, and as the battle started in earnest, the sounds of clanging metal rang through the building. As I watched them fight, I understood why the name of The Righteous had caused that flash of fear across the leader's face; they were surely the stuff of Evil's nightmares.

The sight of Michael in battle captured my full attention. I knew now what Devlin had seen that night at Falkirk. He moved like a symphony of death. Every step was calculated and precise; no thrust of the sword was wasted. Three of the vampires were on him. He blocked one's sword and his fist shot out and smashed into the vampire's jaw. Michael spun, his foot catching the vamp across the side of the head, bringing the beast to his knees. Michael plunged his sword deep into his attacker's heart and rode him to the ground.

He jerked the sword free, the blade slicing upward, catching the next vampire in the stomach. The vamp raised his sword, but when it fell, Michael was no longer there. Quicker than my eyes could follow him, he was behind his enemy, the great claymore falling across the vampire's neck, severing its head. As he turned to face the next man, I noticed that the whole time a small smile lingered on his lips. He was good at this and he enjoyed it, enjoyed facing an enemy and besting him with nothing but his cunning and his steel. He was made for this, his lithe, lethal body fairly humming with the thrill of battle.

A movement caught my eye. The master was moving toward the door, attempting to escape. I thought about staying where I was and trying to stop him, but Devlin was right, I didn't yet know how to fight, and if I got into trouble with the master, the distraction could get one of my friends killed. I eased away from the door, staying in the shadows and skirting the battle in the opposite direction. The chained man moved, swaying slightly. I supposed I could be useful and check on the old fellow, see if I could get him free.

I crept past the wooden crates lining the wall, trying

to be as unobtrusive as possible, and knelt before the man. His head still hung forward, his hair falling to cover his face. I put my hands in his hair and pushed it back. It was far softer than it looked, sliding through my fingers like silk. I gasped at the face looking up at me. I'd thought he was old, because of the gray in his hair, but his face was young, perhaps ten years older than me. He was handsome, not unearthly beautiful like Michael or starkly masculine like Devlin, but handsome nonetheless. His brows were dark and his eyes were an odd shade of deep amber. The utter loathing I saw in those odd-colored eyes made me rock back on my heels.

"Don't be afraid," I said. "I'm here to help you."

"Who are you?" he asked, his voice raspy, as if he needed water.

I squared my shoulders. "The Righteous."

I got the feeling that the name meant something to him as his gaze traveled over me from head to toe in frank disbelief. He looked out into the center of the warehouse, and what he saw there must have satisfied him because he nodded and then, with a clinking of chains, pointed one long finger past me. "The key," he said.

I looked over my shoulder and saw the large silver key dangling from a hook on the side of the master's carved throne. I sprinted across the open space, grabbed the key from the hook, and ran back. Kneeling once again in front of the man, I opened the shackles. His wrists were raw and bloody, the flesh eaten away where the cuffs had chafed him. I took his hands in mine.

"We need to get you to a doctor," I said, looking at the jagged, open wounds.

"Let me go," the man said, pulling his hands from mine.

"Don't be afraid, please, we need to get you some help," I said, reaching again for his hands. Perhaps I could bind his wrists with some clean fabric until we could get him out of here.

His face was suddenly very close to mine. A growl sounded low in his throat. An honest-to-goodness predator's growl, like I'd heard from Michael the night I'd first summoned him. Whoever the chained man was, he wasn't human. Nothing human had ever made that sound. My eyes flew to his. I was suddenly very aware of how close I was to him, how vulnerable.

"What are you?" I whispered. He didn't feel like a vampire to me.

"I am something best left alone, vampire," he snarled, his breath hot on my cheek as he shoved me backward.

I landed in a sprawling heap and looked up to see the man jump ten feet straight up to land on top of one of the stacks of shipping crates. He lifted one of the large crates and sent it smashing through the blackened windows. In one fluid movement he vaulted through the jagged hole in the glass. Dear Goddess, what had I unleashed?

A roar of denial swept through the building and I turned to see the master staring in disbelief, frustration, and anger at the broken window where the chained man had disappeared into the night. And then his gaze came to rest on me. Fury contorted his features as he grabbed his sword and advanced across the room toward me.

Oh, damn, I thought as he came at me with murder in his eyes. I scooted back toward the crates as if I could melt into one of them and be safe. I kept my gaze locked on the master's, afraid to look away, and he stared right back at me. His eyes finally left mine as he neared the spot where Michael was still fighting two vampires. The master's path veered and he took a few steps toward Michael, his sword raised.

"Michael!" I shouted. "Behind you!"

Instead of turning around, Michael's head came up and he looked in the direction of my voice. The distraction was enough and the master's sword plunged into my lover's belly. Michael looked down and then looked up at me, confusion marring his perfect features, and then he fell to his knees and pitched forward.

"No!" I screamed and vaulted to my feet. No, this couldn't be happening. I'd just found him.

Justine was near, just a few feet to my right, and one of the master's henchmen was between us. The barrel-chested vampire saw her attention waver when I screamed and he raised his sword. I grabbed his wrist as his arm drew back to strike and felt his bones snap and break under my fingers. He yelled and I took the sword from his limp grasp. Swinging it two-handed, I severed his head in one clean blow.

I never slowed but advanced on the master, my eyes locked on his face, vengeance vibrating through every inch of my being. He snapped his fingers at the two vampires who had been fighting Michael, and the men came toward me. I held my hand out, power and rage flowing through me, and the first man flew backward as if I'd struck him. His companion turned briefly to look back at the fallen man and that was all the opening I needed. The blade sliced through his neck and I stepped over the body, never breaking stride, my gaze still locked with the master's. The vampire on the floor was just staggering to his feet, and I buried the sword hilt-deep in his heart as I passed him.

Fear passed through the master's eyes and he took a step back. I smiled. Caught in his cowardice, his eyes narrowed with hatred and he advanced again, raising the sword stained with Michael's blood before him. He yelled wordlessly and ran toward me, his sword held out in front of him like a battering ram.

I stopped. Raising one hand, I willed my power out into the night, and the sword in his hand exploded into a cloud of little silver-gray moths. His eyes widened even as his momentum propelled him forward. I grabbed his head as he crashed into me, intending to snap his neck. I wrenched the head to one side, but my anger and my new strength were a powerful combination, and his head came off of his neck with a thick sucking sound of broken bone and wet meat. I stared in horror as the skin shriveled and faded away, as if decomposing before my very eyes, until I held nothing but a skull with a few patches of hair attached to dried skin.

"Ugh," I groaned and dropped the thing next to its already decomposed body.

I ran to where Michael lay on his back on the cold floor, his eyes staring straight up, one hand pressed to the hole in his stomach. I threw myself across him, weeping, my hands moving over his face.

"Michael, no," I cried, "please, no. I've just found you and I think I might even love you and you can't die, do you hear me? You can't die."

Devlin walked over and stood staring down at us. His booted foot kicked Michael none too gently in the shoulder.

"Are you going to lie about all night," he asked, "or are you going to put the poor girl out of her misery?"

Michael glared up at him and then turned his head to smile at me.

"Oh, you wretch!" I said, and pushed away from him. "I thought that blasted man had killed you."

Michael struggled to sit up. "It takes a lot more than a sword through the belly to kill me now, lass." He leaned over and put one hand behind my head, pulling me to him, and whispered, "But I'm flattered that you care so much and I think I might even love you too."

A thrill of excitement went through me as he kissed me.

"That's enough of that," Devlin groused. "We've had enough earthquakes for one week."

I looked up at him in confusion. "What?"

Michael chuckled. "Apparently it wasn't just us who felt the earth move the other night."

My hand went to my mouth and I blushed furiously.

"Just so," Devlin chuckled. "People must have felt that for miles around. You are going to get that under control at some point, aren't you?"

I laughed. "Yes, but I really don't know how I'm going to broach that subject with my aunt."

Michael grunted in pain and I stood and helped him to his feet. He looked down at the bleeding wound.

"Bugger it. I could go another seventy years without *that* happening again."

"I'm sorry I distracted you," I said. "I was trying to help."

Michael shook his head. "The last time I saw him he was heading for the door. Why would he come back when he could have escaped?"

"That was my fault too," I said sheepishly. "I released the chained man and the master saw it. He was coming for me and you got in the way."

They all turned to the now-empty chains.

"Where is he?" Devlin asked.

"Gone," I said.

"Gone? What do you mean gone?"

I motioned to the broken second-story window. "Gone."

"Was he a vampire?" Justine asked.

I shrugged. "I don't think so. I don't know what he was, other than rude and ungrateful, but I don't think he was one of us."

"He's no longer any concern of ours," Devlin said with a shrug, and then turned to me and took my shoulders in his large hands. "You did well tonight. With a little training, you'll make a fine warrior."

"Really?" I said. I had a feeling that was a great compliment coming from Devlin.

Michael pushed my loose hair back over my shoulder. "You were magnificent."

I smiled at him and then I noticed the lines of strain around his eyes and mouth. I glanced sharply at Devlin.

"Is he going to be all right?" I asked.

"He needs blood. Come."

It wasn't until we'd reached the end of the alley that I thought to ask, "What are we going to do about the bodies? We can't just leave them there."

Devlin winked at me. "Watch."

At the corner of the building Justine stopped and took a deep breath. Tears welled up in her eyes and she started to scream. She ran to the door of the tavern and wrenched it open, screaming, "Murder! Murder! Oh, my God, come quickly! Please!"

The tavern emptied itself of its rough-looking clientele. In fact men poured out of two other taverns down the street as well. Justine led them to the corner and pointed down the alley.

"Bodies!" she shrieked. "The whole warehouse is full of bodies!"

The men trooped down the alley to investigate. Someone stopped to help Ned to his feet. The drunk's face was ashen as he touched his neck, his eyes darting frantically around the alley. Devlin and Michael and I moved back into the shadows. As soon as she was able to slip away unnoticed, Justine joined us.

"Good job, my sweet," Devlin said.

"I thought my screams were particularly good this evening," she said, smiling up at him.

"I always enjoy your screams, *cherie*," Devlin murmured as he kissed her temple.

Michael motioned to the alley, now teeming with people. "They'll find the bodies and fetch the authorities."

Devlin nodded. "And now, my friend, we need to find someplace a little quieter and get some fresh blood in you."

Michael looked at Justine. "Will you take her back to Pendergrass's?"

"But I want to come with you, Michael," I protested. "Let me help you."

He shook his head. "I don't want you to see me like that, to see me feed. Not yet. You've had enough shocks for one night. You don't need to see your lover drink someone else's blood. Let Justine take you back to the shop. I'll be fine and I'll return later. Besides, Mr. Pendergrass is eager to share with you what he's been working on."

I looked at him for a moment. "You'll come back safe to me?"

He kissed my forehead. "You have my word on it."

I nodded and let Justine lead me away.

Chapter Twenty-nine

I stood in the open doorway of Mr. Pendergrass's large, windowless attic. Fiona was sitting on the bed, her chin resting on her tucked-up knees. I stared at her and she stared back, confusion and distrust in her eyes.

"Fi," I said, but she just winced and said nothing. I could feel the tears well up deep within me.

"Oh, Fi, you know I'd never hurt you. I was . . . not myself, but I'm better now. It won't happen again." I glanced sharply at Justine and demanded, "Will it?"

She shook her head and gave me a sad smile. *"Non."*

I crossed the room and knelt in front of Fiona, a girl I'd known all my life, who had been like a sister to me. She looked so young and innocent and I suddenly felt so old. There was a gulf between us now, and we would never be the same again, but maybe we could become something else if she could only forgive me. She swung her legs over the edge of the bed and reached out to catch the tear that rolled down my cheek. She looked at the wetness on her finger, felt of it as if to make sure it was real. Was she wondering if monsters cried?

"Hard night?" she asked.

I choked on a laugh and laid my head on her lap and cried. I knew I needed to be strong, but I took a moment to cry, for scaring her, for scaring myself a dozen times tonight, for the loss of everything I had been and would never be again. Mrs. Mackenzie came and sat next to her daughter. She took my hand gently in hers and I cried harder.

The heavy footfalls of a man running echoed up the stairs. I looked up, worried, and glanced at Justine. She lounged with her hip propped up against one of the tables, looking vastly unconcerned. Archie appeared in the doorway.

"Did I miss anything?" he asked, glancing from the three of us to Justine, then to Mr. Pendergrass.

We all silently looked at one another, no one knowing quite how to answer the question, and then Fiona started to laugh. Her laugh was infectious and soon we all joined in. Poor Archie was left standing in the doorway, staring at us like we'd all gone mad.

"Where have you been?" I asked. It suddenly occurred to me that he hadn't been here earlier.

He blushed and looked at his feet. "Kitty came back from her mother's this afternoon."

I smiled at him. "You should go home and be with her."

"Well, I can't stay long. I told her I needed to come check on Mr. Pendergrass since he's getting quite feeble in his old age," Archie said with a wink.

Mr. Pendergrass snorted. "Watch yourself, boy."

"Have you told her yet?" Archie said to Mr. Pendergrass.

"Told me what?" I asked.

"No, I haven't. I've not had the time but now that everyone's here . . ." He glanced around the room. "Where are Devlin and Michael?"

"Oh," I said, "we ran into a bit of trouble, nothing to do with Kali or Sebastian, but Michael was wounded.

He'll be fine but the two of them will be back a little later."

Fiona patted my hand and I smiled at the gesture.

"Well," Mr. Pendergrass said with a shrug, "I suppose there's no sense in waiting, nothing the two of them don't already know. Tell her, Mrs. Mackenzie."

I looked up at Mrs. Mac, confused.

She shook her head. "We can't find the book."

"What do you mean? It's not at Ravenworth so it's got to be in the townhouse."

"We've spent the last three days packing up all your mother and father's personal effects, and yours as well, but that book isn't there."

"Three days?" I shrieked, turning to Justine. "I've been gone for three days?"

She shrugged in that French way. "Did Michael not tell you it would take three nights for you to rise?"

"No, it seems he skipped that part. Then again," I said, chewing my lip, "I never really asked. But Mrs. Mac, the book has to be there. Mother never sold a book in her life. Mr. Pendergrass, what exactly does it look like?"

"About so big, red leather binding, no title on the cover. It's a hundred-year-old Book of Shadows belonging to a witch from Lewis. It's written in Gaelic, which is why I thought your mother might be interested in it."

I shook my head. "It's not one I remember. If it's not in the townhouse, then the only other place it could be is in Scotland at Glen Gregor with Aunt Maggie, in which case, we're in big trouble." I sighed and rubbed the bridge of my nose. "Mr. Pendergrass, what have you figured out about the talisman?"

"Ah," he said, turning to one of his many tables,

"I've cleansed it as well as I'm able, but considering what it is, it will always have negative energies attached to it. Blood magic is bad business, indeed."

He pulled out a small, black leather pouch that contained the necklace, the leather acting as a barrier to keep it from collecting the energies around it. He also pulled out several other small pouches and set them next to the talisman.

"These are as many of the ingredients of the spell as I can remember, but I must be missing at least three or four. The additional ingredients that should bind her into an object of your choosing are here as well."

"What are you using that isn't in the original spell?" I asked.

"I think it's best if you don't know," he replied.

"I have to know, otherwise how will I know how much to use in the spell?"

He lifted a red fabric bag. "One pinch," he said and lifted a blue bag. "Two pinches of this. The rest is listed in the spell book."

I didn't argue with him. I probably didn't want to know what was in those bags. I walked over and weighed the individual pouches, looking over the contents of Mr. Pendergrass's worktable as I did so. Jars of all colors and sizes were filled with colored stones, various feathers, and dried herbs. When I was a child, I'd loved to help my mother hang and dry the herbs for her potions. When I was a child . . .

"Ha! I know where the book is!" I crossed the room and pulled open my valise, rummaging through it until I found my black beaded reticule. I checked to make sure the money I had put in it was still there, and then added the small pouches containing the herbs and the talisman.

"Justine," I said, "we need to catch a hack to Mayfair."

She frowned. "We should wait for the men."

"It's a waste of time. They can't accompany us anyway," I said. "I'm in mourning, and even if I wasn't, I can't possibly show up on my cousin's doorstep in the middle of the night in the company of two strange men who aren't relations. No one will raise an eyebrow if my companion is another woman. Mrs. Mackenzie, what did you tell Thomas?"

"That we'd come to move your personal things out of the house. They invited you to stay there, in your old room, but I told them that we were staying at Grillion's Hotel, and that you'd come down with a cold and would visit as soon as you were feeling better."

"Grillion's?"

"Well," she said, "that's where Devlin and Justine and Michael have rooms and it's quite the nicest hotel in Mayfair."

"Yes, I know, but it's rather close to the townhouse. I hope they didn't stop by to call on me. At any rate, it doesn't matter right now. You and Fiona and Mr. Pendergrass wait here. Tell Michael and Devlin where we've gone when they return. We'll be back shortly with everything we need."

I reached up and kissed Archie on the cheek and whispered, "Thank you, my friend, for everything. Now, go home and make love to your wife."

He blushed and I winked at him. Grabbing Justine's hand, I led her down the stairs.

Chapter Thirty

It took longer than I'd thought to find a hack. We walked for several blocks and still there were none in sight.

"Justine," I said. "Would you sing for me?"

"Now?" she asked.

I shrugged. "Why not?"

She looked at me as if I were mad and then smiled. She hummed a few bars and then her voice rang out, clear and lovely in the still night. I walked along, swinging my reticule from my wrist, and listened to her sing Donna Anna's aria "*Or sai chi l'onore*" from *Don Giovanni*. As we passed the Union Arms on Panton Street, several of the pub's patrons came to the door to listen. By the time we reached Haymarket at the end of the block and Justine broke into Zerlina's "*Vedrai, carino*," nearly the whole population of the pub had moved into the street to listen to her. We had just rounded the corner when a small, wiry man stumbled into me as he rushed past. Annoyed more than anything, I scowled at the man's retreating figure until I realized with a start that the heavy weight attached to my wrist was suddenly gone.

"Justine!" I shouted, as if she weren't standing right next to me. "He's cut my purse!"

She never missed a beat of the aria, simply swept aside her cloak, pulled one of the sapphire-tipped daggers from inside her boot, and threw it at the man. It hit him in the back of the leg and he fell to the sidewalk. I ran up and snatched my reticule from his grasp and then pulled the knife free. He stumbled to his feet, one hand reaching back and coming away with blood.

"You'll be sorry you did that," he snarled.

"Really?" I said. "And why is that?"

"Because," came a voice from the shadowed alley, "I can't have you stealin' from me brother."

Three large men came out of the alley, stepping into the circle of light cast by the street lamp. One of them stepped forward. "Now hand over the purse."

I threw my hands in the air. "Good gods, not twice in one night! Do you people have nothing better to do than skulk in alleyways and attack lone females? And what do you mean, steal from him? He cut my purse!"

He shrugged. "Man's got to eat."

"Get a job," I snapped.

"But this is so much easier," he replied with a smile.

The cutpurse stumbled over to the group, hiding behind the bulk of his brother. I looked over at Justine. Her eyes were fixed on the man in front of her, her body vibrating with excitement.

Seeing the look on Justine's face, I said, "Do yourself a favor and walk away."

"Not without the purse," he said, cracking his knuckles. "And I'll be havin' the shiny dagger as well."

Justine reached out and I handed her the purse instead of the dagger. I felt much more comfortable armed with a weapon and I knew that the sapphire-tipped blade wasn't the only weapon she had on her. She didn't argue; she simply swept her cloak aside and tied my purse to the thick leather belt she wore.

One of the men nudged the other. "Lookee there, mate! She's wearin' breeches!"

His black-haired companion grunted and laughed. "Maybe we'll be takin' more than the purse, eh?"

Justine raised her arms away from her sides. "If you want my purse or my dagger, *mes amies,* come and get them."

"Ooh, and a Frenchie, too," the black-haired man said.

He started forward and, quicker than my eyes could follow the movement, Justine reached behind her head and drew her sword from her spine sheath. The black-haired man stopped, eyes widening, and glanced back at his companions. The cutpurse's brother shifted uneasily.

"Naw, miss," he said. "You ladies be on your way. No trouble here."

The black-haired man glanced over his shoulder. "They're just two women," he whined.

Justine smiled. "Want to bet your life on that?"

The brute paled and stepped back. "What are you?" he whispered.

Justine sheathed the sword and reached for the bloody dagger. I handed it to her without question. She took it and held it under her nose, her eyes closing briefly as she inhaled, and then she very slowly opened her eyes, looked at the man, and licked the blood from the dagger.

"I am the Devil's justice," she said, and even I shivered.

The men paled and stumbled over one another in

their haste to flee into the dark depths of the alley. Justine's laughter chased after them as she tucked the dagger back into her boot. Seconds later the clatter of hooves echoed through the night and I looked down the street to see, finally, a hack approaching. I hailed the driver and gave him the address of the townhouse as I climbed into the carriage. Justine glanced back, looking down the shadowed alley almost wistfully, and then climbed in after me.

She laughed. "That was fun."

I shook my head in wonder.

"You didn't think that was fun?" she asked.

I shrugged. "Earlier tonight, when I was alone, there was a man who came up to me outside that tavern—"

"The unconscious man in the alley? The one you fed from?"

"Yes. When I led him into that alley and bit him, I enjoyed his fear, Justine."

"And that scared you. Cin, if you had been merely a defenseless human woman, he would have ravished you, you know that."

"I suppose so."

"There is no harm in feeling joy in victory, Cin."

"It wasn't merely joy in victory, Justine. It was something much darker than that."

"There is darkness in all of us. Men find it in the rush of battle, the thrill of a well-fought brawl, but women rarely get the chance to feel it for themselves. It was power you felt tonight, the power of your own strength, and it is nothing to be ashamed of."

I frowned and settled deeper into my cloak, wrapping my arms around me as if the small gesture would bring me some comfort.

"Then what makes us any different than the monsters?" I asked softly, thinking of the vampires in that warehouse, the floor littered with bodies. Had they felt joy in their victories?

"You could have kept that man, fed from his blood and his fear until he was nothing but a dead, empty shell. You didn't though, did you?"

I shook my head.

"You took only what you needed and left him with his life, even though he might have gravely harmed you, might even have killed you, if you hadn't had the power to stop him. That is the difference."

She leaned forward and looked me in the eye. "The ability to temper power with mercy, Cin, is what separates us from the monsters."

Chapter Thirty-one

The hack stopped in front of the South Audley Street townhouse in Mayfair, and Justine and I disembarked. As I paid the driver, I noticed the figure of a tall, black-haired woman standing under the street lamp across the street. She was well-dressed with sharp, angular features . . . and she appeared to be simply standing there watching us.

"Justine?" I said, turning to catch her eye.

When I looked back, though, the woman was gone. I scanned the street in both directions but found no sign of her.

"What is it?" Justine asked, moving to stand behind me.

"Nothing," I said, shaking my head. "I suppose it was nothing."

We turned and climbed the steps to the front door. This had been my family's London residence since before I was born and it was as dear and familiar to me as Ravenworth Hall. Justine looked up at the three-story structure appreciatively.

"It is very nice," she said.

"Thank you. Now, don't forget to keep your cloak closed at all times. I don't think Masterson's old heart could handle the sight of a woman dressed in breeches," I chuckled.

"And how is it you think you can find this book that Madame Mackenzie and Fiona cannot seem to find?"

I smiled. "Because they were looking in the wrong places. I think one of the girls has pinched it. Magic is fascinating to a child, you know. My money's on Sarah Katherine."

I raised my hand to clasp the large brass knocker on the door and paused. Laying my hand on the door, I stood very still and reached out with my senses, feeling what was beyond.

"What is it?" Justine asked, glancing around.

"Do you feel that?" I whispered.

"Feel what?"

"Evil," I said. Whether it was part of my magic or some of the intuition that my father had had, I knew something was terribly wrong inside that house. "Come, let's slip around the back."

We were headed for the servants' entrance when I spotted a light on in one of the second-story bedrooms. I knew that room well; it had once been mine. I studied it for a moment and tugged at the ivy that climbed the trellis below.

"Justine, can you climb that?" I knew I'd never make it in my dress.

Justine crouched low and then sprang into the air, vaulting onto the balcony with barely a whisper. The movement reminded me of the chained man in the warehouse. Had he been one of us? Justine leaned over and reached out a hand. I attempted to jump as she had but I didn't make it quite as far. She grabbed my wrist and hauled me over the balustrade in a very unladylike manner.

I crept to the balcony door and laid my hand on it, listening. I sensed nothing out of the ordinary. Knocking lightly, I waited for one of the girls to open the door.

It was fifteen-year-old Sarah Katherine who pulled back the thin draperies an inch or two and stared out at me, her face streaked with tears. Recognition dawned and she jerked open the door, launching herself at me.

"Aunt Dulcie! I'm ever so glad you've come. Something's the matter downstairs. Mama and Papa are in the salon with a man and a woman and I heard Mama scream. I'm a terrible coward, Aunt Dulcie. I should have gone down but I was hiding the little ones."

I looked over her shoulder to see thirteen-year-old Claire and ten-year-old Will huddled together on my four-poster bed. Sarah Katherine stepped back into the room, expecting us to follow. I started forward but was stopped at the doorway by an invisible shield, unable to walk any farther into the room.

"Oh, you've got to be joking!" I muttered, reaching up one hand to test the barrier. "This is my bedroom!"

But of course it wasn't, not anymore. The minute my father had died, the townhouse and Ravenworth Abbey had become Thomas's. I gritted my teeth.

"Sarah Katherine, you'll have to invite us in, love."

She looked at me in confusion and then blushed. She thought I was reprimanding her manners and I suppose that was just as well. If she'd truly known what she was inviting into her home, she might have left us standing there on the balcony. Squaring her shoulders she said in her best debutante voice, "Forgive me. Ladies, would you please come in?"

Justine and I crossed the threshold.

"Children, this is my good friend, Mademoiselle Justine."

Justine smiled but lingered near the door. I drew Sarah Katherine to the bed and sat with her and the other children, holding them and murmuring promises I wasn't sure I could keep.

"Sadie Kate," I said, taking her hands in mine, "tell me, did you see the couple when they came in?"

She shook her head. "Only from the back. They both had black hair and were dressed in evening clothes."

I glanced sharply at Justine, who cocked one blonde brow at me.

"Children, listen to me. My mother, your aunt Lora, had a book somewhere in this house, and it's very important that I get it back. It's fine if one of you has it but I need it back now. It will help me get rid of those people downstairs."

Sarah Katherine blushed and then crossed the room to the wardrobe and rummaged in the bottom of it, finally producing the red leather-bound volume. She handed it back to me with a sheepish smile.

"I'm sorry, Aunt Dulcie. I didn't mean to steal it. Mama said we weren't to go into Aunt Lora's workroom but Claire and I slipped in one night. There were all kinds of interesting things in there, and I took the book back to my room with me, but when I opened it, I realized that it was in Gaelic. I meant to put it back, but then Mrs. Mackenzie and Miss Fiona came and I was afraid they'd catch me. I'm very sorry, Aunt Dulcie."

"Think nothing of it, my dear, it's perfectly fine," I said, relieved that I'd been right about the location of the book. Of course, the children weren't supposed to know anything about witches, especially about the Macgregor women *being* witches, but children always know more than anyone gives them credit for.

I leafed through the pages of the book until I found the binding spell Mr. Pendergrass had described. I read it through once and then asked Justine for my purse. She opened her cloak and untied the purse from her belt. The children gasped. Justine looked up sharply and then back down at her breeches. She rolled her eyes and threw me the purse.

"Mademoiselle Justine is a pirate," I said, digging through the contents and pulling out the little pouches of ingredients, "like Grainne O'Malley." It was the best I could come up with on such short notice.

Sarah Katherine and Claire looked at Justine as if she were some pagan goddess of high adventure. Will simply looked at her as if he'd fallen in love. I smiled at him as I opened each pouch and checked the contents against the spell in the book. Only three ingredients missing, and nothing exotic at that. I could work with that.

"Are the people downstairs evil pirates?" Claire asked in an excited whisper.

"Yes, are they Captain Justine's sworn enemies?" Will chimed in.

I nearly groaned aloud. Ye gods, what had these children been reading?

"Something like that," I muttered, folding down the corner of the page to mark my place. "*Capitaine* Justine, may I speak with you outside for a moment?"

I stepped to the door and paused, "If we walk back out, do they have to invite us in again?"

"*Non,* they need do it only once."

We slipped out onto the balcony and I pulled the door closed.

Justine arched one brow at me. "A pirate?"

"It was all I could think of at the moment. Now, focus, *Capitaine*. Kali and Sebastian are downstairs doing Goddess knows what to my cousin Thomas and poor Amelia. What do we do?"

"We should go back for Devlin and Michael," she said.

I shook my head. "That will take too long. What if they take Thomas and Amelia somewhere? I can't let anything happen to them, Justine. Besides the fact that I love them both, I'm all the family those children have. If their parents die, how the bloody hell am I supposed to raise three children?"

Justine paled at the thought. I paced the balcony.

"All right, here's my plan," I said. "I have nearly all the ingredients for the binding spell and the ones I'm missing are common herbs I can get anywhere. I walk down the stairs and Kali takes me. She's probably only here to use Thomas and Amelia and the children as leverage so that I will cooperate with her. If I go with her, then she'll leave them be. I hope."

Justine frowned. "And what am I to tell Devlin and Michael?"

"Tell them we had no other choice. I want you to stay here and guard the children until we've left the house, and then find Devlin and Michael."

"And how are we to find you again?"

"I don't know. The spell requires it be performed in a sacred place, I just haven't figured out where that is yet."

She shook her head, crossing her arms defiantly over her chest: "*Absolument non*. I will not agree to a plan that puts you in their hands and leaves us with no idea where you are."

"Justine, the plan has always been to work the binding spell. I have to get close enough to her to do that. You know that."

"*Oui*, but we are supposed to be near to hand when you are with her, in case something goes wrong."

"So what should we do? We can't very well drop the children off the balcony and take them with us to find Michael and Devlin. If we leave the children alone, then eventually Kali is going to come looking for them. Justine, she only needs one hostage, the other four are expendable. Tell me, what other choice do we have?"

She pursed her lips. "She could kill the parents anyway, once she has you, or she may take them along to ensure your cooperation."

"Then bring Mrs. Mac and Fiona and Mr. Pendergrass back here. Mrs. Mac and Fiona can watch over the children, and I want Mr. Pendergrass to find some sort of spell to revoke the invitations issued to the undead."

"Even you?" she asked.

I frowned and nodded reluctantly. "Yes," I said, "even me. This is no longer my home. I have no right to be here."

She shook her head. "You risk your life for them and yet you think you have no right to be a part of their lives?"

I looked at her and arched a brow. "Did you not do the same for your sister?"

A pained look crossed her face for a fleeting moment. "What do we tell the children?"

I smiled and winked. "Leave that to me."

I called Sarah Katherine out to the balcony. Justine stepped inside to stay with the other children and I closed the door behind her. I looked down into Sarah Katherine's face. She was so lovely, with her mother's dark blonde hair and her father's sparkling blue eyes. I remembered holding her just after she was born, when I was little more than a child myself. I would not, could not, lose her or any of them, not while there was one ounce of fight left in me.

"Sadie Kate," I said, using the nickname I'd called her as a babe, "I need you to be my grown-up girl tonight, can you do that?"

She nodded.

"The people downstairs are very bad people. They want me to do something for them, and I think they mean to hold your parents captive so that I'll do as they wish."

"Are you going to do it? What they want?" she asked, chewing her bottom lip.

"Yes, I'll do whatever I can to keep your parents safe. To do that, though, I'm going to have to pretend that I'm on their side. Whatever you see or hear tonight, whatever anyone tells you I did, I want you to know that it was all pretend. I love you and I'll lay down my life to protect you and your family, do you understand?"

She nodded again.

"Justine is going to stay with you and the little ones until the bad people leave. They may insist on taking your mama and papa with them. I promise you I'll do everything I can to keep them safe and bring them home to you, all right?"

"If you and Mama and Papa leave with the bad people, will Miss Justine stay with us?"

"She'll leave for just a little while to get help. Mrs. Mackenzie and Fiona will come and stay with you. Also a very nice old man named Mr. Pendergrass. He's a wizard—"

"Like Aunt Lora was?"

"Yes, and he'll make sure the house is safe for all of you. Now, if your Mama and Papa go with us, the minute Miss Justine leaves, go down and tell Masterson what I've told you and tell him that Mrs. Mackenzie and Fiona and Mr. Pendergrass are on their way. And Sarah Katherine, this is very important," I said, taking her by the shoulders, "do not open the door for anyone but Mrs. Mackenzie, do you understand? I don't care if the king himself comes calling, do not open the door or invite anyone in but Mrs. Mackenzie. Do you understand me?"

"Yes, Aunt Dulcie. I promise. What do we tell the children?" she asked.

"Mostly the truth," I said. "I know this is frightening, but I need you to be brave for the little ones, all right? So that they aren't afraid."

I took her hand in mine and walked back into the bedroom. Claire and Will looked up at me with large, expectant eyes.

"Children, I've just spoken with Sarah Katherine," I said. "It seems that two evil pirates, arch enemies of my friend *Capitaine* Justine, have taken your parents captive."

Will's bottom lip trembled and Claire twisted the hem of her nightgown in her hands.

"But have no fear," I said. "We'll rout the villains and return your Mama and Papa to you safe and sound. Just think of the tales of adventure they'll be able to tell you! Now, I'm going to go downstairs and pretend to be one of the evil pirates myself, but it's all just a ruse to get them out of the house so that you three will be safe."

"Why doesn't *Capitaine* Justine just slice them up with her cutlass?" Will volunteered.

"Well," I said, "because the fair *Capitaine* must go and find the Pirate King and his first mate, and the three of them will ride to our rescue and save us all!"

"Aunt Dulcie?" Claire said. "You don't look very much like an evil pirate to me. Are you sure it's going to fool them?"

I looked down at my dress with its long sleeves and modest cut. There were blood stains on the dove-gray silk but the heavy black lace covering the dress hid them well. Truly, I didn't look much like an evil pirate, though.

"Maybe I'm a lady pirate?"

Claire looked at me doubtfully.

"Well," I sighed, "we'll just have to make do with what we have. Maybe when this is all over, *Capitaine* Justine will take me to wherever female pirates get their wardrobes made?"

Justine smiled and winked at me. I sat on the edge of the bed and pulled all three children into the circle of my arms.

"Good-bye, my babies. Always, always remember that Aunt Dulcie loves you. Promise me?"

Three faces nodded back at me, three faces with excitement and fear written all over them. I would have to be strong and very powerful to keep their parents alive for them and, Goddess help me, I hoped I could do it. I held the lives of everyone in this household in my hands tonight.

I stood and squared my shoulders. I would do this. I would fight her and I would taste victory. After all, this was what I had died for, and by all the gods in heaven, I would not let it have been in vain.

Chapter Thirty-two

I walked calmly down the stairs, more calmly than I felt. Inside I was shaking. The scene in the foyer below was one of barely controlled chaos. The drawing room doors were firmly closed. Masterson lay bleeding but alive on the tile floor, several nearly hysterical maids hovering over him. Cook was ringing her hands and the footmen seemed to be waiting for instructions from Masterson.

Silence fell throughout the hall as they all looked up at me in surprise, and then every one of them rushed me, tripping over themselves and talking rapidly. No one seemed to wonder how it was that I'd come to be upstairs; I suppose they were simply accustomed to my presence in the house. Finally I called for silence and knelt down, easily helping Masterson to his feet. There was a gash on his temple but it didn't look too alarming.

"Miss Dulcie, Lord Montford and a woman came to call. He cracked me over the head, he did, and they spirited Lord and Lady Craven into the drawing room and locked the door!"

"I could hear the missus screaming but I couldn't get the door open," one of the parlor maids said. The poor little mite looked like she was about to swoon.

"Has no one gone for the magistrate? Or the Bow Street runners?" Masterson chided, staring down each of the footmen who were standing about. Three of them made for the door but I called them back.

"No, Masterson," I said softly. "Trust me when I tell you that the magistrate can't help us with this." I addressed the crowd, "I want all of you to go to your rooms. Lock your doors. There's nothing more to be seen here tonight. You can gossip about it all you want to in the morning but not a word about this leaves this household. If I hear even a whisper of this night's events in Town, I'll sack every last one of you just so I know I got the right one. Do I make myself clear?"

Everyone nodded and shifted uncomfortably. Thankfully no one remembered that it wasn't my house anymore and I no longer had the right to terminate anyone's employment.

One of the footmen spoke up, "Miss Craven, we can't leave you here alone and defenseless."

I laughed. "Of all the people in this house, I am the least defenseless. Now, seek your rooms and good night to you all."

One small, dark-haired woman in a deep blue dress caught my eye. "You," I said and she turned to me with a rather vacant look on her face. "I don't know you. Who are you?"

"The governess, miss."

I pursed my lips. "Did it not occur to you that the children might need you?"

A look of shocked horror came over her face, as if she'd just wakened from a dream. "Oh, dear Lord!" she exclaimed.

"Go up and stay with them, they're all in my . . . in Sarah Katherine's room. A friend of mine is with them. She's made up a game of make-believe, pirates and the like, to keep them occupied. Do whatever she asks of you."

"Yes, miss," she stammered and flew up the stairs.

I rolled my eyes at her departing figure and turned to Cook and Masterson, who had stayed behind in the foyer. I glanced at the closed doors of the drawing room, thinking how much more sensitive my hearing was now that I was a vampire. I was almost certain Kali knew I was here but I didn't want to tip my hand completely.

"Cook," I whispered, "take him back to the kitchen and tend that wound. After I've gotten these people out of the house, my friend will send Mrs. Mackenzie and Fiona over from the . . . hotel."

"Oh, thank the dear Lord," Cook said. "Mrs. Mac'll fix things up right and proper."

"Very good, miss," Masterson said, dabbing at his head with his handkerchief. "Miss Craven, these . . . guests, are they—"

"They're evil, Masterson, that's all you need to know."

At the very last second I leaned down and kissed his weathered old cheek. He blushed and stammered and Cook shooed him off toward the kitchen like a large mother hen. I set the Book of Shadows down on the hall table and stared at the drawing room door. I tried the doorknob but it was locked, just as the parlor maid had said. I drew my arm back and slammed the palm of my hand into the door, just above the lock. It exploded inward with a cracking of wood.

Thomas and Amelia sat huddled together on the sofa. They were pale and terrified. Amelia's hair hung around her shoulders in disarray, as if she'd been dragged by it, but I couldn't see or smell any blood on them. It was more than I could have hoped for. Sebastian lounged negligently against the mantel on the opposite wall, his black evening clothes spotless, a lit cheroot dangling from his long, slender fingers. I gritted my teeth. I should turn him into a toad for daring to smoke in my mother's drawing room.

Kali stood before me in the center of the room, resplendent in a gold silk evening gown. Her hair was artfully arranged, but there certainly seemed to be less of it than there had been the last time I'd seen her. On the whole, the two of them looked remarkably well for having been burnt to a crisp four nights before.

"Did the grand lady get the servants all sorted out?" Kali asked, her voice light and airy as if she'd just offered me a cup of tea.

I inclined my head but didn't answer. She stalked over to me, hips swaying, and her eyes widened a bit. She leaned in and smelled me. I stiffened but didn't step back. I would not allow her to see how scared I truly was.

"Oh, you've been a naughty girl, my little witch," Kali purred.

Sebastian straightened and walked to me, his eyes never leaving my face. "What have you done?" he whispered.

"Ensured my survival," I said, "much as you did, I'll wager."

I snatched the cheroot from his fingers and snubbed it out into a small, rather ugly candy dish that must have been Amelia's.

"If you'd wanted to talk, all you had to do was say so," I said, wandering through the room and trailing my fingers absently over the furniture. "There was no need to go to all this trouble."

I stopped in front of Thomas and Amelia, my back to Kali and Sebastian. I tucked a lock of Amelia's hair behind her ear and winked at her. She stared at me, frozen with terror, but Thomas seemed to understand. That understanding flashed momentarily in his eyes and then was gone. He squeezed his wife's hand and patted it, but the expression on his face never changed. He'd been a soldier once; I was hoping that training would help him keep a level head through this ordeal.

"Forgive me, but you have been quite unreceptive to my invitations thus far. Besides, we have *talked* enough, you and I," Kali hissed, one hand reaching up subconsciously to touch her hair. "Now you either do my spell, or you die, but not before I make you watch as I kill everyone you love."

I shrugged, as if what she'd just said meant less than nothing to me. "Yes, well, that no longer works for me. I've come to renegotiate."

Her eyes narrowed. "Renegotiate?"

"Your terms," I elaborated.

"I don't recall offering you any terms."

"Yes, I suppose you didn't. 'Do it or die,' 'I'll make you crawl,' and all that rubbish. But, you see, that was when I was weak and human. You have no power over me anymore, Kali. Sure, you could kill me outright, cut off my head, stake me through the heart." I flounced down in one of the wing chairs and smiled up at her. "But I'm the only one who can get you what you want. So, I've come to renegotiate."

Fury boiled just below her skin but she kept her temper in check. "What do you want? You want me to promise I'll leave? Go back to my world and spare your precious humans?"

I waved a hand absently. "I couldn't give a badger's ass what happens to the lot of them. No, I'll do your spell for you, and I'll get your crown back, but in return I want you to make me your High Priestess."

Kali stared at me. Sebastian laughed. "I know her, she's lying. It's some trick."

"No trick, Sebastian. It's called self-preservation, an instinct I'm sure you know quite well. I realized the other night that I couldn't stand against her. If she makes me her High Priestess, then I'll be at her side and not caught down here in the muck when the apocalypse comes about."

Sebastian stared at me and I gave him my best blank debutante smile, that perfectly pleasant, slightly patronizing smile I saved for clumsy dance partners and boring dinner companions.

"Done," Kali said, though she still didn't look like she entirely trusted my change of heart. Smart demon, but, really, what choice did she have if she wanted her full power back?

"Excellent," I said, and bounded up from the chair. "Now, let's leave here. No sense standing about in Mayfair when we have places to go and spells to cast."

"Indeed," Kali said, "but they come with us."

I looked over my shoulder at Thomas and Amelia, trying not to panic. "Are you serious? I thought you were a woman of stronger appetites than that. Let's go find something more sporting. I know this cutpurse and his gang over in Piccadilly—"

"They are not to eat," she said in that tone of voice one reserves for small children and lunatics. "They are for the spell."

I looked at her in confusion. "The spell?"

She pulled a folded piece of parchment from the depths of her bodice and handed it to me. One edge was ragged, as if it had been torn from a book, and the paper was yellowed with age and crackled under my fingers. I glanced at the words and paled.

"This is blood magic," I whispered.

"Yes, it is. It requires the blood of two. We have two here so we might as well use them."

I stared at the paper. This was blood magic, human sacrifice. Dear Goddess, the binding spell I intended to work on her was darker magic than I had ever thought to perform, but this, this was something that would stain your soul for eternity. Of course, I had absolutely no intention of going through with this spell, but the thought of what she expected me to do sent a shiver up my spine. Kali watched my reaction closely.

"You hesitate. Why?"

I gathered my wits. "I've never done this sort of magic before. It's going to require a sacred place to perform the ritual. I don't know where yet. I'll have to think about it."

"Perhaps that is why you hesitate. Then again, perhaps it is not," she said softly, her hand reaching out to caress the side of my face, her nails raking my cheek. "Did your magic die with your human body, little witch? Is this just a ruse after all? Tell me now and I'll kill you quickly. Lie to me and I'll see you suffer for eternity."

"I still have my magic."

"Prove it," she said.

I snapped my fingers and the lights flickered out, plunging the room into darkness. I sent my will flowing outward and the candles flared back to life. Kali looked unimpressed.

"Parlor tricks," she spat.

"Well, it is a parlor." She didn't laugh. Ah, well. "Fine, what would satisfy you? Perhaps it would be amusing to turn him into a weasel again?" I said, gesturing to Sebastian.

"Here, now," Sebastian spoke up, "there will be no more of that!"

I smiled and stepped close to the Destroyer, much closer than I'd ever wanted to get again. Mere inches from her lips, I whispered, "We really don't need a show of strength, do we? As powerful as you are, you can feel my magic."

Something flickered in her eyes and she nodded. I don't know if she could truly feel my power or if she just didn't want to admit that she couldn't. Either way, it saved me from having to turn someone into a weasel. I still hadn't a clue how I'd done that and I wasn't eager to have to prove myself.

She glanced at Sebastian. "Bring the humans and come."

I faltered. One swift glance back but she'd seen it. She turned on me, her power beating at me, her eyes filled with fury. "On second thought, maybe I'll kill them now, just to test your commitment."

I waved a hand in their direction. "Do what you like, but we're going to have to get out of the city to work this spell, and it'll be much easier to travel without them slowing us down. We could find two nice plump virgins when we get to the country that would do just as well or better."

Kali stared into my eyes as if she were trying to crawl into my mind and snoop around inside. I'll bet it just galled her that she couldn't tromp freely through my head anymore. Finally she nodded to Sebastian.

"Bring them," she said and walked from the room as regal as any queen, or demon goddess. "Besides, have you *tried* finding virgins in the country these days?"

Chapter Thirty-three

The dark coach rolled to a stop as we walked out into the night, almost as if it had been waiting in the shadows for its mistress's summons. The driver had the look and smell, the dead eyes, of one of Kali's walking corpses. I clutched the Book of Shadows in my hands, helpless, as Sebastian shoved Thomas and Amelia roughly inside. Kali glanced back at me and snatched the book from my grasp, leafing through it impatiently.

"More of your Gaelic?" she said, her tone harsh and cool. "I do not think I will allow you to keep this since I do not understand what it says. Get rid of it."

"It's a witch's spell book, nothing more. It has information in it which will be helpful in working your spell. I returned for it, and if you want your spell done properly, it would be wise to let me keep it. As I said before, I've never done this sort of magic."

She watched me for a long time, studying me, looking for any indication that I was being untruthful. Whatever she saw on my face must have convinced her.

"Fine, but if anything should happen to catch fire," she said with great meaning, "I will burn that book and you with it."

"Understood," I said.

She looked at me through narrowed eyes. "I do not yet trust you, witch. Tread very carefully with me."

"I could say the same to you but we need each other, so let's just make the best of it, shall we?"

She regarded me carefully and then nodded. "You said we needed a sacred space to work the spell. Where should the driver take us?"

I hadn't thought that far ahead so I said the first thing that came to mind, "Stonehenge."

"What?" Sebastian roared. "That'll take days!"

"Look, this isn't a simple spell. It requires a great deal of power and ritual. Samhain is three nights from now. If we perform the spell on the holy night in that sacred place, then we have a good chance of succeeding. We could attempt it tonight someplace closer but I can't guarantee the outcome. To put it succinctly, this is our best chance. The choice is yours."

"What is this Stonehenge?" Kali asked.

"A circle of giant standing stones on Salisbury Plain. It's an ancient site of great power, built before even you walked this earth."

"And it'll take at least two bloody nights traveling without stopping to get there," Sebastian grumbled.

"Enough," Kali said shortly. "I would like to see this place. It intrigues me. However, we must stop at the hotel. I will not travel so long without a change of clothing. Come."

Sebastian held the coach door and assisted Kali and me inside before climbing up with the driver. The thought of Thomas and Amelia in their tender care for three days and nights made my blood run cold, but I had little choice. Perhaps I could find a way to help them escape between now and then, during the day when the vampires would be powerless to pursue them. Then again, would they be able to get far enough away, hide well enough, that Kali couldn't find them once the sun set? That would go even worse for them.

As the coach rumbled on, Amelia leaned forward and grabbed my hands. "For God's sake, Dulcie," she cried. "Help us!"

I shook her hands loose. "No one can help you now, Amelia."

If I had the chance, should I tell them what I planned? One wrong gesture from either of them, one misspoken word, and the whole ruse could come crashing down around us. I knew it would be better if they thought that I was in league with the Destroyer. I sighed and looked out the window to avoid Amelia's tearful pleading and racking sobs. Dear Goddess, I couldn't stand three days and nights of that. No matter the danger, I would have to tell them the truth.

I nearly laughed aloud when our carriage stopped in front of Grillion's Hotel on Albemarle Street. If only Devlin and Michael knew that Kali and Sebastian had taken rooms in the same hotel as them! It took some persuading to get the clerk to tell me which rooms they were in, but he finally succumbed to my charms.

"What are you about, witch?" Kali asked as we climbed the stairs.

Sebastian had remained out front with the coach. I wondered if Kali would pack a bag for him. I didn't think Sebastian would fancy wearing the same clothes for a week, either.

I did laugh then. "Do you realize that you're staying in the same hotel as The Righteous?"

She paused on the stairway and glanced around.

"Don't worry, they're not here. The last I saw of

them, they were bleeding all over each other in a warehouse down by the docks."

She glared at me. "I do not *worry*, witch, but I haven't lived this long by being incautious. Did you kill them?"

"No, they ran afoul of about a dozen grumpy vampires while they were chasing me through the city. They're wounded, and by the time they recover enough to limp back to the hotel, we'll be long gone. I asked for their rooms so I could steal some clothes from Justine."

We found the first of the rooms. The door opened with a cracking sound as I shoved hard against the lock. Half a dozen dresses and other ladies' things lying strewn across the gilded furniture told me I'd found the right room. Kali surveyed the empty chamber and then turned to me.

"If you even think to cross me, witch—"

"I have no intention of crossing you, Kali. Since I woke up as a vampire, I've realized that I've been wrong about many things, not the least of which are my former companions. I've been through too much not to end up on the winning side of this. I do not intend to cross you. I intend to stand at your side. I've found that I rather like the taste of victory."

She looked unconvinced. "I think you are a liar, little witch, but regardless of that, you will do as I wish. You feel powerful now that you are a vampire, but remember, I can kill you just as easily now as I could when you were human."

She walked through the door and I called to her, "Kali, another thing. My name is Cin Craven, High Priestess of the Destroyer. I would appreciate it if you used it instead of referring to me as 'witch.'"

Her eyes narrowed for a moment and then she inclined her head and turned to walk down the hall.

I closed the door behind her, listening until she reached the end of the hall, and then sank to the floor, shaking. I must be mad. How could I possibly keep this up for three days?

Stealing clothes from Justine, I soon realized, presented a bit of a problem. I needed a change of clothes because I'd had to rip the back out of my lace mourning gown, since I couldn't reach all the buttons, so the dress was hardly wearable anymore. Even if it was, the blood in the silk would soon begin to smell. But the new problem I hadn't exactly counted on was just how differently shaped Justine and I were.

The hems of her dresses dragged the ground because she was at least four inches taller than my five foot five. Her waist was also a bit narrower, but at least the current fashion of waistless gowns was in my favor on that score. No, it was the bodices I was having the most trouble with. All of Justine's gowns were low cut and my breasts were larger than hers. Getting them squished into the dresses was one thing, but if I so much as moved the wrong way, they threatened to pop right back out.

I flipped open the lid of another trunk and found more dresses, none of them any better than what I was currently bursting out of. A third trunk contained lingerie, chemises, and an astonishing variety of the scandalous new pantalettes from Paris. I held one of the delicate undergarments to my waist and looked in the mirror, shaking my head. Flinging the pantalettes on the bed, I regarded the last trunk.

There had better be something useful in that one.

Did the woman not own one modest gown? I opened the lid and nearly crowed with delight. It contained all of Justine's masculine attire.

The breeches didn't fit much better than the dresses but they were a bit of an improvement. They stretched tight across my hips and thighs, but as I moved around the room, the fabric gave enough to make them almost comfortable. I selected a loose shirt of beige linen that was obviously custom-made for Justine and clung a little more than I would have liked, but it would do. I found one pair of boots that probably came to just above Justine's knees but on me they rode to mid-thigh. I emptied out a valise and shoved several pairs of breeches and five shirts of varying colors and fabrics into the bag.

Crossing to the desk I saw one of Justine's sapphire-tipped daggers lying there. It must be a spare, I thought, and wondered how many of them she had. I picked it up and weighed it in my hand. Very nice balance. I tied the sheath to my thigh so that my boot hid the knife, just as I'd seen Justine do. Then I pulled a piece of paper from the desk drawer and scribbled a quick note.

Stay well behind. If she senses you near, we are all dead. I need a sacred place to work the spell—we have gone to Salisbury. If all goes well I will find you afterward. If not, then may the Goddess help you all. And thank you, Michael, for everything. I think I may truly love you.

Cin

I tucked the note inside the bodice of my discarded dress. Perhaps they would return to the hotel and find it but I didn't hold out any great hope.

The door opened without a knock and I stood up quickly, trying not to look guilty or call attention to what I'd been doing. Kali stood in the doorway, her golden gown exchanged for one of jade green shot through with gold. Her eyes widened when she saw me. She stalked around me, looking me up and down. I stiffened when she moved behind me and I could no longer see her, but I didn't turn around.

She pressed herself against my back and whispered in my ear, "I like it. Very much."

I shivered, and not in excitement.

"You've had one of The Righteous in your bed," she purred, "I can feel the change in you. Not the blonde woman, I think. Was it Devlin or his Archangel? Perhaps both? It matters naught. I will teach you to love the touch of a woman. You have no idea the pleasures I can bring you."

"What about Yasmeen?" I asked, stalling, avoiding having to tell her that I certainly had no intention of ever coming willingly to her bed.

"What about Yasmeen?" she asked, confused.

"I thought you planned to get her back."

"And so I do."

"Won't she be jealous?"

Kali laughed, a sound of pure delight. "Oh, my dear, Yasmeen will enjoy you also."

Damn. This night continued to get scarier and scarier.

Apparently Kali couldn't travel for a week with less than two large trunks. She ordered the porters about as they secured the trunks to the top of the coach, snapping at one of the young men to be careful. I felt like a poor relation with my single small valise as I handed it to one of the porters and climbed into the coach.

"Listen quickly," I whispered to Thomas and Amelia. "I'll get you out of this, I swear it, but you need to be strong. This will not be pleasant or easy. I have to act as though I'm on her side and I cannot help you if you do something foolish. The best thing you can do is be quiet and do not draw attention to yourselves. Do you understand me?"

They nodded and Amelia sobbed, "My babies?"

"Shh. They're safe with Mrs. Mac by now. Don't worry about them."

Weeping, she buried her head in Thomas's shoulder and he looked at me, his chocolate brown hair as disheveled as his wife's, his pale blue eyes filled with worry.

"We'll do as you say, I promise," he said softly. "Thank you for seeing to the children."

I nodded to the door. "She is a demon and a killer, never forget it."

"And you?" Thomas said softly. "What are you?"

I saw Kali moving toward the door and knew my time was up. Reclining in the seat, I let my cloak fall open to reveal my breeches and propped one booted foot on the seat next to him. Kali climbed into the coach and the porter shut the door.

"I am a vampire," I replied. "I am no longer the girl you knew."

Kali smiled smugly at Thomas and he lowered his eyes, not meeting her gaze. I turned my head to look out the window.

Yes, I was no longer the girl he'd known and I never would be again. I'd given myself to Michael, for one night and for all eternity. I only hoped I'd live long enough to be held in his arms once more, to feel his hard body above me, inside me, to gaze up into his beautiful face. The thought was what sustained me through the next few hours.

Chapter Thirty-four

We made it only as far as Chiswick the first night. It was still full dark as the coach pulled into the inn yard, but I could feel dawn approaching as I never had before, as if some instinct deep inside me was screaming to find shelter. I watched through the window as Sebastian jumped down from the box, tossed a coin to the sleepy lad who came out of the inn, and opened the coach door with a flourish. Kali leaned forward and looked Thomas in the eye.

"Behave yourselves in there. If you cry out or invite attention, I will simply slaughter every soul in that inn. Their lives do not matter to me. Do they matter to you?"

Amelia looked out the window at the young boy and gripped Thomas's hand. Thomas nodded and we exited the coach.

"Philip, come," Kali called to her driver, and we all trooped into the inn.

The innkeeper, Mr. Hughes, was a round, jolly-looking man. He smiled and nodded as we walked through the door, his gaze resting on Kali in appreciation. I didn't blame him; she was a beautiful woman, if you didn't mind the fact that she was a demon and a killer. Kali requested one large room.

"Two rooms," I said. "And a cot."

She narrowed her eyes at me. I shrugged and whispered, "I'm tired and I am not going to lie awake all day worrying about what the two of you may try to do to me if I fall asleep. I'll take the two of them," I said nodding to my cousins, "and you and Sebastian can have the other room."

She stared at me for a moment, distrust showing in her eyes, but I stood my ground. Finally she gave an irritated sigh and requested two rooms. We all followed her up the stairs like peasants trailing in the wake of a queen. Mr. Hughes stopped in front of the first room. Opening the door, he motioned to me. I walked in to find a spacious room with two beds, a wardrobe, a wash stand, and a comfortable chair by the fireplace.

"No need for a cot," he said. "This ought to do nicely, eh?"

"Very nicely. Thank you, Mr. Hughes," I replied.

He let Kali and Sebastian into their room and then asked if we'd like some breakfast sent up.

"No," Kali answered.

"Yes," I said. "The three of us would very much like some."

Hughes glanced at Kali as if seeking her permission and she smiled icily and inclined her head. He walked off, humming as he went. I motioned Thomas and Amelia into the room as Kali crossed the hall from the doorway of her own room.

"They have to eat," I said simply.

"Why?" she asked, as if she really didn't understand the purpose of feeding them.

"What do you mean 'why'? They're human, Kali. They need to eat and drink."

"Perhaps," she said, looking into the room where Thomas and Amelia huddled together on one of the beds. "And you? Will you be in here drinking while Sebastian and I sleep?"

I snorted. "Of course not. They can't be touched, you know that."

Her eyes snapped to mine. "What do you mean?"

"I thought you knew," I said, my eyes wide in mock surprise. "They must be pure for the sacrifice. We cannot feed from them or they're useless to us."

She gritted her teeth; I could almost hear the grinding. "Fine, keep your pet humans. Philip will stand guard outside the door today. He has orders to rip the arms off of anyone who tries to leave this room, is that clear?"

I nodded.

"Good. Rest well, High Priestess. Tonight we feed and then we must travel. I am anxious to see this Stonehenge of yours."

"Rest well," I replied and walked into the room, closing the door behind me and leaning against it with a sigh of relief.

"Dulcie—," Amelia said.

I put my finger to my lips. "Quietly," I whispered. "I have no idea how thin these walls are."

She glanced nervously at the wall separating our room from Kali and Sebastian's and nodded. "Dulcie, let us go," she pleaded softly.

I shook my head and crossed to close the blessedly heavy drapes over the room's one window. Pushing the other bed to the farthest corner of the room, I replied, "The coachman is one of her creatures. She meant it when she said that he'd rip the arms off of anyone who tries to leave this room."

"But there are three of us and only one of him," Thomas argued.

"I've fought them before," I said, setting the Book of Shadows on the chair and throwing my cloak over it. I removed the knife from my boot, laying it across the top of my cloak. "You can hack them to pieces and they just keep coming."

Amelia stared at me in horror. "Dulcie, dear God, what have you been doing up there at Ravenworth?"

I slowly managed to remove my boots and then stretched out on the bed. "It's a very long story," I sighed. "If there's any way I can get you two away from her before we get to Stonehenge, I'll do it, but if we try and fail, she'll kill us all. It's better to bide our time."

"Dulcie, what did you mean when you said you were a vampire?" Amelia asked.

"The walking dead is what she meant," Thomas grunted. "The Devil has stolen her soul and now she's nothing more than the walking dead."

"That," I propped myself up on an elbow and pointed to the closed door, "is the walking dead. I am much more. And he wasn't the Devil and he didn't steal my soul. He's a good man and he and his friends will come for us. Until then, I'm the only thing standing between the two of you and a very horrible death, so I think I deserve a little respect."

"Of course," Thomas said, looking ashamed. "I apologize, Dulcie, truly. But what are we to do?"

I explained the plan to them. We would go to Stonehenge. Kali would think that I was performing her spell but in reality I would work the binding spell against her. I had to get another look at the paper she had with the instructions for her spell, compare it to the binding spell, and figure out a way to mesh the two so that she wouldn't notice anything was amiss until it was too late. At the moment, though, I was too exhausted to think about it. A knock sounded at the bedroom door and I rose to answer it.

Philip stood aside, eyes staring blankly ahead, as the boy from the inn yard stepped inside with my valise. A pretty young maid appeared behind him with a heavy tray of food and drink. She set the tray on the table in front of the fireplace, bobbed a curtsy, and left. The boy set my valise on the end of the bed. I fished a coin from my reticule.

"The others I'm with," I said, "they'll sleep until dusk. Make yourself scarce by then, understand?"

He looked at me with more wisdom in his eyes than any young boy should have. "Aye, miss. The swell in the other room, he's one of *them* type of dandies, eh?"

I had no idea what he was talking about but I smiled indulgently and nodded. When he was gone and the door closed firmly behind him, Philip standing like a statue at his post, I turned to Thomas.

"What did he mean?" I asked.

Thomas blushed and looked down at his eggs. "You really don't want to know," he muttered. "He'll stay well away from them, though, trust me."

I shrugged and slipped into my bed. "Eat well, wash up, do whatever you wish, only under no circumstances are you to open those drapes or set foot outside that door. Use the day to rest," I advised. "It'll be a long night."

Chapter Thirty-five

Kali breezed into the room at sunset. I'd just finished helping Amelia with her hair and was putting the comb back in my valise. Kali's gaze swept the chamber, satisfied that we were all where she'd left us.

"I thought you might like to come next door. I've ordered something to eat," she said with a wicked laugh.

"I thought I'd go out," I replied.

"And I would like you to stay in," she snapped.

"I meant no offense," I said, as humbly as I could manage. "This is all very new to me and I prefer to feed in private. For now."

She crossed the room in a blur of movement, grabbing my hair and twisting it in my fist.

"You always have such a ready answer, a logical reason to defy me at every turn. It grows tedious."

She released me with a small shove and I held my hands out, palms up. "I'm not trying to deceive you in any way. It's just my personal preference."

"One would think you would have a care for *my* personal preference," she snapped. "Go feed, but take Sebastian with you. I've taken great pains to acquire you, I'd hate for any misfortune to befall you."

That was ridiculous. What harm could possibly come to me? She wanted her lap dog to watch over me, nothing more.

"I didn't dine with Sebastian when I was alive and I have no intention of starting now."

"You will do as I say!" she shouted, her fury rolling off her in waves, making my teeth hurt with the power of it. "I am the master here, little girl, not you."

"Fine," I said. "Tell him I'm ready."

Sebastian appeared in the doorway, an easy smile on his lips. He'd probably been eavesdropping.

"Take her out to eat," Kali ordered.

Sebastian bowed, every inch the gentleman, and offered his arm. I cringed but accepted the gesture. I had pushed Kali far enough for one night; I would play along. Besides, if I took Sebastian out to hunt, then no one would die at the inn tonight. I hoped.

The high street was still crowded with people and I let Sebastian steer me toward the taverns at the far end.

"So tell me, Sebastian, what did you sell your soul for?"

"What do you mean?" he asked.

"Kali. What did she offer you that was worth your life?"

"You don't think I did it simply for eternal youth?" he teased.

"Somehow I doubt it," I muttered. "I get to live, to be her High Priestess. I did it for power and freedom and, yes, I'm woman enough to admit that eternal youth was a rather attractive prospect. What did you do it for?"

"England," he said simply.

"England?" I asked incredulously. "What the devil do you mean by that?"

"I mean that when her hordes overtake the earth, I get two things: England and you."

"Then you made a very bad deal, Sebastian. I won't

be yours, I can guarantee you that. I will be her High Priestess and I'll not be bartered away like chattel. As for England, there will be nothing left after she's finished here."

"Of course there will. She complains a great deal but in truth I think she likes this world. She'll have her bit of fun but it won't be total destruction. She'll leave the strong so that they may repopulate the world."

"And she's promised you England?"

"Yes," he said, triumph in his voice.

"I still don't understand. You want to be king?"

Sebastian looked at me as if I were mad.

"That would be treason," he hissed.

I stopped and stared, and then nearly laughed in his face. He was completely serious and utterly horrified. The thought that he would care a whit about treason when he'd murdered without conscience made no sense to me.

"I fought the French under Wellington," he said. "Did you know that?"

"No." I knew he'd been on the Continent but somehow I'd never imagined Sebastian actually in battle.

"Whatever I am, Dulcinea, I love my country. To suggest that I want to be king is ludicrous and treasonous. The monarchy will stand as long as England does. I merely wish to be the power behind the throne. The country will be mine and I will make her so strong that no one will dare to stand against her again."

I shook my head in wonder. He was absolutely mad, there was no doubt about that, but could there be a glimmer of something noble and patriotic underneath that insanity? There was such a look of fear and determination on his face. It was the look of someone who's been thrown from a horse and is determined to get back on, not because they wanted to, but because they can't just walk away.

"Sebastian, what happened to you over there?" I whispered. What was it that he couldn't just walk away from?

His jaw clenched and all emotion bled from his face until there was nothing left but a blank mask. "Nothing that concerns you, my dear," he growled and grabbed my arm, pulling me faster down the high street.

We stopped in front of a rather rough-looking tavern called The Cock and Bull. I laughed softly.

"Go around the back," I said. "I'll meet you there in a moment."

"I'm not supposed to leave you alone," he countered, crossing his arms over his chest.

"Sebastian, please, how am I to get one of those men to leave the tavern with you hovering over my shoulder like a jealous husband?"

"I'll give you five minutes," he growled.

I walked into the tavern and paused at the door for effect, scanning the crowd inside. A hush fell over the common room. I remembered Michael saying that I could drink liquids in small amounts so I walked to the bar and ordered a whiskey. I'd taken only a sip when two men walked up, one on either side of me. They were obviously brothers, tall and blond, dirty from a hard day harvesting in the fields. I felt guilt shoot through me for what I was about to do, but if I didn't do this, then there was no telling where Sebastian's appetites might stray.

"Hullo, love," the one on my right said. "My name's Nick Bridges and this here's my brother Dick. And who might you be?"

I smiled up at him. "I might be interested," I replied. "Why don't you two handsome men come with me and have a stroll in the moonlight?"

I turned and they both offered me their arms. Laughing, I linked my arms with theirs, steering them out the door. We came around the corner, me with my two blond bookends, to find Sebastian lounging negligently against the building. He flicked his cheroot into a puddle and smiled.

"My dear, you amaze me. How quickly you've managed to procure our little evening snack."

"Here, now," one of the brothers said, "I think you've got the wrong idea. We're interested in the lady, not you, mate."

"No," I said sadly, "it's you who have the wrong idea."

I pushed him toward Sebastian and turned on the other, grabbing his arms and shoving him against the wall. His head snapped back and hit the brick, knocking him unconscious. It was probably for the best. Hunger growled through me and I felt my canines lengthen. I sank them deep into his neck, mentally asking forgiveness for what I was about to take. I drank deeply but not enough to harm him. Pulling back, I let him slide gently to the ground.

His brother was struggling futilely against Sebastian. Sebastian stood behind him, his mouth fastened on the man's neck and his arms wrapped around him to hold him still. When the man stopped struggling and his eyes fluttered shut, I walked up and shook Sebastian off of him.

"Enough," I said.

Sebastian removed his handkerchief from his pocket and dabbed his lips. He then grasped my chin in one strong hand and wiped a spot of blood off the corner of my mouth. I jerked my head away and he shrugged, refolding the linen and returning it to his pocket.

"Are you old enough yet to bespell them while you feed?" I asked, glancing at the two men on the ground.

"No," Sebastian replied.

"I'll be glad when I reach that age. I hate it when they fight me."

"Really?" Sebastian said with a smile. "That's my favorite part."

I scowled at him. "It would be," I muttered. "Come on, then. The Destroyer awaits."

Chapter Thirty-six

The floor of the bedroom at the inn in Amesbury had a squeak near the window. After listening to that squeak for the fifteenth time, I sat up from the bed and looked at Thomas as he paced. He was nervous and I didn't blame him. We'd spent yesterday holed up at an inn in Basingstoke. Tomorrow night was Samhain. We would go to Stonehenge and we would defeat Kali, or we would die. He had a right to be nervous but that infernal squeaking was driving me mad. I had to get out of the room.

I needed to acquire the remaining supplies necessary to perform the binding spell and I still hadn't gotten another look at Kali's spell. Crossing to the door, I opened it. Philip of the dead eyes stood in the doorway. He turned, regarding me with a lifeless expression, as if it didn't really matter to him if I stayed or if I walked through that door and he got to tear my arms off. It probably didn't.

Since it mattered a great deal to me, I closed the door and walked over to the wall. I pounded on it three times. Kali and Sebastian were in the next room, I could feel them. A minute later she appeared at my door wearing a long black velvet cloak with silver buttons marching up the front. I had no idea what was underneath it.

"What is it?" she snapped.

I blinked. She was grumpier than usual tonight. That couldn't be good.

"I need to see a copy of your spell and find a merchant who has the supplies we'll need for tomorrow night."

"You also need to hunt. You didn't feed last night."

I hadn't and hunger now gnawed at my belly. She had been in a strange mood last night and I hadn't wanted to leave Thomas and Amelia unprotected. Tonight's mood wasn't much better but I didn't have a choice tonight. I needed supplies and I needed blood, or I'd be useless to them tomorrow night.

"Yes, I need to feed and I need to find an apothecary. May I see the spell again so I can be sure I get the right ingredients?"

"Yes, give me a moment and I'll go with you," she said.

"That's not necessary—"

She narrowed her eyes and I shut my mouth. I really, really didn't want to go anywhere with her, but I also got the distinct impression that I did not want to make her angry tonight.

"All right," I whispered.

She turned in a swirl of black velvet and I let out the breath I hadn't realized I was holding. My stomach was knotted up in hunger and fear. I turned to Thomas.

"I'll be back in an hour, perhaps two. Don't worry, Sebastian won't harm you. He wouldn't risk her displeasure."

Thomas nodded and I hoped that I was right.

The air was cool and crisp, moist from the rain that had fallen that day. I hoped the weather would hold tomorrow night. I couldn't think of anything more miserable than having to work this spell in the rain out on the wide, unprotected expanse of Salisbury Plain. I turned my head to the west. The henge was two miles outside of town. I inhaled deeply as if I could perhaps smell it or sense it. I couldn't, of course. If I were closer, I could feel it, but two miles was too far away.

I did sense something else though. I turned and scanned the nearly empty street but saw nothing out of the ordinary. Still, I could feel eyes out there, somewhere. Someone was watching us. Was it Michael?

"What are you searching for?" Kali asked.

My attention snapped back to the demon next to me. "Oh. I was just seeing if I could sense the henge from here."

"Can you?"

"No, it's still too far away."

"Tell me about these stones of yours."

I tore my thoughts from Michael and shrugged. "They're old and very powerful. I wish I could have seen them before they fell to ruin; they must have been magnificent. My mother brought me here to see them when I was a child."

"Ah yes, your mother. A beautiful woman. I thought she was my witch, at first."

Something very cold spread inside me and I stopped and turned to Kali. She'd seen my mother. She'd been near, even before Sebastian had come to me, and we hadn't known. Had I been wrong about the coach-a-bower? Had Kali been the one responsible for my parents' deaths?

"What do you know about my mother?" I said, my voice sounding harsh and threatening, even to me.

Kali raised a brow. "I have been watching you."

"How long?"

She shrugged. "Weeks before I sent Sebastian to you."

I clenched my hands into fists to keep them from shaking. "Did you kill my parents?" I asked very slowly.

"Of course not," she scoffed. "That was truly an accident."

I narrowed my eyes. "Why should I believe you?"

She laughed. "Why would I lie? Honestly, child, do you think I care enough about your feelings to lie to you?"

"I am not a child and, yes, I think you would lie if you thought I wouldn't cast your spell for you if I found out that you'd killed my parents."

Anger radiated from her. "You are a child, a squalling infant. You are what? Twenty-two? I have seen more millennia than you can begin to imagine. I was ruling over millions when your precious Stonehenge was nothing more than a dream. I don't care about your tempers or your feelings. They are nothing to me. It was my intention to take you at a ball, but then your custom of mourning fouled that plan. I didn't want to wait another year so I turned Sebastian because he said he could procure you. That is the truth, but it matters little to me whether you believe it or not."

There was something in her voice that told me she really did care whether or not I believed her, and yet, Goddess help me, I still believed her. Foolish maybe, but I did.

"Why Sebastian?" I asked suddenly. "I would have thought you'd have chosen someone . . ." Someone female, but I didn't say it aloud.

"The last lieutenant I had was Yasmeen. I didn't expect her betrayal, and it . . . hurt," she said finally, as if she were surprised by the emotion. "I chose a man this time because I expect a man to betray me. When he does, and he will, I won't have to feel those unsettling emotions again. Also, he was powerfully motivated to get you. In his own way, he loves you, you know. He was very cross when you gave yourself to the swordsman."

I glanced at my feet and continued walking down the high street. I didn't want to comment on my feelings about Sebastian, and especially not on my feelings for Michael.

"I told him he was a fool," Kali continued, oblivious to the fact that I wasn't encouraging the conversation. "Virginity is highly overrated. Do you know that there are men in this world whose god promises them they will have many virgins in heaven?" She laughed, a high, trilling sound of mirth. "Can you imagine anything more tedious? An experienced woman in your bed is undeniably more satisfying."

I looked at her, amazed that she truly thought I cared about Sebastian's views on my chastity.

"Will this do?" she asked.

I blinked and looked around. We were standing in front of an apothecary shop with large windows and a sign over the door that read SILAS SIMMS, APOTHECARY. I peered in the darkened windows at the rows of bottles and herbs. It appeared well-stocked.

"This should do," I agreed.

She grabbed the knob and pushed. There was a sound of breaking wood and the door swung open. I stepped inside and looked around, my list clutched tightly in my hand. One good thing about being a vampire, I didn't need to light a candle to see in the dark.

"The spell," I said.

Kali turned and looked at me questioningly.

"I need to see the spell in order to make sure I have the right ingredients."

She reached into her pocket and pulled out the small, folded piece of yellowed parchment. I took it from her and read over the ingredients, surprised at how few there were. Then again, when you have human blood charging your magic, I suppose you don't need much help.

I laid the paper on the counter and slipped behind it to gather what I needed. I picked out the herbs for Kali's spell and then moved on to find the ones I needed, hoping she wouldn't notice the extra ingredients. Glancing up, I watched her wander through the shop, picking up jars and scanning the contents of the shelves, seeming not to pay me any attention. I wasn't fooled. I quickly placed the rose oil, rue, and rosemary in the bag and then began to look for Silas Simms's stash.

Generally every apothecary will have a cupboard or drawer that contains things only a witch would want. Openly supplying witches isn't advisable, but it is lucrative. Back in the Burning Times, most people who stood at the town square and watched a witch burn had gone to her for charms or cures themselves, the hypocrites. I had just found the supply of black candles and was slipping several into my bag when an angry voice startled me.

"What the devil are you doing in my shop?" the man shouted, brandishing an iron fire poker.

Damn. Mr. Simms must live above his shop.

"Look at me," Kali said softly.

He turned, surprised. He hadn't seen her there. He looked at her beautiful face and was lost. She bespelled him at a glance. The fire poker slowly lowered to his side and then clattered to the ground as he stood staring at her, a vacant look on his face.

I felt a horrible sense of guilt as I moved around the end of the counter. I'd broken into the poor man's shop, stolen from him (not that I wasn't planning to leave him three times what the supplies were worth) and now I was going to take his blood. My guilt was overcome only by my hunger. I wouldn't hurt him, after all, and many lives depended upon my strength.

I walked up behind him. He was short for a man, only about my height. I wrapped one arm around him and pulled down the collar of his shirt with the other. His blood called to me and my canines lengthened and sharpened. Kali watched as I sank my teeth into his neck, his blood flowing into me, rich and hot, filling me and energizing me. I could feel her eyes on me, feel the tension strum through her body, but I couldn't stop.

When I had drunk my fill, I released the man. Kali came up in front of him, her dark eyes staring at me while she licked the wound and then sank her own teeth into the holes I'd left behind. I nearly jerked the man back from her, afraid she'd kill him if she drank from him after I had, but she released him after only a taste. I blushed when I realized she'd done it so the wound would close and disappear. Remembering Sebastian's bite on my neck, I knew I was too young to not leave the telltale marks behind.

"Go up to bed and sleep well," she whispered.

The man shuffled off up the back stairs as if he were walking in his sleep.

"You thought I was going to kill him," Kali said.

I shrugged. What could I say? My momentary guilt for thinking that she had intended to kill him was lost when I remembered who and what she was. She hadn't done it out of mercy or pity. She'd done it because we had to spend one more day at the inn and she didn't want a mob of villagers with torches dragging us out into the daylight. Come to think of it, I wasn't sure if a mob would have bothered her. She'd probably only done it because massacring an entire village would take too much time.

I moved back behind the counter and collected my bag of candles and herbs. Before I could reach for the spell, Kali picked it up and slipped it back into the pocket of her cloak. I laid a substantial sum of money on the counter, not that it would ease my conscience.

"Let's get out of here," I said. "You need to feed and then I need to get back to the inn and charge the herbs and go over the spell again."

"Then by all means, let us return to the inn. I don't need to feed. Sebastian and I have something arranged for later."

I really didn't want to know what it was, so I smiled and nodded and led the way back to the inn.

Chapter Thirty-seven

I stopped at my door. Philip of the dead eyes didn't move an inch, blocking my way quite effectively. I turned to look at Kali. She smiled in an odd sort of way.

"Come to my room," she practically purred.

I took a step back. "No," I said, "I need to work on the spell."

She cocked her head to one side. "But you don't have it."

I shrugged. "You seem reluctant to give it to me so I thought I'd write it out from memory."

"Can you do that?"

"Most of it."

"Well, that won't do. Come to my room for a few moments and I'll give you the spell. You may take it with you when you go," she said, as if she were bestowing a great boon.

I wasn't stupid and neither was she; there was no way she was giving me the only copy of that spell. I followed her to her door, deciding not to point out that the spell was in her pocket and she could easily give it to me in the hall. Something was off. She was tense, not anxious but excited. She practically floated through the door.

I followed her in, my eyes taking a few precious seconds to adjust to the dim candlelight. It was long enough for her to shut the door behind me. I whirled around but she wasn't paying any attention to me, she was looking over my shoulder and smiling. Turning around slowly, I realized that I was in deep trouble. I also figured out what that little "something" was that she and Sebastian had arranged.

Sebastian was on his knees in the middle of the bed, his face shadowed in profile. He was stark naked, pale and possessing quite a bit more muscle than I would have thought was under those dandy's clothes. On her hands and knees in front of him was the plump blonde barmaid from downstairs. Sebastian's eyes rose slowly to mine, raking over my entire body, as he moved in and out of her. Her eyes were glazed over, not be-spelled because he wasn't old enough for that yet, but drugged perhaps. Still, she looked like she was enjoying herself. I took a step back toward the door.

"Not so fast," Kali said. "Stay awhile."

"No, really," I stammered, trying to look anywhere but at the bed. "I'll give you some privacy."

Kali grabbed a handful of my hair and tossed me a few feet from the door.

"I said stay," she commanded and turned back to the bed, breathing in a deep breath. "Ah, Sebastian, look what you've brought me. Just what I needed."

Her black velvet cloak fell to the floor and I was astonished to see that she was naked beneath it. The whole time we had been out together, she hadn't had a stitch on! She stalked toward the bed, hips swaying seductively. She was like some wild, beautiful, exotic jungle creature; you knew it would eat your face off if given half the chance, yet you couldn't help but stand and stare. Her dusky skin seemed to glow from the inside as she sat on the bed, leaning over to fondle the girl's breasts as they rocked gently back and forth with each of Sebastian's long strokes. Kali quivered and I didn't think it was necessarily in lust.

"What kind of demon were you?" I asked. It was like drawing the attention of a coiled cobra but I couldn't stop the words.

Kali smiled, her eyes watching me as she ran her tongue up the side of the girl's throat. "Succubus," she purred and gently drew the blonde's earlobe into her mouth, as if to emphasize the point.

Succubus, a demon that assumed female form and fed off of sex. No wonder she'd gone to such lengths to keep that body. And no wonder her power was so much stronger than a normal vampire's. She was siphoning energy by feeding off of sex. That explained a great deal, most especially how Devlin came to be her prisoner. I wondered if he knew what she was.

I watched in fascinated horror as Kali maneuvered herself beneath the barmaid's planted hands. She was quite a bit taller than the girl which put her generous breasts flush with the girl's face. The barmaid bent down to take one of Kali's dusky nipples into her mouth, tugging gently and then harder. Kali moaned and planted her feet solidly on the mattress, lifting her hips until her dark curls brushed against the blonde's.

Sebastian never took his eyes from me. His pupils were enormous, making his eyes appear solid black. He pulled out of the girl, his member long and wet. She moaned and moved back a little, as if her body were searching for him. He did look down then. He slipped his thumb deeply into her, at the same time plunging three long fingers into Kali's waiting slickness. The two women before him cried out in pleasure. He turned again to me, stroking himself with his free hand, sweat running in rivulets down his chest.

"Come here," he said firmly.

"No," I whispered and then more forcefully, "No!"

It was too much to ask me to stand there and watch that. I'd never even heard of anything like this. I turned and ran to the door, Kali's voice stopping me just as I reached it. Pain ripped through me like razor blades in my brain as she shouted for me to stop. I did so, leaning my palms and my forehead against the cool wood of the door. I moved through the pain, grasping the door knob and nearly crying when I found it locked. Had she been able to lock it from across the room? Or had I just not noticed that she'd locked it behind me when we came in?

"Do as he asks," she commanded coolly.

"No," I said. "You cannot make me. You'll have to kill me first, and you won't do that because you need me."

"I have given you more free rein than I have anyone else in centuries . . . witch." She spat the word at me and my bones began to ache from the power she was emanating. "Now, this time, you will do as I tell you."

"I won't do that," I repeated.

"You will do it or I will go next door and kill those two humans you seem so fond of."

"You're going to kill them tomorrow night anyway," I stated, carefully removing any sort of emotion from my voice.

She laughed. "Yes, but if you don't do as I say right now, then Sebastian and I will rape the woman and make you and the husband watch. Now. Come. Here."

I turned slowly, my eyes blazing with a mixture of hatred and fear. I walked across the room, sweating, shaking. When I was close enough, Sebastian reached out and grabbed my wrist, jerking me onto my knees on the bed. I struggled until I could feel the bones of my wrist grind together under his fingers.

"You have no idea how long I've waited to have you on your knees," he growled. "Now, get down and open that pretty mouth of yours."

"What?" I asked, confused.

Kali laughed, a sound of true pleasure. "Oh, Sebastian, I think perhaps you should start slower." There was a sly smile on her face as her hands roamed over the girl's body.

"Fine," he said, pulling me toward him until I was flush against his side.

As his fingers moved furiously in and out of both women, his free hand grasped mine, placing it on his swollen shaft. I cringed; it was slick with her juices. He curled my fingers around himself, placing his hand over mine. We both stroked, the rhythm keeping pace with his other hand. He squeezed and loosened, teaching me what he wanted. Moisture grew on the tip of him, and he ran my palm over it, spreading it down the hard length of him. He moved my hand between his legs, gently rolling his sac between my fingers. Goddess, I would have crushed him if I hadn't thought that Kali would kill me for disrupting her sport, or perhaps carry out her threat against Amelia as punishment.

I closed my eyes, nearly choking on bile as he moved against my hand in a frenzied pace. Kali and the barmaid were making soft, mewling sounds. Suddenly Sebastian grunted and jerked away from me. Grasping the blonde's hips, he drove into her in one hard motion, threw back his head, and shouted. The blonde screamed and Kali gave a throaty groan, sinking her teeth deep into the girl's neck. The three of them spasmed together in a wave of pain and pleasure. Sebastian's hand shot out, grabbing my hair and pulling my face toward his. Before I knew what he intended, he pressed his lips to mine, and the power that was coursing through the three of them spilled into me as well.

It was comfort, like chocolate and whiskey and warm sheets. It was power, like calling the elements and feeling the enormous strength of nature rushing through your body. It was lust, like watching Michael across a room and then suddenly having his hands on me, his lips against my bare skin. It was all that and much, much more. And underneath it was something dark and evil and laced with tainted blood.

I jerked free of Sebastian and stumbled across the room, my head spinning, my stomach churning, my legs numb and tingly. I fell against the dressing table and leaned against it for a moment, my stomach heaving as if I would vomit. From the bed I could hear Kali begin to laugh. As I stood there with my hands braced and my head hanging down, I noticed that her discarded cloak was on the floor next to my feet. Reaching down, I fished the folded spell out of her pocket and ran to the door. To my surprise, it opened for me. I spilled from the room like a drunk from a tavern, the tangy smell of sex clinging to me, and Kali's mocking laughter chasing me down the hall.

Chapter Thirty-eight

The coach clattered along in the evening mist. I stared out the window, wondering if Michael was out there somewhere, watching over me. Had it been him I'd felt watching me last night? I sighed to myself. I wanted this all to be over. I wanted to curl up in bed, safe in his arms. I rested my forehead on the coach wall.

The first thing I'd done when I returned to my room last night was ring for a bath. Thomas had been a complete gentleman and kept his back to the room as I'd soaked in the small copper tub behind an ancient, nearly transparent screen. I'd stayed there, shaking and scrubbing, until my skin was all wrinkly and the hot water had turned frigid. Amelia had brought me a towel, which she had warmed by the fire, and she brushed my hair and mothered me, though neither she nor Thomas asked me what had happened. I think it was more because they didn't want to know, rather than out of any regard for my feelings.

The rest of the night and part of today I'd worked on the spells, trying to figure out how to incorporate the components of both so that I could change from one to the other in mid-spell without Kali realizing it, and without jeopardizing the end result. I'd figured out everything except what I was going to do about Sebastian if I managed to trap Kali in one of those stones. I'd have to fight him, of course. The problem was that he had his sword and he had Philip, who may or may not take orders from him, and all I had was one of Justine's daggers hidden in my boot.

Laying my head back against the seat, I closed my eyes. Perhaps with enough magic, I could hold him off until the reinforcements arrived. Perhaps.

A hand on my knee drew me bolt upright. Kali was leaning across the seat, her proper English dresses of the past few days now replaced with the houri's costume she'd worn on our first meeting. Of course, it wasn't the same skirt. That one had burned, I thought with more than a little satisfaction. The new one was deep red to match the rubies in her necklaces. We looked like a matched pair, she and I, all in black and red.

My hair hung in loose waves down my back in its natural scarlet. Justine's thigh-high black boots and snug black breeches encased my legs. I wore my black cloak with the crimson lining, which matched the silk shirt beneath it. The shirt had little gathered pleats around a modest neckline and long, flowing sleeves caught at the wrists in a fall of crimson dyed lace. It fell in a whisper to the tops of my thighs. The shirt was the most modest of all of the clothes I'd taken from Justine, and after last night, I felt that I needed all the modesty I could get.

"Nervous, my priestess?" Kali purred, her hand gently squeezing my knee. The ends of her black hair brushed her nipples where they peeked through the many strands of wrought gold. "Perhaps when this is all over, we can finish what we started last night?"

I thought of the blonde barmaid. Joan had been her name. She hadn't shown up for work this evening. The whole inn was rife with gossip that she'd run off with a lover. I knew who her lovers were and I wondered where they had hidden her body. I wondered if anyone would ever find her and give her a proper burial. I looked at Kali's hand on me, knowing that she and Sebastian had used that poor girl and then taken pleasure in killing her, and something inside me snapped.

I grabbed her wrist and threw her across the coach, landing on top of her in the far corner, my fingernails digging into her flesh. My other hand wrapped around her throat and squeezed.

"If you ever," I said with tightly reined fury, "ever try anything like that with me again, I will cut your heart out, burn your body to ashes, and mount your head over my fireplace. Do you understand?"

"You can die trying," she whispered.

"Then we'll both burn. I'm not afraid to die. Are you?"

She shuddered and her eyes went liquid black. Dear Goddess, I realized, she's aroused by this! Smacking her head once against the wall, I released her and retreated to the opposite corner. Amelia regarded me with wide eyes. I'd just broken every one of my own rules: Keep your head down, be inconspicuous, don't make her angry, and you may live to see another dawn.

What the hell, I thought, we were probably all going to die anyway.

If I'd had a stake, I probably could have driven it though her heart as she stood transfixed, staring at the wonder that was Stonehenge. The strong, silent, stone sentinels rose majestically from the flat earth of Salisbury Plain, the light of the full moon gilding them a glowing silver. Kali cooed and ran her hands over the stones, walking around until she stood under one of the still-standing lintels. Stretching her hands out, she breathed deeply and threw her head back.

"Such power. Can you feel it?" she whispered.

"Yes," I replied.

"When I rule this world, I will restore this place to its former glory. The ground will run red with blood from the sacrifices we will perform here."

"Sacrifices to whom?" I asked, wondering what god Kali prayed to.

"Why, to me, of course. It will be my temple."

She strode through the upright sarsen stones and into the inner circle as if it were already her temple. I followed behind, Sebastian and Philip coming after with Thomas and Amelia in tow. Sebastian smiled at me and winked, a promise in his eyes of things yet to come. I turned away from him and ran my hands down the legs of my breeches, as if I could wipe away the memory of last night.

"There," Kali said, pointing to two smaller upright stones inside the great horseshoe of trilithons around the altar stone.

Philip stood guard while Sebastian forced Thomas to his knees and tied him to the stone, then moved to do the same to Amelia. Poor Amelia, who had been so stoic until then, started screaming and crying. The look on Thomas's face was pure torture. I turned my back as I set my bags of herbs, vials of oil, and jar of salt water on the altar stone, trying to ignore her cries. I would do the best I could to save us all, but at the moment I needed to concentrate.

I measured my charged herbs and oils carefully

into my little stone bowl: rose oil, dragon's blood, rosemary, rue. The little pouches that Mr. Pendergrass had given me contained what looked like ash and I was grateful that I didn't know what they really were. The herbs I had brought were not the ones listed in Kali's spell but I didn't think that she knew rosemary from ragwort. At least I sincerely hoped she didn't. If she realized I was using the wrong herbs, we were all doomed.

I glanced up, cautiously, but she paid me little attention, much too occupied with walking around, gazing at the henge. When my herbs were ready, I gathered my black candles and walked around the outside of the horseshoe, placing them on top of the smaller bluestones that ringed the inner trilithons. Kali followed me like a noisy shadow, her glittering jewels swaying and tinkling with each swing of her hips. She laid a hand on one of the bluestones and quickly stepped back from it, holding her hand against her chest.

"It's warm," she said, more as a question to me than the statement it was meant to be.

"Yes, strangely, those are always warmer than the others," I replied and continued around, placing my candles where I could.

Something moved out on the Plain and I froze, turning my head to look out past the standing stones. There was a dark shape out there, low to the ground. As if it had felt my gaze on it, it stopped moving and blended into the mist and shadows. Could it be Michael? No, surely he and Devlin knew better than to come this close. There were no trees nearby, nothing to provide cover. Besides, it had seemed too small to be a man. I watched as long as I thought I could without someone noticing, but the shadow didn't move again so I walked back to the altar stone.

"Kali, I'm ready to start but I need Sebastian and Philip to move outside the circle."

"No," she said. "They have been loyal to me and deserve to be here when I regain my crown."

"They can see just as well from outside the circle," I argued.

"You have pushed me as far as you can for one night," she said through clenched teeth. "They stay. The matter is closed."

I hadn't thought I could get away with that but it had been worth a try. "Fine, but once the circle is cast, no one can cross it. If anyone breaks the circle, then the spell is ruined, understand?"

"No one will interfere," she assured me. "Proceed."

I took my jar of salt water and walked the perimeter of my circle, cleansing the area as I had when I'd done the spell to summon The Righteous. I walked it three times more, closing the circle, and then starting in the north, I called the quarters. The candles blazed to life, just as they should, and I felt a small triumph that I'd been able to do it all without anyone else's help.

Perhaps it was just a matter of time, or perhaps it had something to do with becoming a vampire, but I had felt more in control of the magic inside me since I had woken in Mr. Pendergrass's attic. The magic didn't feel alien to me anymore; it felt like it was a part of me. I still had a great deal of work ahead of me, learning the extent of the power I possessed, and how to harness and control it, but tonight I felt strong. Of course, the full moon, the night of Samhain, and the sacred stones lent me power beyond my imagining. As I walked back and stood upon the altar stone, I could feel the power coursing through me. Magic had been performed here from time immemorial and the earth remembered. Power rose up from the ground below me, beating through me like a drum.

This was Samhain, the night when the veil between the living and the dead was the thinnest, the night when all those who had died during the year were finally able to cross over into the spirit world. Being both living and dead, I felt the charged atmosphere of this night more acutely than most. I stood there on the altar stone for a long time, soaking in the power and gathering my will.

Finally I opened my eyes, floated gracefully off the stone, my cloak swishing behind me, and walked to Thomas. Amelia was a quivering mass of hysterical womanhood, and I couldn't use her for what I needed to do now. Thomas knelt with the Craven family arrogance, looking tall and proud in the face of certain death. He knew I didn't mean to kill him, and that made him braver, at least until I reached down and pulled the sapphire-tipped dagger from my boot and raised it high. He turned several shades paler at that.

I raised the dagger and paused. Creasing my brow in what I hoped looked like thoughtful confusion, I lowered the dagger and turned to Kali.

"No," I said, "the spell is wrong."

"What do you mean it's wrong?" she spat. "It cannot be wrong. It was written by witches much more knowledgeable than you."

"No, I'm sorry, I don't mean the spell is wrong, I mean your interpretation of it is wrong."

I thought her head might actually explode, she was so angry. "What?" she snapped, stalking toward me.

"The blood of two, it's not they who need to bleed."

She paused, cocking her head. "What do you mean?"

"It's not their blood, it's ours. *Their* blood isn't going to call forth *your* crown. Their blood isn't going to have the power to do it, only our blood, yours and mine."

"Yes," she said slowly, "I see your logic."

"Come," I said and walked back to the altar stone. I think Amelia actually fainted when I turned my back on her and Thomas. That was probably for the best.

I knelt on the stone, placing her in front of me. She offered me her wrist.

"Your knife," she said, gesturing to her exposed wrist.

"No," I said, shaking my head. Here was the dangerous part. I remembered when I had drunk from Michael the night I was made, remembered being in his mind as his blood flowed into me. I saw myself as he'd seen me, felt what he'd felt. I was hoping that if I bit her, I would get a similar result. What I needed was an image of that crown, one flickering image from her thoughts, something I could use to draw her into the binding spell.

"No," I repeated. "I want you to offer me your neck."

Her eyes widened in shock and perhaps a little fear. "No," she replied. "I don't trust you enough for that."

"Do you want your crown or not?"

"I have offered you my blood," she argued, holding her wrist out to me again.

"I don't need your blood solely on the stone," I said softly. "I need it inside me, flowing through me."

Her lips parted and she stepped closer.

"Be honest," I whispered, pushing her ebony hair back over one shoulder to expose her neck, "you've wanted the same thing since the first night we met."

She said nothing but tipped her head to the side, offering me her neck.

I took a deep breath, bracing myself for the unpleasant task ahead of me. I wrapped my fingers around her shoulders and bent down. Against the dusky perfection of her skin, I whispered, "Now, think of your crown, what it looks like, what it feels like. Call to it as your blood moves through me so that I may bring it home to you."

She shuddered and I felt her nod. I took a deep breath and cleared my mind, for if even one glimpse of what I meant to do passed to her during the exchange, then all was lost. I drew back and tore into her throat. I wasn't gentle, and by the soft mewling sound she made, that was what she preferred. Images flashed through my head, brief vignettes of a large, ornately worked crown of polished white bone, red stones set throughout it like the stone in Kali's talisman, which was hidden in the pocket of my cloak. It was enough. I drew back and she swayed into me, her eyes liquid black with lust. I pushed away from her and stood.

"It's done," I said, raising my arms and gathering my power once more. The letting of blood swelled something dark in the power that rolled up from the earth, and I wondered exactly what had been done here all those centuries ago. Pushing it down, I moved to the standing trilithons opposite Thomas, Amelia, Sebastian, and Philip. They were about to experience something none of them would ever forget.

At my gesture Kali moved with me. I reached out and wiped some of the blood off her neck, smearing it on the stone. Then I took the dagger from my boot and made a shallow cut on my left forearm. I squeezed the cut until blood welled up and then I spread my blood on top of hers on the face of the stone. I didn't think this was exactly blood magic, it was my own blood and hers, freely given, but it was very close. I sent a silent prayer to the Goddess for understanding.

I moved back to place her between me and the stone and then I pushed my will into the stone. It would have been much easier if I'd been able to say the words I needed aloud, but I couldn't. I had to make a space in the stone to trap her. It was like calling the elements, for the stone was part of the earth, only this was much harder. I pushed my will out into the stone, feeling what I wanted from it, calling to the earth to do my bidding. Sweat beaded on my forehead and the veins in my head throbbed. Finally, just when I felt dizzy with the effort, the face of the stone shimmered and appeared to fall in on itself.

The opening looked like the narrow hall of some ancient castle, a small tunnel lit with flickering light, and inside that tunnel was Kali's crown. It wasn't really her crown, but a simple glamour imposed within the stone, a picture that I projected from the memories she had given me. Kali's breath caught and I wished I could have seen her face. She reached out one hand, stepping forward to reclaim what was hers. Her hand moved through where the stone should be. It swirled like mist around her, the crown just out of her reach. *Come on,* I thought, *just a little farther*. And then she did it. The minute she stepped fully into the stone, I allowed my concentration to break.

The solid face of the giant stone flicked back into reality, trapping her within. An unearthly scream sounded from within the rock as I reached into the pocket of my cloak, pulled Kali's talisman out, and smashed it against the rock face. Sparks flew from the disc as the conjured ruby burst like a ripe melon. A backlash of wind flew from it, sending my hair flying out behind me. The blood from inside the ruby rolled down the face of the stone, mixing with the two streaks already there.

I gathered my power and shouted over the wind and the screaming rock, "Kali, the Destroyer, by blood I bind you! By the power of this circle I bind you! By the power of my will I bind you! I bind you behind this stone door. Until the end of days, walk no more. So mote it be!"

There was a snap of power, like the clicking of a lock, and the wind that was streaming uninterrupted from the stone reversed itself, sucking back into the rock and sealing her inside. I'd done it. Dear Goddess, I thought as my body quivered with exhaustion and I fell to my knees, I'd really done it!

And then from behind me I heard Sebastian's roar of denial.

Chapter Thirty-nine

"What have you done?" Sebastian screamed. He rushed at me and I braced myself for the attack.

Michael, I silently pleaded, *now would be a good time to arrive.*

The breath I'd been holding exploded in a grateful whoosh when Sebastian brushed past me and went to stand before the rock, pounding on it with his fists, pacing around it, calling to her.

I glanced across the circle and saw Thomas staring at me with his mouth open, his eyes gone wide with amazement, or possibly horror. Amelia was still blessedly unconscious. Philip lay on the ground, well and truly dead now that Kali's power was no longer there to animate him.

A shadow caught my eye outside the circle. I watched, as if I had nothing else in the world to worry about, as the shadow moved behind the stones. *Wolf,* I thought and then chided myself. Wolves had been extinct in England for centuries. Still, this animal didn't move like a dog. I watched it, its head down and its hackles raised, as it trotted around the edge of my circle. The way it moved, that floating suspended motion between each step, told me it was no dog. It truly was a wolf, and it was looking for a way inside. Until one of us inside the circle broke it, though, nothing else could get in. I turned my head back to Sebastian and wondered if I wasn't safer out there with the wolf.

"What have you done?" Sebastian growled, turning toward me. "It was the talisman, wasn't it? I knew you had it but she swore it must have burned in the fire. She said you didn't have the guts to take it from her. She said she'd be able to feel its energy if you had it. You bitch, I'll kill you for this!"

I sat there in the grass, shaking and weak from the power it had taken to work the binding spell. He rushed me then, hands outstretched, fingers bent like claws. I just sat there, waiting. The second before he fell on me, I rolled backward and kicked up with my legs, hitting him in the stomach and throwing him over my head. Pushing myself upright, I turned to see that he'd landed not a foot from the edge of the circle. The wolf was growling now and throwing itself at the invisible barrier of the circle behind me.

Sebastian pulled himself up. "Bring her back," he snarled.

I shook my head. "No."

"Bring her back or I'll kill both your pet humans," he said, drawing his sword, "and then I'll kill you."

I sighed. "If I have to sacrifice all of us to save the world, then I will do it, Sebastian." I reached behind me and used one of the bluestones to pull myself up. The muscles in my legs quivered but I managed to stay on my feet. "Now, if you want to fight, then put down your sword and fight me. Or are you so much of a coward that you need a weapon to fight one unarmed female?"

The muscles in his jaw clenched. He turned his back on me, to show that I posed no threat to him, and sank the tip of his sword into the ground . . . and damn the man if he didn't reach right through the edge of the circle to do it. The invisible shield fell with a pop that made my eardrums hurt.

"Sebastian, you fool!" I yelled as a warmth of fur brushed my right thigh.

Sebastian had turned and taken several steps toward me before he registered exactly what he was seeing. The large gray and black wolf raced through the center of the stone circle, bounding onto the altar stone and springing into the air with a growl, its teeth flashing white and deadly in the moonlight. Sebastian had just gotten his arms up to defend himself when the wolf slammed into him, knocking him to the ground. Sebastian's screams broke the stillness of the night.

"Dulcie!" a female voice called from across the circle. My head snapped up and around. At some point Amelia had regained consciousness and she and Thomas were frantically tugging at the ropes that bound them.

"I'll get you free," I shouted. "The knife! Where's the blasted knife?"

I crawled on hands and knees, searching through the grass for the dagger I had dropped. I had to get them free. Once the wolf was finished with Sebastian, it would turn on the rest of us. I couldn't let them die like this. I was so intent on my search, I didn't notice when Sebastian's screams stopped.

"Dulcie, behind you!" Thomas shouted.

I whirled and the wolf was coming toward me at a slow walk. I screamed and scrambled to get my feet underneath me. I crab-walked backward, but there was no place to go. The wolf was panting, its tongue hanging out of the corner of its mouth. Blood stained its jaws and yet it didn't seem inclined to eat me. I stopped moving, my breath coming in shallow gasps. I fixed my gaze on the ground in front of it, not looking it in the eye, hoping that if I didn't do anything to threaten it, then perhaps it would go away.

When it was inches from me, it gave a little hop, its front paws coming up and hitting me squarely in the chest, knocking me back to the ground. Amelia screamed. My gaze involuntarily flew to the wolf's face, its amber eyes blazing with intelligence. And then its head bent toward mine . . . and licked my cheek.

I lay there in a cold sweat, blinking at the black, starry sky. A thousand thoughts and emotions flooded through me, not the least of which was shock that I wasn't screaming and bleeding. The wolf sat on its haunches and waited, its head tilted to one side. I rose up on my elbows and looked at the animal. There was something about those eyes . . .

The wolf threw back its head and howled, standing every hair on my body straight up. And then I felt it. Power. Power and a nebulous shimmering of magic that tingled along my skin. The wolf walked into a spill of silver moonlight and its body convulsed, its legs lengthening, its muzzle shortening, its hair seeming to pull into its own skin. In the space of a heartbeat or two, the wolf was gone and a naked man stood where it had been.

He was tall and solid, his muscles large and well formed, quivering slightly from the stress of the change. My gaze flew to his face as heat crept into my cheeks. He was still handsome, his face having neither Michael's beauty nor Devlin's stark masculinity, but somewhere comfortably in the middle. His hair was still too long, still black streaked liberally with gray, just like the fur of his wolf pelt.

"I knew it!" I crowed. "They asked me when you disappeared from the warehouse if you were a vampire, and I said no but I knew you weren't human, either." I laughed.

"Woman," he said, "I don't have a great deal of time. Do you know how much energy it takes to hold my human form under the full moon?"

"I'm sorry," I muttered, trying to keep my eyes from wandering away from his face. "How did you get here?"

"I've been following you," he said, as if that explained anything.

"But . . . why?" I asked, realizing it must have been him and not Michael I had sensed watching me the night before.

"You saved my life and now I've saved yours. My debt is repaid, vampire, and honor is satisfied."

I nodded. I wasn't going to waste time arguing that he didn't owe me anything for saving his life, especially when he considered it a matter of honor. Men are very particular about that sort of thing.

"Is he dead?" I asked, jerking my chin toward where Sebastian lay unmoving in the grass.

"No, but he will be. His life is not mine to take though," the werewolf said. Turning his head as if he'd heard something I hadn't, he inhaled deeply. "Your mate comes."

I spun around. "Michael?" Distantly I could hear horses' hooves. Relief spread through me. He was coming.

When I turned back the man was gone and the wolf stood in his place.

"Damn," I muttered. "I wish I'd asked your name."

The wolf let out a small *woof*.

"Woof, eh? Well, Woof, would you watch Sebastian while I untie my cousins, please?"

Woof loped over and jumped up on the altar stone, lowering his head and soundlessly showing his teeth. It looked vaguely like a canine grin. I found the dagger in the grass and crossed the circle as quickly as my shaky legs would carry me. It took longer than I'd expected to saw through the ropes but I soon had Thomas and Amelia free. Amelia fell into her husband's arms, weeping hysterically. He held her close and smiled at me over the top of her head, but the smile didn't quite reach his eyes. There was a sad distance to it.

I felt my chest tighten but I nodded back before I turned away. No, things would never be the same again. No matter how much I loved them, no matter how much they may still love me, they were human, and somewhere deep inside they would forever think of me as one of the monsters. It was part of the sacrifice I had made, I knew that, but it didn't make it hurt any less.

I walked to the edge of the stone circle, my arms wrapped around myself. I could see Michael now, riding at an insane pace across the Plain. When he saw me, he pulled the horse up. Its head tossing violently, he trotted it through the obstacle path of stones that littered the area.

It was a testament to Michael's will to get to me that he had gotten on the back of a horse. The poor animal was clearly terrified of him. He managed to maneuver the horse to a stop and slid off its bare back. Quickly unhooking the bridle, he slapped the horse on its rump and the poor thing tore off across the Plain, sending divots of earth flying behind it. The bridle fell to the ground with a clinking of metal, and I gathered the last of my strength and ran to him.

His face was etched with strain and worry, but he slid his hands inside my cloak, grabbed my thighs, and lifted me. My legs locked around his waist, and I stared into those blue-gray eyes, ran my fingers over his cheekbones and down across his lips as if to make sure he was really real.

"I know you said to stay back but when I heard you scream . . ."

"It's all right," I said, unable to hold back the tears that I had been pushing down for days. "Everything is all right. Thomas and Amelia are alive and the spell worked, Michael. Kali is trapped in the stone. It worked."

He spun me around and kissed me. If I live another hundred years, I don't think anything will ever feel as perfect as that kiss. His lips were warm, moving softly but urgently against mine, and I kissed him back as if I wanted to crawl inside him and stay there where it was safe and nothing could ever harm me again.

"Dulcie!" I heard Thomas shout from the stone circle. "He's moving!"

I pulled back and looked at Michael's confused face. Eyes wide, I whispered, "Sebastian."

Chapter Forty

Michael swung me down and set me firmly aside. Flinging off his greatcoat to reveal his high black boots, breeches, and a black shirt similar to the one he'd worn the night we first met, he pulled his sword free and stalked with lethal purpose toward the center of the circle. What greeted him there made him pause.

Thomas held Amelia close, his eyes going wide when he saw Michael approach, the wicked-looking claymore firmly in his grasp. The wolf was crouched on the altar stone, teeth bared, and Sebastian was sitting on the ground below. His throat had been nearly torn out. It wasn't a wound that would kill him, but it would take a long time to heal, and it would hurt like hell in the meantime. I hoped he'd enjoyed his sport last night because I didn't think he'd be drinking again any time soon. I suppose that just goes to show that any evil you do will come back and bite you in the ass, or the throat.

"Cin, darling," Michael said warily, "do you know there's a wolf in your circle?"

"Oh, yes, that's Woof. Don't hurt him, he's a friend," I said, rushing to Michael's side, the muscles in my legs and arms still shaking with slight tremors.

Michael arched a brow at me, and Woof blew out a puff of air, which I supposed was the canine version of a snort.

"Well, all right, maybe not a *friend*, but he did attack Sebastian and save my life. I'll explain it all later, but he's on our side so don't hurt him."

Woof grunted and looked pointedly at Sebastian and then at Michael before turning his amber gaze to me. It was as if he was saying that after what he'd done to Sebastian, he doubted that Michael could harm him either.

"Oh, please," I said to the wolf, "he's one of The Righteous, not some newly-made lackey. Give him some credit."

Woof looked at Michael, did his doggie snort again, and lay down on the altar stone, resting his head on his front paws. I wasn't fooled. He looked at ease but his hind legs were tucked under him in case he needed to leap up on a moment's notice.

"If you two are quite finished?" Michael asked.

I opened my mouth to reply but he cut me off. "Forget it. Tell me later. Right now, however, I have some unfinished business to attend to."

He stalked around Sebastian, every muscle in his body quivering with deadly intent. Sebastian stumbled to his feet and pulled his sword from the ground. The two circled each other and I moved to put myself between them and Thomas and Amelia.

"No threats, Montford? Not so brave without your mistress to fight your battles, are you? What's the matter?" Michael mocked. "Wolf got your tongue?"

A wet, bubbly growl came from Sebastian's ruined throat and he lunged at Michael. The strength of their clashing swords sent sparks flying from the steel. They moved around the inside of the stone circle with a speed that even I had a hard time following. Sebastian may have fought the French on the Continent but he was no match for Michael. After several minutes, it was clear that Michael was just toying with him, much as Justine had done with me in the dining room at Ravenworth. Sebastian knew it too. He was learning firsthand why the sword of the Devil's Archangel was feared among the undead.

I kept moving Thomas and Amelia out of the way, their human eyes unable to follow the quick movements of the two vampires. Finally I shooed them both toward the outer edge of the stone circle and away from the fight. Woof leaped down from the altar stone, keeping himself near me. I reached down to stroke his fur but he let me know with a quick snap of teeth that it was unappreciated. It was hard to remember that he was a man inside that furry coat and I didn't know him well enough to be so familiar with him.

"I could do this all night," Michael called out, "but you're looking a wee bit peaked. Why don't you just give up? I'll make it quick, though you don't deserve it."

Sebastian was clearly tiring, his retreating steps faltering, his sword lashing out wildly. Michael, however, moved like a wraith over the ground, fluid, graceful, each movement exact in its precision. He could have taken Sebastian at any time but I think he wanted the other man to surrender. As they neared me again, I jumped up on the altar stone to get out of the way. Sebastian's gaze flicked briefly to me, his foot caught on a rock, and he sprawled at the base of the stone, his sword flying from his hand to land uselessly in the grass, out of reach. Michael laughed softly and stepped forward, the tip of his sword coming to rest at Sebastian's torn throat.

"I am the sword of vengeance," Michael said, his

voice low and dangerous. "You have violated the rules of the Dark Council and now you must forfeit your life."

Michael raised the great claymore and Sebastian turned his head to me, his hair falling over one eye. Gone was the look of sly cunning, the malice and arrogance and cruelty that had marked his features for far too long. His eyes found mine, silently pleading. They were soft and brown, and in that moment reminded me so much of the little boy I had once known, that lonely little boy who had desperately needed a friend. Goddess help me, for the first time I truly understood why Archie had said that I couldn't fight him. And I recalled what Justine had said to me about mercy being what separated us from the monsters.

"Michael," I sighed, just the barest whisper on the wind, but he heard.

I couldn't bring myself to ask him to spare Sebastian but Michael had come to know me well. Whatever he saw on my face made him groan and lower his sword. With one quick motion he shoved the tip into the gaping wound that was Sebastian's throat. Sebastian squealed and turned terror-filled eyes up to Michael.

"Mark me well, Montford," he said. "You're lucky it was me here tonight. The Dark Lord would give you no quarter, not for the love of any woman."

I winced at that, for it was true. Devlin wouldn't have done what Michael was about to do. Of course, Justine would never have asked it of him.

"Look at her, Montford. She is mine, and it's my bed she sleeps in, now and forever. It is my sword that protects her. Never come near her again, because the next time we meet I will kill you without preamble. Do you understand?"

Sebastian nodded and Michael stepped back, his sword resting against the side of his leg.

"She gives you a precious gift tonight, Montford; it's called mercy. Be worthy of it."

Sebastian stumbled to his feet. He moved to retrieve his sword but Michael slapped the flat edge of the claymore against Sebastian's arm and silently shook his head. Sebastian's eyes widened and, faster than a weasel in the dark, he scurried to Kali's waiting coach, jumped up on the box, and snapped the reins. I stood and watched, not quite believing it was finally over, until he'd vanished into the shadows to the north.

"Michael," I said, hopping down from the stone and moving into the shelter of his strong arms, "I shouldn't have asked that of you. It's just that he was such a sweet little boy once and we were . . ."

"Shhh," he said. "A week ago you were human. I can't expect you to become as hard as we are overnight."

"But Devlin—"

"I'll take care of Devlin."

I raised my head from his shoulder and looked around. "Where are Devlin and Justine anyhow?"

"Oh, they're on their way from Salisbury Cathedral. They should be here soon."

"What were they doing at the Cathedral?" I asked.

"Well," Michael hedged, "the next time you get kidnapped and leave a note, you might want to be more specific."

"I was!" I gasped. "I told you exactly where we were headed!"

"No, you said you were going to a sacred spot at Salisbury. They naturally assumed it was the Cathedral. I have to admit that it took me a while to figure out that a sacred place to a witch wouldn't be a Christian church."

"Hmmm," I purred, snuggling into the solid wall of his chest, "you're a very smart man."

He sighed and held me close. "I don't know about smart, but I am a very lucky man."

Chapter Forty-one

Devlin's large black town coach rumbled to a halt outside the henge, Archie's familiar voice calling out to the horses. Michael and I were walking toward it as the door burst open and Devlin and Justine emerged. Justine rushed to me and grabbed my shoulders, looking me over as if to make sure I was still whole.

"The spell?" she asked.

"It worked," I replied with a satisfied grin.

"That was a foolish thing you did, *mon amie*," she scolded, shaking me once.

"I did what I had to do. You of all people should understand that."

She regarded me for a moment and then nodded solemnly. Looking me up and down, she pursed her lips. "My clothes do not fit you well."

Michael ran a hand inside my cloak to caress my hip. "I think they fit just fine."

I laughed. "Perhaps, Justine, when we get back to London, you can take me to your modiste?" I looked down at the breeches and boots I wore. "Or perhaps your tailor?"

"But of course," she replied.

"Come," I said, "I want you to meet my cousins."

I led them over to where Thomas and Amelia were

standing, eyeing the newcomers with interest and a healthy dose of suspicion.

"These are my friends, Devlin and Justine. Mr. Archie Little, a good friend from London. And this is Michael, my . . ." I realized I didn't have a clue how to introduce him.

"Her consort," he supplied, and made an elegant bow.

I blushed. "May I introduce Thomas and Amelia Craven, Viscount and Viscountess Ravenworth?"

Murmurs of greetings were exchanged, but after the past few days, Thomas and Amelia were understandably wary of anyone who wasn't me. I could see the knuckles on Amelia's hand turning white where she gripped her husband's sleeve.

"Amelia," I said softly, "Justine is the one who kept the children safe while I tried to get Kali and Sebastian out of the house. She also went to fetch Mrs. Mackenzie and Fiona to stay with them while we were . . . gone. Sarah Katherine knows nothing more than that Sebastian and Kali were evil people who took you so that they could try to force me to do something for them. The young ones think that Justine is a pirate and we're all on a grand adventure."

Amelia's eyes widened. "Thank you," she said. "Thank you for taking care of my babies."

Thomas took my hands. It was the first time he'd touched me voluntarily. "We owe you our lives and we owe you for protecting our children. All of you," he said, looking from me to the others in turn.

I shook my head. "If it weren't for me, you would never have become a part of this walking nightmare. I can't ask for your forgiveness but I want you to know how horribly sorry I am."

Devlin stepped in before he could answer, laying a hand on my shoulder. "I'm sure that her ladyship would like nothing better than to get back to the inn and have a nice hot bath, a change of clothes and a good night's sleep. If you would indulge us for but a moment, I'd like to see what Cin has done with the Destroyer."

"Of course," I said and led them through the outer ring of stones.

"Cin," Michael asked, "where's your wolf?"

I gasped and looked around but Woof was long gone. Not a shadow moved anywhere on the Plain that I could see. I wondered if I would ever cross paths with the werewolf again, or if I really even wanted to. "I can't believe I forgot about him in the melee. I suppose he's gone."

"Wolf?" Devlin scoffed. "We don't have wolves in England anymore."

"We have werewolves," I replied. "You remember the chained man who escaped the warehouse through the second-story window? Werewolf. He followed me from London because he said I'd saved his life and he was honor-bound to repay the debt. If he hadn't shown up when he did, Sebastian might have killed me."

"The werewolf killed Sebastian?" Devlin asked, looking around the inner circle, his gaze traveling over Philip's inert body but seeing no other.

"Not exactly," Michael said.

"He got away, actually," I interjected.

"Got away?" Devlin said, incredulous. "How is that

possible? You never leave an enemy at your back, Michael, you know that."

"Later, old man," Michael said, his eyes turning cold. "I'll explain it all later."

"What about him?" I asked, motioning to where Philip lay very dead in the grass.

"I'll send someone from the village to fetch him and give him a proper burial in the churchyard. Now, show me, please."

I stopped in front of the great trilithon stone where Kali was trapped. Our blood still stained the face of the rock but it would wash away with the first good rain. I had no illusions that the stone would hold her forever. She was so strong; eventually she would find a way out. As Mr. Pendergrass had said, an entity will always find its way back to its natural form. That's why I hadn't been able to keep Sebastian a weasel. But my magic was strong now, especially tonight, and especially in this place. The power of the circle would hold her for a very long time. I knew though that one day I would have to fight her again. But by then I would be smarter, stronger, my power greater. I'd beaten her once and I'd do it again. I laid my hand against the stone. I could feel her, not with my flesh but with my magic. She felt like a moth trapped in a jar, its wings beating against the glass.

"We are The Righteous," I said.

Devlin moved to stand at my left. "We are the defenders of the innocent."

Justine moved to my right. "We are the hand of justice."

Michael stepped up behind me. "We are the sword of vengeance."

I leaned forward, putting my lips near the stone, just so she could hear me. "We are what Evil fears."

Devlin's town coach was a massive thing, large enough to fit six people comfortably. The windows had been painted over in thick black paint. Archie had explained that they hadn't found my note until the night after my disappearance, so to make up for lost time, he'd painted the windows black to keep out the sun and they had driven day and night in an effort to catch up.

Although the coach was big enough for all of us, Devlin offered to ride up top with Archie while we made our way back to the Red Lion Hotel in Salisbury, to give my cousins a little breathing room. Devlin had told them that he would hire a second carriage for their return trip to London. He'd taken enough rooms for all of us at the Red Lion and I felt a surge of pride that they hadn't doubted I would be able to work the spell and get Thomas, Amelia, and myself out alive.

Thomas was holding up well enough but I worried about the strain of the last few days on Amelia. That is, until she paused climbing into the carriage, looked at my head, and said, "Dulcinea Macgregor Craven, whatever have you done with your hair?" I hadn't bothered with my glamour in days and she hadn't even noticed. I figured if she was feeling well enough to scold me about my hair, she'd be all right. A nice hot bath and a new dress would do us both a world of good.

Before I climbed into the carriage after her, I pulled the door halfway closed and took a closer look at the crest on the side. Someone had painted a silver pentagram above the falcon. I smiled. The three of them were a family and now I was a part of them. I traced the coat of arms with my finger, the Jacobite rose, the fleur-de-lis, and the pentagram forming a triangle around the falcon with its outspread wings. The motto that curled around the edge was Latin. I'd looked up its meaning in the library at Ravenworth.

Non Sum Qualis Eram: I am not what I used to be.

Chapter Forty-two

I snuggled my head into the crook of Michael's shoulder and sighed. We'd returned to Ravenworth last night and it felt good to be home. Devlin and Justine had stayed behind in London with Mrs. Mackenzie and Fiona to give us some time alone together. They would return in a few days with the trunks that Fiona and Mrs. Mac had packed up from the London townhouse.

Thomas and Amelia had gotten home to their children safe and sound, just as I'd promised. Again, I said a silent prayer of thanksgiving for that miracle. An anonymous note had alerted Lord Lindsey to the fact that he might want to search the Montford estate in connection with the village murders. They'd found bodies littering the manor and the grounds and four terrified servants locked in the cellar, babbling incoherently of demons and vampires. There was a massive search to apprehend Sebastian but it was believed he'd fled England for the Continent. I certainly hoped so. I'd sent a letter off to Tim and John Coachman advising Tim that he and the boys could return and that John could follow in the spring when his leg had healed.

As for myself, I couldn't remain here for long with Michael, Devlin, and Justine under my roof while I was supposed to be in mourning. Eventually people would find out and there would be talk. We decided to stay at

Ravenworth for a few weeks and then it would be said that I'd gone to stay with my aunt in Scotland. In reality, Michael had promised me that he would take me for that gondola ride in Venice. In the spring we would take a ship to Inverness, or possibly Edinburgh, and spend a few months with my aunt Maggie. There was still much for me to learn from her, but I wouldn't take vampires, even myself, into the haven of Glen Gregor.

I'd asked Thomas to send my father's solicitor to Ravenworth next week so that I could draw up my will. At some point I would have to "die" in the eyes of the world. By that time the bulk of my fortune would be in houses and accounts across Europe and America. Michael, with his Scottish sense of frugality, would manage my finances as he managed Devlin's and Justine's. I was, however, going to leave Ravenworth Hall and an obscenely large annuity to Mrs. Mackenzie and Fiona. The property and the money would be passed from Fiona to her eldest daughter and so on, much as my magic had come to me. Fiona wasn't made to be a servant. Now she would be the lady of the manor. She would have enough money to make polite society accept her, if that's what she wanted, and she and her daughters and granddaughters down through the generations would be rich enough to marry well, and financially independent enough to do it for love alone. It would be my legacy.

I ran my hand down the solid ridges of Michael's bare chest.

"What are you thinking about?" he asked, caressing my leg where it lay draped over his thighs.

"Everything," I murmured.

"Are you sorry?" he asked softly.

I didn't know what he wanted me to say. Did I miss the person I'd once been? Yes, sometimes. Did I miss the things I'd lost? Often. Was I sorry that I'd put my cousins through a nightmare that would haunt them for the rest of their lives? Of course I was. Did I regret what I'd become?

I looked up and pushed Prissy's fluffy white tail out of Michael's face for the fifth time tonight. She'd taken to sleeping curled up on the pillows of our bed and he didn't have the heart to make her move. I smiled. Lord and Lady, when had he become so dear to me? At what point had I given my heart to him? In that moment I knew without a doubt the answer to his question.

"No, my love. I'm not sorry," I said, sliding my body over his.

Did I regret what I'd become? No. I am Cin Craven. I am a witch. And now I am also a vampire, one of the undead . . . and my life is just beginning.

Read on for an excerpt from Jenna Maclaine's next book

Grave Sins

Coming soon from St. Martin's Paperbacks

Love. Such a small word, really. Four little letters. And yet it is the axis upon which our lives revolve. We live for it, die for it . . . kill for it. It is the impetus that propels us to do extraordinary, or terrible, things. It has created and destroyed lives, kingdoms, empires. It is the light and the darkness within us all. It is the best of us, and the worst of us.

Love is, in short, the most powerful magic in the world. And I know a little something about magic. . . .

Ravenworth Hall, near London
October 1828

I looked down at the child, her face flushed in sleep, and smiled. Reaching out, I ran the backs of my fingers over the old gray cat sleeping next to her. The cat meowed softly and scowled at me before tucking her nose back into the fluff of her tail and closing her eyes.

"Grumpy old lady," I whispered. "Don't worry, Prissy, I won't disturb your girl."

I bent down and kissed Janet's forehead. I was tucking the covers more snugly under her chin when I heard a soft laugh from the doorway.

"Any other mother would die of fright to see a

vampire bending over her sleeping child," Fiona said, settling her shoulder against the door frame.

"I would sooner stake myself in the heart than harm a child, especially *your* child, Fi, and well you know it," I scoffed.

I crossed the room and looked down at eight-year-old Ian, shaking my head. "By the gods, he even sleeps like a boy."

Ian's covers were in a wad at the foot of his bed, his arms were flung over his head, and one leg was trailing off the edge of the mattress. I gently moved his leg back onto the bed as Fiona straightened the blankets. When her child was tucked tightly back into bed, Fiona walked over and put her arm around my waist. I put my arm around her and leaned against her.

"You've done well for yourself, Fi," I said. "You have a lovely family and a good life."

"Yes, well, I can thank my cousin Dulcie for dying and leaving me this estate and a substantial income."

"You're welcome," I laughed, "but I didn't have anything to do with these babies."

Fiona shrugged. "No, but thanks to your legacy, I was no longer the housekeeper's daughter and I was considered a proper enough wife for Lord Bascombe's youngest boy."

I snorted. "John Bascombe could have married any girl he chose, be she a duke's daughter or a scullery maid. It's not as if he needed to worry about his father disowning him."

Fiona smiled wickedly. "Yes, who would have thought that scrawny John Bascombe would return home from years in India all grown-up and handsome as the devil," she said, holding up her hand so that the candlelight flickered and danced off the huge sapphire in her wedding ring, "and rich as Croesus to boot?"

"Ah, so now we know the truth! You married him for his money, did you?"

"Ha. John has qualities much more . . . compelling . . . than his money."

"Oh, stop," I said. "I'm getting very naughty mental images of the rising young star of the House of Commons."

Fiona elbowed me in the ribs. "Be naughty with your own husband."

"Oh, I am," I said with a wink. "Frequently."

We giggled and walked arm in arm to the door. It was as if we were children again, as if I'd never left. As if I'd never . . . I stopped and looked back at the children. Fiona smiled and squeezed my hand.

"Do you ever regret it?" she asked.

Did I? Even in the quiet moments when I couldn't lie to myself?

"No," I said, honestly. "I did what I had to do, or Kali and Sebastian would have killed us all. You have a good life, Fiona. You have the life I was supposed to have. But it's not my life anymore and I'm happy with the one I chose. I have an incredible man who loves me. I have adventure and purpose. And every year I get to come home for two weeks and see my family."

I didn't add that every year it killed something inside me to see them grow up and age when I would never grow old, would never die. I didn't add that it worried me that some day we would get caught, sneaking off to Ravenworth for two weeks of solitude every year, that one year John or someone else who knew that I was "dead" would find me here. I didn't add that sometimes I missed being plain Dulcinea Macgregor Craven, only child of Viscount Ravenworth, instead of being Cin Craven, the Red Witch of The Righteous, judge, jury and executioner for the Dark Council of Vampires.

"You've never wished you had children?" Fiona asked.

I snapped my head around, pulling myself out of my reverie, and smiled. "Not really," I replied, cocking my head to one side. "Especially when your youngest screams his head off day and night."

"I don't hear him," Fiona said, frowning.

"You don't have a vampire's sense of hearing," I replied. "I can hear him all over this house."

"I'm sorry, Dulcie. I'd better go see what the problem is. I swear he is the neediest child I have. He's such a boy, just like his brother. Janet slept through the night from the beginning, but not my boys. He wears me out, that one," she said, but she smiled as she said it. "Apparently no one told Mackenzie Bascombe that thirty-five was entirely too old for his mother to be having more babies."

"He was something of a surprise," I agreed.

"We have another surprise," Fiona's mother said as she came down the hall. "And I'm not sure it's one you're going to like, dear."

Fiona's mother, Jane Mackenzie, had been my nanny and, later, Ravenworth's housekeeper. She had been there for everything in my life. She had been at my mother's bedside when I was born, and she'd been at my bedside that night, thirteen years ago, when I had risen as a vampire. I'd left Ravenworth Hall and a sizeable annuity to Fiona in my will, and now Mrs. Mackenzie was no longer a housekeeper. She still ruled Raven-worth as she always had, but money now bought her the respect due to a dowager.

Mrs. Mackenzie was still a beautiful woman at fifty-two. Her chestnut hair was graying at the temples and her face was softly lined around her eyes and mouth. Those lips that had kissed me good night every evening of my twenty-two human years were now pursed in consternation.

"What's wrong?" I asked.

"There's a man at the door."

"A man?"

"A vampire. Well, I'm practically positive he's a vampire. He's asking for Devlin."

My whole body stiffened. "You didn't invite him in, did you?"

Mrs. Mac snorted. "Of course not."

I relaxed somewhat. Devlin and Justine were out hunting with Michael, but they should be back soon.

"Fiona, go check on the baby. Mrs. Mac, stay here with the children. I'll handle this."

I strode down the hallway, my temper rising with every step. By the gods, I got two weeks of peace and quiet a year, and I wondered what sort of suicidal idiot would be foolish enough to show up at my door, unin-vited, with my family in residence. He would be lucky to leave Ravenworth with his head still attached to his body.

The idiot was definitely a vampire; I could sense that within moments of opening the door. He was old too, even older than Devlin, perhaps. He had dark hair, and his skin looked tanned, which meant that he was originally from somewhere far more exotic than England. He was of average height and build. In fact, there was not anything about him that wasn't average. He wasn't beautiful like Michael or overwhelmingly masculine like Devlin. He wasn't anything out of the ordinary . . . until he turned his pale eyes to mine and smiled.

"Miss Craven," he practically purred as he raised my hand to his mouth. "A pleasure to make your acquaintance."

He brushed his lips across my knuckles and I breathed a soft, involuntary "Oh." No, he was not classically handsome, but there was something so raw and earthy about him, that you didn't really notice. Watching his lips linger on my fingers made me think of those lips moving across other, more intimate, places. *So this is what it feels like to be bespelled*, I thought. No. No, that wasn't right. One of the good things about being a vampire is that another vampire, no matter how old he might be, cannot use mind tricks against you.

I jerked my hand from his, frowning, and narrowed my eyes. "Who the bloody hell are you?"

"I am Drake, Sentinel of the Dark Council." His voice was rich with an exotic accent, eastern European perhaps. It gave me mental pictures of shadowy castles and dark, misty mountains. "I've come to speak with Devlin, indeed with all four of you. I have a personal request from the High King himself."

"You'll have to wait. The others are out at the moment." My voice sounded hollow, even to my own ears.

"Then I shall wait. May I . . . come in?"

The inflection of his voice when he said "come in" sounded almost like a proposition, and I had no doubt that he'd meant me to take it that way. For a moment it was tempting, but the faraway sound of Fiona's baby crying brought me sharply back to my senses.

"Actually, no," I said with an icy smile, and then I shut the door in his face. I leaned back against the wood and rubbed the chill bumps from my arms. Lord and Lady, what was that all about?

"Who was it, dear?" Mrs. Mac asked from the landing of the stairway.

"Trouble," I said, simply. When she frowned in confusion, I elaborated. "He says he's from the Council. Let Devlin and Michael take care of it when they return."

"You're just going to leave him out there?"

"I am. You and Fiona go on to bed. You're the only ones who can invite him in and I don't want him in this house under any circumstances. He may very well be a good man but he . . . disturbs me."

I passed her on the stairs and leaned over to give her a good-night kiss on the cheek.

"Oh, and Mrs. Mac? When are you going to marry that man?"

She flushed and stammered, "What? What are you—"

"Don't bother to deny it. I've smelled him on you for the last eight summers. Lord Bascombe's been a widower for ten years now. Don't you think it's time you made an honest man of him?"

I smiled wickedly and floated up the stairs, leaving Mrs. Mackenzie on the landing with her mouth open and her face a charming shade of pink.

I stood at the window of the empty guest room across the hall from my bedroom and watched as Michael,

Devlin, and Justine came from the woods and approached the house. Devlin, the leader of our group, had his arm around his consort and was whispering something into her ear, her blonde hair caressing his face. Michael was laughing with them until his gaze snapped toward the house and his hand came to rest lightly on the sword strapped to his hip.

Good man, I thought.

Drake walked from the shadows of the house and was greeted by Devlin and Justine as if he were an old friend. Drake and Michael simply exchanged respectful nods. Well, that was interesting. Perhaps I wasn't the only one who was disturbed by our unexpected guest.

As they talked, Drake motioned toward the house, and Devlin frowned. Michael's head came up, and his eyes scanned the windows of the second floor. Even though I was standing in a darkened room on a moonless night, I knew he could see me. He arched a brow at me, and I crossed my arms over my chest and shook my head slowly from side to side. Michael gave an imperceptible nod and turned back to Drake, smiling and putting one arm around his shoulders in a brotherly gesture. I watched as he steered Drake toward the kitchen garden, Devlin and Justine following along in their wake. There was a comfortable little gazebo out there that would do nicely for whatever business they had to conduct.

I breathed a sigh of relief as I returned to my room. Michael was my consort, my lover, my partner. He would respect my wishes in this but eventually I would have to explain myself. That, I did not look forward to. I flopped down on my bed and stared at the ceiling.

What was it that disturbed me so much about Drake?

That I found him attractive? While a rare thing, it was hardly a crime. I could barely remember the faces of the two men that I had been physically attracted to before I'd met Michael, one a lord and the other a footman in my father's house. Each of them had once made my heart race, but now they were both no more than a blurry watercolor in my memory. Michael fired my blood now, and only Michael. Feeling an attraction to Drake, even if I had no intent or interest in doing anything about it, somehow seemed like a betrayal. Justine would tell me that I was being ridiculous, that there was no harm in looking as long as your lips didn't follow your eyes. She was a one-hundred-fifty-year-old vampire and former courtesan, so I tended to take her word in such matters. I had nothing to feel ashamed of, truly, but there it was all the same.

What should have concerned me more was what kind of power Drake wielded. I knew he couldn't bespell me. Certainly Drake was old, but even Kali, who had been well over two thousand, hadn't had that power. It just wasn't possible, which meant that whatever magnetism Drake possessed had little or nothing to do with being a vampire. It made me wonder what Drake had been as a human.

Everyone has some sort of innate talent, and there is something in the magic that makes a vampire that amplifies what we were when we were human. My magic is stronger now, though different in some ways, than it had been when I was alive. Michael's skill with a sword is greater. Devlin had been a soldier, a knight and a champion, and few in the undead world could claim to equal his skill and leadership, on and off the field of battle. Justine had been an opera singer and courtesan to kings.

I'd often wondered if her incredible voice had been
made more perfect by the transformation when Devlin
had turned her, but it had always seemed too rude a
question to ask. It was her past as a courtesan, however,
that put me in mind of Drake. I'd seen the way men, and
women for that matter, looked at Justine when she
walked into a room. She was sex incarnate, and Drake
had that same appeal, in a masculine form, vibrating off
him in waves.

Yes, it definitely made me wonder how our Sentinel
had made his living when he'd been human.

When Michael walked in, I was sitting in the middle of
my bed, wearing only my green satin nightgown, my
knees tucked under my chin and my arms wrapped
around my legs. I was staring at the painting on the
wall. I hated that painting, though I'd never tell
Michael that. He had painted it for me the first year after he'd made me a vampire. It was a nearly life-sized
portrait of me, wearing the scandalously-cut red courtesan's dress I'd had on when we'd first met (which
was why it was hanging in here and not in one of the
public rooms). The technique was flawless. Michael
had once told me that, given ninety years to practice,
one could become accomplished at almost anything. I
had yet to master the piano, so I assume that, unlike me,
he'd had some talent to begin with.

The painting was so realistic that it seemed as if I
could have walked right off the canvas. No, it wasn't his
skill with a brush that I'd taken exception to, it was the
cold, arrogant look he'd given me. The set of my chin,
the arch of my brows, the look in my eyes, all screamed

"bitch." Michael and I had had a huge fight about it. He had never quite come to terms with the fact that he was a poor crofter's son and I was a viscount's daughter. From the beginning he had not felt himself worthy of me. When our relationship was new, the subject had come up frequently, but in the intervening years it had become less of an issue between us. I'd been horrified when I'd first seen the painting and asked him if this haughty creature was truly how he saw me. He had been genuinely shocked at my dismay and to this day we agreed to disagree about that painting. He'd once told me that it was my strength he had painted, and that one day, when I was ready, I would see it, too. I'm still waiting for that to happen.

I tore my eyes from the canvas, laid my cheek on my knees, and looked at Michael lounging against the closed door. By the gods, he was beautiful. Even after all these years, he still took my breath away. His dark blond hair was cut shorter than it had been when we'd met, and the shorter length gave it a bit of curl. His neatly trimmed sideburns accentuated the knife-edge sharpness of his cheekbones. His blue eyes were dark with worry as he pushed away from the door, his hard, lean body moving with supernatural grace. He sat down behind me, gently pulling me between his legs and against his chest as he reclined against the pillows.

"Tell me," he said simply, his lips briefly caressing my ear.

I leaned my head back against him and relaxed in the protective circle of his arms. The warm summer air clung to him, along with the spicy fragrance of his lime-scented soap and the barest coppery hint of the blood he'd drunk tonight. He smelled like home, he felt like a god, and I nearly laughed out loud that I'd even given Drake a second thought.

"I don't like that man," I said.

"Drake? He's very old and very powerful. He's the messenger of the High King and not a man who's accustomed to being insulted. He is trustworthy, Cin."

"Well, I thought Sebastian was harmless, too, once upon a time. He was a childhood friend of mine and nothing more than an unwanted suitor until the night he tried to kill me."

"I understand why you did it, we all do. You had Fiona and Mrs. Mackenzie and the wee ones to protect. Drake understands this."

As if I gave a damn one way or another whether or not I'd offended the man. "That wasn't the only reason I wouldn't let him in," I said coldly.

I could feel Michael stiffen behind me. "Did he attempt to seduce you already?"

"Well, I wouldn't go as far as to say that, but he certainly made me uncomfortable."

"Rotten bastard," Michael muttered.

I laughed. "I got the impression the two of you aren't exactly great friends. You might as well tell me all of it because something tells me that Drake will anyway."

Michael was quiet for a moment. He and I talked to each other about everything and his reticence made me sure this story involved a woman. I had long ago ceased asking him about the women who had come before me. On some level I was grateful to them for making him such an amazing lover, but secretly I was just as content to pretend he'd been a monk before he met me. Hearing anything about his previous lovers always sent me into a jealous pout, which frustrated Michael and accomplished nothing but making me think less of myself for it. Therefore, past loves were a subject we both avoided.

Finally, Michael said simply, "I took a woman from him once."

"Really?"

"Don't sound so impressed. He didn't really want her or I probably couldn't have had her. I was young and foolish. This was after the war," he said, as if there'd only ever been one and I should know which one he was talking about. I assumed that he meant the Jacobite Rebellion of the last century when Devlin had found Michael mortally wounded from an ambush by English soldiers and had turned him into a vampire to save him. I nodded silently, encouraging him to continue. "Oh, he wasn't really angry with me, still isn't, but his pride was wounded, and he'll try to even the score with me by having you, if he can."

I laughed. "Well, since I haven't seen pigs flying around the estate recently, I don't think you should worry. Besides, now that your business has been concluded, we may not see him again for years, if not decades."

"Well, as to that . . ." Michael said, running his fingers slowly up and down my arm in a nervous gesture.

I turned in his arms until I could look him in the eye. "Michael?"

He sighed. "We have a job."

I narrowed my eyes. "When?"

"We leave tomorrow at dusk."

"Michael, you didn't agree to that!"

"Cin, it's an order from the High King himself. It cannot be ignored simply because we're on holiday."

"Two weeks, Michael!" I yelled, poking my finger at him. "Two weeks! All year we travel the whole of Europe, hunting down rogue vampires, bringing death and destruction in our wake, and all I ask is two weeks of peace and quiet with my family. You promised! We've only been here for five days," I said, with a firm jab to his chest.

He reached out, grabbed my wrist, and in one smooth movement, I found myself flipped onto my back with Michael's body pinning me to the bed, his hands shackling my wrists above my head.

"Quit poking at me, woman," he growled. "I'll talk to Fiona in the morning and schedule a time when we can come back for a full fortnight. I did promise you, and I'll make good on it, but we have to do this." He buried his face in my hair and kissed my neck. "Ah, darling, you know I wouldn't take you away if I didn't have to."

Yes, I did know that. I sighed. "Damn Drake anyway. I should have followed my instincts and cut his head off the minute I opened the door."

Michael laughed against my neck and pushed himself up, his hands pressing my wrists into the pillows. "So, lass, other than rescheduling your holiday, what can I do to make this up to you?"

I smiled at the devilish way his eyebrow arched as he said it. Sliding my legs around him, I pressed myself against him. Well, he was certainly ready to make amends!

"Hmmm. . . . We could start with this." I closed my eyes and called up my magic. An instant later we were both naked, his hard body flush against me, and our clothes were in a pile on the floor beside the bed. Michael chuckled and began to explore my newly exposed skin with his mouth.

"I'm so glad you finally mastered that," he said between kisses. "I was getting tired of ending up on the floor while our clothes stayed in bed."

"It is a handy bit of magic," I agreed, my breath catching in my throat as his mouth closed over the peak of my breast.

"How would you like me to make it up to you?" he murmured as one extended canine grazed my nipple back and forth, back and forth. "Quickly or slowly?"

"Michael," I whispered.

He knew me well enough to know my moods, my every whim and desire. He released my wrists, grasped my hips, and drove into me in one deep stroke. I arched my back and braced my palms against the headboard as a low moan escaped from somewhere deep in my soul.

The sheets were tangled in a heap at the foot of the bed, there was dried blood on both of our necks, and I was so bonelessly content that I could have purred. I rested my head on Michael's chest and traced my fingers across the square muscles of his stomach.

"I love these little ridges," I muttered, absently. "Michael, you never told me what the job is. Where are we going?"

His mouth tightened, and he laid back and closed his eyes. Finally he said simply, "Marrakesh."

It was enough. That one word tied my stomach in knots. I dug my nails into his biceps. "You're not serious."

He opened one eye and looked down at me. "I wish I weren't."

I laid my head back down on his chest, thinking, "Dear Goddess. Marrakesh."